STAR FALL

STAR FALL

A Bill Slider Mystery

Cynthia Harrod-Eagles

This first world edition published 2014
in Great Britain and 2015 in the USA by
SEVERN HOUSE PUBLISHERS LTD of
19 Cedar Road, Sutton, Surrey, England, SM2 5DA.
Trade paperback edition first published
in Great Britain and the USA 2015 by
SEVERN HOUSE PUBLISHERS LTD.

British Library Cataloguing in Publication Data

Harrod-Eagles, Cynthia author.
  Star fall. – (A Bill Slider mystery)
  1. Slider, Bill (Fictitious character)–Fiction.
  2. Murder–Investigation–Fiction. 3. Police–England–
  London–Fiction. 4. Detective and mystery stories.
  I. Title II. Series
  823.9'2-dc23

ISBN-13: 978-0-7278-8460-2 (cased)
ISBN-13: 978-1-84751-561-2 (trade paper)
ISBN-13: 978-1-78010-609-0 (e-book)

All Severn House titles are printed on acid-free paper.

Severn House Publishers support the Forest Stewardship Council™ [FSC™],
the leading international forest certification organisation. All our titles that
are printed on FSC certified paper carry the FSC logo.

Typeset by Palimpsest Book Production Ltd.,
Falkirk, Stirlingshire, Scotland.
Printed and bound in Great Britain by
TJ International, Padstow, Cornwall.

ONE

Hairline Pilot

Slider went back to the bedroom to say goodbye to Joanna. He murmured, 'I'm off, now,' but she didn't stir, so he didn't kiss her, in case it woke her. It was early, and she hadn't been sleeping very well lately. Actually, he had an idea she was only pretending to be asleep, but either way . . . He listened a moment to her quiet breathing, then left.

Outside, the icy air romped into his lungs like something with claws. After a mild, wet Christmas and New Year the wind had gone round and was now hurtling with malicious glee straight from Siberia. *Too cold to snow*, he thought. It was still dark, the pre-dawn black and glittering as obsidian. No-one about, the houses shut tight, the cars sleeping nose to tail along both kerbs. When he started the engine it sounded offensively loud. He imagined cross stirrings in warm beds with still an hour to go before the alarm.

He was going in early to try to get a jump on the paperwork. He could get through a lot with no-one around and no telephones ringing. He turned on to the Chiswick High Road, the only moving car in sight, drove in the sickly lamplight past the shuttered shops and empty pavements. The traffic lights, all green, were round alien eyes watching him. The naked trees bent to the wind; a sheet of newspaper like an albino fruit-bat flapped across the road and wrapped itself round a lamp post.

He was aware of a low-level sense of dread. Getting up in the dark always made him uneasy. It was no coincidence that all the old religions had feast days in the dead of the year, involving lights and fires. The primitive part of the brain was still Stone Age, huddled in its bone cave, afraid the sun would not come back. *Oh, let me not die in the black of night.*

Other traffic was beginning to appear by the time he reached

Shepherd's Bush; early birds were waiting at bus stops, huddled in the wind, or hurrying towards the tube. Mike's coffee stall, at the end of the market, showed yellow light, a haven of steam and comfort in the hollow dark. A couple of taxi drivers were shifting from foot to foot in the mean wind, hands clasped round mugs as thick as sanitary ware. Slider stopped at the kerb alongside and bought himself a takeaway styrofoam cup of tea and a bacon roll.

He parked in the station yard and went straight in and up the stairs without seeing anybody. The smell of the bacon neutralized the reek of rubber flooring and disinfectant. The only sound was a faint buzz from a mildly defective strip-light. *No phones*. There would be no-one up here but him – the Department was not manned at this hour.

He stepped into his own office, and for an instant before he put on the light he looked through the far door to the main office beyond, lit by the street lamps outside. For a while, Hollis, one of his sergeants, had been practically living there after his wife had thrown him out, sleeping in a chair and washing and shaving in the gents. Slider had turned a blind eye to this unauthorized occupancy. It had been comforting, somehow, to have Hollis there to greet him at whatever hour he came in, like the family dog. Recently, Hollis had found himself lodgings of some kind, and the CID room was empty, a place of shapes and shadows.

He clicked down the light switch, banishing ghosts, and padded towards the Matterhorn of papers waiting for him on his desk.

Connolly was the first one in. The light went on next door, and she crossed his line of vision, came back to his door, then went away again without speaking. A good chap, that Connolly: knew he did not want to be disturbed. He heard the pattering, clacking sound of her keyboard. Hollis was next. He heard his greeting and Connolly's low reply. The sounds of occupancy gradually accumulated, phones began to ring, daylight arrived grey and apologetic outside the window, but no-one broke into his concentration. He was deep down, occupied – safe.

Atherton, his other sergeant, and also his friend and bagman, arrived in the early afternoon, having been on a half-day awareness seminar about cyber-crime. Slider, who was just surfacing, heard him before he saw him. He was singing the Toreador song from Carmen:

> *Toreador, please don't spit on the floor.*
> *Use the cuspidor –*
> *Whaddaya think it's for?*

Tall, elegant, beautifully suited, he lounged in to Slider's room like a refugee from a more gracious age. Slider stretched, crackingly, and registered that he was hungry. He hadn't stopped for lunch, and the bacon roll was a distant memory. 'How was the seminar?' he asked.

Atherton considered, searching for the right word. 'Technical,' he said at last. 'You wouldn't understand.'

'Oh, thank you. What am I, your granny?'

'They liked *me*,' Atherton said with a faux-modest smirk. 'In fact, I got the impression the unit boss wants to poach me.'

'I don't know about poaching. Many people would like to boil you,' Slider mentioned. 'In oil.'

'You woke up from your nap cranky. Don't worry, I'm not tempted.'

'Afraid of the competition?'

'I couldn't hack the uniform,' Atherton said, with a shudder. 'Facial hair, cargo pants, and a T-shirt that makes a statement.' He sat down on the window sill, crossing his feet at the ankle, folding his arms, ready for a chat. 'I met your friend Pauline's new boyfriend, by the way. Bernard Eason.'

Slider and Pauline Smithers had started out at Hendon together, but she was now a Chief Superintendent in a specialist unit in SCD1. They had teetered on the edge of romance for many years before he had married someone else and she had shot up the career ladder. They met for a drink now and then, and there was still a warmth between them.

'What's he like?' Slider couldn't help asking.

Atherton thought. 'A bit like you.'

'Stop that!' Slider said sternly.

'Not to look at. I don't know . . . just something about him.

I liked him. So what's going down in Groove Town?' He bent a slat of the Venetian blind and peered out. 'It's quiet out there,' he intoned. 'Too quiet.'

'Bite your tongue,' Slider said.

On cue, his phone rang. It was Nicholls, the relief sergeant downstairs, his north-west-coast Scottish accent soft as a sea breeze.

'There's a call coming in, Bill. A homicide. I thought you'd want a head start. I know how you've been longing for a corpus.'

'Now look what you've done,' Slider said to Atherton when he put the phone down and immediately it rang again.

The long post-Christmas lull was over.

There was something indefinably unkempt about Hollis. He was tall, skinny, with thinning fuzzy hair and a scrawny moustache that seemed to grow in random tufts, like a lawn mowed with blunt blades. Today his eyes looked red and his face pouchy, as though he hadn't been getting much sleep. Slider wondered if he was drinking too much – a common hazard, particularly in coppers with domestic troubles.

Hollis immediately offered to be office manager, which was a relief all round. It was not generally a favoured job, staying in the office, recording and keeping track of all the information that came in. People joined the CID for the freedom of the open road, not for the clerical duties.

'Thank you. Right then,' said Slider, looking round his assembled troops.

Before he had got further than announcing the shout, Porson, their superintendent, bustled in. In the low winter light his worn face looked grey and craggy, eroded by the cares of leadership. 'Got a bit more griff for you, 'fore you head off,' he said without preamble. 'It appears deceased is some sort of telly personality, name of Rowland Egerton. Anybody know him?'

'He's one of the experts on *Antiques Galore!*' said Atherton.

Porson gave him a 'trust you to know that' sort of look. 'Never watch it,' he said quellingly.

Atherton couldn't take a hint. 'He's also the presenter on *Going, Going, Gone.*'

'Whatever that may be,' Porson growled.

'I know,' said Mackay helpfully. 'My missus likes that. These two dealers get given a monkey each to buy antiques, then they auction 'em to see who makes the most profit.'

'When I want your input I'll ask for it,' Porson withered him. 'Point is, telly is telly, even if it *is* daytime pap for old ladies.'

Mackay looked hurt.

'The press are going to be all over this like a nasty rash. I'll do my best to keep 'em off your back, but you'll all have to be on your best behaviour. Absolutely no leaking, is that understood?' He looked round the troops. 'I don't want any juicy titbits getting out. Nobody says dickie to anyone – not your mum, your best girl, and especially not the friendly bloke down the pub who wants to buy you a pint.'

'We don't leak,' Swilley objected.

'You want to talk to Mr Carver's firm about that,' McLaren muttered resentfully. 'They leak like a French toilet.'

'What's that?' Porson barked, his eyebrows crashing together like fighting rams.

'I said we don't leak, sir.'

Porson maintained the glare for long enough to drown the defiance, then said, 'See you keep it that way. All right, what are you standing around for? The early bird gathers no moss. Get on with it.'

He stumped out. In his impatience, it was his way to fling words at meaning and see what stuck. The results made the intellectual Atherton wince; but Porson was a good boss, and on their side, so Slider was always willing to cut him some slack.

Blenheim Terrace was a row of early Victorian houses, in yellow London stock brick, now weathered to a tasteful grey, with white stone copings. Two storeys and a semi-basement with railings. A black and white tiled path led to the front door, and a steep flight of steps went down into what Londoners called 'the area'. Slider noted that the door down there, which once would have been the servants' entrance, had been bricked in. The area contained a number of antique-looking plant pots and urns, bare at this time of year except for a few browning ferns.

Built in the 1840s, they still had the Georgian proportions inside and, where they had not been horribly modernized, handsome fireplaces, panelled doors, cornices and ceiling roses. What they didn't have was anywhere to park. Luckily, it was daytime so a lot of the residents were out at work, leaving their kerbside spaces empty. Uniform had taped off the whole road and roused the neighbours who were in to move their cars to the next street, making room for the working vehicles. It had the benefit of keeping the ranks of the press at a distance, bunched up at either end of the street like a dangerous accumulation of water behind an inadequate dam. Though, with the long-ranges lenses they had these days, distance was hardly an object.

'Maybe it'll be a suicide and confound them all,' Atherton said, digging his hands deep into his pockets.

'Not likely, said Bob Bailey, the crime scene manager, arriving beside them. 'Not easy to stab yourself in the neck. You know who it is, don't you?'

'Rowland Egerton, darling of daytime TV,' Atherton supplied.

'Right,' said Bailey. 'My wife reckons him. Him and his poncey suits and his long hair! Its funny how females go for the type.'

'Yes, you'd think they'd prefer a hairy chested caveman like you,' Atherton said with deep sympathy.

Bailey sniffed. 'Got up on the wrong side of the web this morning, did we?'

'Who found him?' Slider intervened.

'His partner, John Lavender. He phoned it in at two thirty this afternoon. He's downstairs in the kitchen if you want to speak to him first.'

'Is Doc Cameron here?' Slider asked.

'On his way. I'll let you know when he arrives.'

'I'll just have a quick goosey, then I'll see Mr Lavender.'

Beyond the front door, the white walls of the rather narrow hall were hung on both sides with photographs in thin black frames. Some were glossy stills of Egerton himself: his lean, aristocratic face, hawk-nosed, was familiar to Slider, as was the trademark swept-back mane of silver hair. It contrasted so well with the tan of his skin and the bright blue of his eyes, making him look younger than his official fifty-eight years. Others looked like press or publicity shots of him with various celebrities – TV personalities, film actors, MPs: he seemed to know everyone, or at least, a sour bit of Slider added, he knew how to get himself photographed with them.

'You recognize him now, don't you?' Atherton said. 'Is it all coming back to you?'

'I'm afraid of it all coming up on me,' said Slider. 'What sort of a man lines his walls with his own face?'

'An intolerable peacock,' said Atherton.

Slider sighed. 'But I suppose if you're on telly, you have to be a bit of a peacock to succeed.'

'You'll rick your neck if you keep trying to see both sides,' Atherton warned.

They stopped at the first door. 'Drawing room,' said Bailey. 'Dining room at the back, small study on the other side. Two bedrooms, bathroom and shower room upstairs. Kitchen in the basement.'

He stepped aside to allow Slider to look in. It was a beautiful room, mouldings all present, fine marble fireplace, antique furniture, Persian carpet on the floor, the walls crammed with paintings, and various ceramics and curios flocking on every surface. 'That'll be fun to fingerprint,' he observed. There was no sign of disorder, nothing knocked over or broken.

The drawing room and dining room were separated by folding doors, at present folded open, and against the wall just in front of them was a gilt and marble console table on which stood a large ormolu clock flanked by vases. The body was crumpled on the floor in front of it.

Egerton was fully dressed in a smart navy three-piece suit and a rather flamboyant tie: muddled dabs of purple, pink, indigo and sea green. There was a pool of blood under the head, and the hair flowed through it, dabbled like a dead rabbit's ears. The carpet was rucked under the body, as though he had struggled or writhed. The wound was in the front of the neck and seemed to be the only one. The eyes were half open, the mouth wide, and there was a little froth on the lips.

Egerton's right hand seemed to be clutching at his collar; his left rested against his stomach, and Slider saw a heavy gold and emerald signet ring on the third finger and what seemed to be an expensive watch peeping out from the crisp band of the cuff.

'No apparent robbery from the person,' Bailey said. 'Doors and windows were secure. And the place hasn't been turned over. If anything was stolen, they knew where it was. Theft to order, maybe.'

'Or he just got in the way,' said Atherton.

'It'll be hard to tell if anything's missing, with all this crap around.' Bailey waved a dismissive hand at someone's lifetime collection of desirable objects.

'Right,' said Slider. 'Let's go and see the partner.'

As was common with this style of house, the warren of basement rooms had been ripped out and replaced with one large one, which in this case had been extended into the garden, with sliding glass doors on to a paved patio. The street end was fitted as a kitchen, the garden end as a dining area, with an enormous oak table and chairs. The walls were white, the flooring dark slate. The kitchen fittings were modern and expensive, with a huge American fridge and sexy concealed lighting. In the dining area there were framed prints – Slider assumed they were prints – of modernist paintings on the walls. He wasn't sure if they were fauvist or surrealist (he must ask Atherton), but the colours were bright and the images clear-cut. He rather liked them: they looked good amid all the black and white.

The one discordant note, being watched over by PC Dave Bright, was the man sitting at the end of the dining table, sniffing and wiping his nose with a Kleenex. A little heap of them, crumpled and bloodied, lay in front of him.

'Nosebleed,' he explained, looking up as Slider and Atherton appeared from the bottom of the staircase. 'It's emotional.' He examined the tissue in his hand. 'I think it's stopping.'

'Mr Lavender?' said Slider.

He was a big, bulky man in a charcoal suit which, even to Slider's inexpert eye, had not the sharpness of Egerton's: it looked like the sort of 'good suit' that a certain kind of man bought to last twenty years. He sat rigidly upright, but there were signs of disorder about him: his conservatively striped tie had been loosened at the knot; his black (too black?) hair was tousled, which was not a good look, since it was both thin and crinkly and must have been carefully eked over the balding top which had now become visible. His face was like something clumsily carved out of granite, greyish, asymmetrical, with deep creases down the sides of the large nose and at the mouth corners; and the bags under his eyes were so big you could have called them steamer trunks. Without the permatan and the styling of the man upstairs he looked ten years older.

With a last dab and inspection he stood up. It was like a building moving. He was taller than Slider, with heavy shoulders and chest and a look of having once been fit: a rugby forward gone to seed. If he had played rugby, it would account for the bumpy immobility of his face. His aftershave was expensive – Slider thought it was one that Atherton wore sometimes. It seemed rather dainty for such an architectural man.

Lavender offered his hand in an automatic gesture. It looked damp and unappetizing, and Slider never liked touching members of the public. He feigned not to see it, and nodded instead, saying, 'Mr Lavender? Detective Inspector Slider – and this is Detective Sergeant Atherton. Please sit down, sir. I'd like to ask you a few questions. Would you like a cup of tea?'

'Coffee,' Lavender said. He was halfway down and started to rise again. 'But I only drink freshly-brewed.' He looked towards the machine on the countertop, shiny and dangerous-looking with its spouts and knobs, like something NASA had designed for taking samples on the moon.

'I can do it, sir,' Bright intervened. 'I got one like this at home.' Lavender stared in disbelief at this statement, but Bright was unmoved. 'Do you like it strong?'

Lavender nodded doubtfully, and though he sat again his eyes kept wandering to the big policeman, looking curiously out of place as he manipulated grounds and machine with calm efficiency.

'Now, Mr Lavender,' Slider said, sitting catty-corner to him and capturing his gaze. 'Please tell me what happened this afternoon. Take your time. Every detail could be important.'

'I got here at twenty-five past two,' Lavender said.

'You seem sure of that time,' Slider remarked.

'I looked at the clock when I came down here,' he said, nodding towards the clock on the wall between two of the prints.

'So you came straight down here?'

'Yes. I let myself in, I called out, "It's only me!" but he didn't answer. He doesn't always, if he's busy with something. He can get very deeply involved with whatever he's doing. I'd been to Waitrose –' he nodded towards the large green jute Waitrose bag on the countertop – 'so I brought the shopping down here first. I was going to unpack it but then I thought I'd see if he wanted a cup of tea, so I went upstairs again and called to him. I looked into the drawing room, and there he was.' He pressed the Kleenex to his nose and inspected it, and seemed surprised it came away clean. 'It was a shock, finding him like that.'

'It must have been,' Slider said kindly.

'We've been friends for over twenty years.' He raised faded eyes to Slider's. 'I suppose it was a burglary, and he came in at the wrong moment.' There was evidently some emotion going on inside, but the granite face wasn't designed for expressing it. It was like watching an Easter Island head do long division.

The smell of coffee was easing out into the air; the machine was gurgling like a happy infant. A background of normality to abnormal emotions which, thank God, most people never had to experience. 'What did you do?' Slider asked.

'I telephoned for the police,' Lavender said. His voice was gravelly, with a cultured accent, but little inflected, as if it had to match his face.

'There's blood on your clothes,' Slider pointed out. 'On the knees. And your cuff, there. How did that happen?'

'I knelt down beside him to check if he was still alive. I

felt for a pulse. But I was sure he was dead. He hadn't moved at all. And I couldn't see him breathing. And as soon as I touched him, I knew. He *felt* dead.'

'What do you mean by that? Was he cold?'

'No, not that – just, somehow, dead. I can't say exactly.' He stared reflectively at his hands. 'So I rang the police.'

'And then?'

'I came down here and waited. I didn't want to stay in the room with him.'

'So from entering the house, you came downstairs to put the shopping down, went up to the drawing room, and came back to the kitchen again. Did you go anywhere else?'

He looked a little blank, as if he didn't see the point of the question. Then he said, 'Just to the lavatory.' He nodded towards the door in the corner. Now Slider saw why they had bricked up the servants' entrance: they had made the little entrance lobby into a downstairs cloakroom.

'And when was that? At what point?'

'After I rang the police. I had to wash my hands.'

'Was there blood on them?'

'I don't think so. But I'd touched a dead body. I had to wash them.'

Slider nodded. *Squeamish*, he thought. It wasn't a pretty trait in a man. 'Did you touch anything else, or move anything?'

'I don't think so.' He seemed to be recovering a little. He reached up and smoothed his hair in what was probably an automatic gesture, guiding the locks to their place, restoring the comb-over. It did little to foster the appearance of youthfulness, but what people saw in the mirror was never what other people saw. Most men were touchy about hair-loss, and it might be especially delicate for a person who hung around with a celebrity.

'So what made you think it was a burglary?' Slider asked.

He looked blank. 'What else could it be?'

'Was there any sign of a break-in? Any disorder in the room? Drawers opened, furniture turned over? Did you tidy up before the police came?'

'No,' he said. 'Everything was just as you see it. I suppose he interrupted them before they got started.'

'Did you notice that anything was missing?'

Something came back to him. 'Yes, I noticed straight away that the malachite box was missing. It always stood on the console table in front of the clock, and it wasn't there. That was why I assumed it was a burglary.'

'Anything else?'

His eyes became stationary. 'I didn't notice anything else. But,' he added quickly, 'I didn't go and look, of course. My mind was on other things.'

Slider nodded. 'When you arrived, was the front door closed?'

'Yes. I opened it with my key.'

'And the doors here,' Slider said, gesturing to the glass doors to the patio. 'Open or closed?'

'Closed. And locked – the policemen checked.'

'Does anyone else have a key?'

'Only Molly – the cleaner. Molly Bean. She comes in twice a week.'

'So who lives here – is it just the two of you?'

'Well, I don't live here all the time. We have a shop in the Fulham Road, and I have a flat above it. But I have a bedroom here and keep some of my things here. I suppose you could say I divide my time between the two places. But the house belongs to him.'

There was something in the way he said the last sentence that caught Slider's attention. He filed it away to be analysed later.

Bright placed a cup of coffee in front of Lavender and he drank from it thirstily, then glanced uncertainly up at Bright, as though wondering what the correct protocol was. 'Thank you,' he said. 'Very nice.'

Bright retreated. Slider was deep in thought, so Atherton, to keep it moving, said, 'We'll need to know who Mr Egerton's next of kin is. Would it be you?'

Lavender looked at him. He seemed not to like what he saw. 'How could it be me?' he snapped. 'I'm not a relative.'

'I thought you might be in a civil partnership,' Atherton suggested.

Lavender's face mottled, and his lips tightened with

annoyance. 'We're old friends, that's all. Can't two men be friends without people assuming they're homosexual? Really!'

'I had heard you referred to as his partner,' Atherton said, unmoved.

'His *business* partner! We have an antiques business. We have the shop, and pitches in various other shops and markets; we do fairs and special events. I'm his *business* partner.' He glared. 'He was married, you know. Damn!' He grabbed another Kleenex from the box. 'Now see what you've done.' He pressed it to his nose. The tissue reddened, and he discarded it and employed another. The eyes, murky blue with yellowish whites like elderly hard boiled eggs, looked accusingly over the top. 'It always starts when I'm upset or under stress.'

Slider rode to the rescue. 'Mr Egerton was married? His wife may be his next of kin, then.'

'They were divorced – oh – must be thirty years ago. She's dead now, anyway. He was very young when he married, and it didn't last long. But they had a daughter, Dale. He didn't see much of her. She's married now. Fellow by the name of Sholto. They live just outside Henley. I suppose she's next of kin,' he concluded indifferently.

Slider said, 'We'll have to get in touch with her. Do you have her address?'

'Upstairs. There's an address book in the office. I can't remember it offhand.' He changed Kleenex again, inspected, dabbed. 'It's stopping,' he said, apparently to himself.

His nostrils were rimmed inside with dark blood. Slider suppressed a shiver. The light was fading outside, night coming again, the unnatural night of winter, and he was in a basement with a man who wouldn't stop bleeding. Dread sat cold and slick on his stomach. He wanted to get out.

'Do you know if Mr Egerton was expecting anyone today?' he asked instead. Doing his duty.

'No, as far as I know he was just having a day at home, catching up. We only came back last night from two days filming. *Antiques Galore!* He was going to cook for me tonight. Just the two of us. It was something we liked – the occasional quiet evening *à deux*.' He glanced towards the Waitrose bag.

'I bought everything for the meal. I suppose I'll have to throw it away now.'

There was nothing to be said to that. Slider was glad when Mackay appeared to say, 'Doc's here, guv.'

Slider stood. 'Thank you, Mr Lavender. I'm going to have to ask you to come to the station in a little while to make a statement. And we will need to take your clothes for examination.'

'What for?' Lavender asked, looking startled.

'Apart from the obvious blood, there might be particles on the cloth that could be useful to us. Fibres, hairs, skin cells. *Someone* killed Mr Egerton, and everyone leaves minute traces of themselves wherever they go.'

Lavender gave him a pained look. 'Yes, yes, don't go on.'

'Someone will fetch you in a little while,' Slider said. 'Meanwhile, Constable Bright here will look after you.'

'I suppose it's necessary,' Lavender said, closing his eyes in martyrdom. 'Oh my God. I can't believe this is happening,' he muttered.

Slider and Atherton trod up the stairs together. 'What was that aftershave?' Slider asked.

'Miller Harris, I think.'

'It's one you use.'

'Don't remind me,' Atherton said. 'What did you think of him?'

'He doesn't like *you*,' Slider observed.

'You know I didn't mean that,' Atherton said, but Slider would not offer any opinions. 'He didn't seem very sorry.'

'I don't think he's the sort to express feelings very much.'

'Hmph. I'm betting it was a lovers' quarrel.'

'He says they weren't.'

'Methinks he doth protest too much. More fey than Weldon.'

'Oh, come on!'

'Seriously. I bet *he's* never been married.'

'Nor have you,' Slider pointed out.

TWO

Friend or Faux?

Freddie Cameron, the forensic pathologist, was kneeling beside the body, and looked up as Slider came in. 'Hello, Bill! You look tired. How's Joanna?'

'Physically, she's back to normal – the doctor's signed off on her, anyway. Mentally—' He shrugged.

'A miscarriage is a very hard thing for a woman,' Freddie said.

'She's stoical. Sometimes I wish she weren't.'

'Give her time. She's a strong woman. She'll make it.'

Slider looked away. *Everyone's an expert*, he thought, even though he knew this was unfair – people naturally wanted to sympathize. Work was the great refuge. It was hard on Joanna, who hadn't any, other than housework and child-minding. 'What can you tell me about the deceased?' he prompted.

'He's a smart dresser,' Freddie said, with perhaps a touch of relief at being back on neutral ground. 'I love this tie. Rubinacci of Mount Street. I want to steal it. I hate to think of it mouldering away in an evidence bag.'

'But as you know where it came from, you can buy one like it,' Slider pointed out.

'I don't have a hundred nicker to spare,' said Freddie.

'And the rest,' Atherton said. 'Wasted on you, anyway – you only wear bow ties.'

'To work,' Freddie said. 'I *do* have a private life, you know.'

'Don't boast. How did he die?' Slider asked.

'Looks like a single, forceful blow with a narrow, sharp implement,' Cameron answered. 'Penetrated the windpipe and nicked a vein. There's a secondary wound to the back of the head, here.' He demonstrated on his own. 'That was from hitting the table as he went down.'

'We've found a trace on the table edge,' Bailey put in.

'A glancing blow,' said Freddie. 'Cut a little flap but there's virtually no bleeding from it. All this red stuff is from the throat.'

'And we think we have the murder weapon,' Bailey said, pleased with himself. He held up an evidence bag, inside which was a paper knife in the form of a Toledo steel dagger, the hilt elaborately chased, the blade narrow and about five inches long. 'It was lying on that little table just there. It's been wiped,' he said, anticipating the next question. 'But with all that scrolly stuff, there might be something left.'

'I can confirm it by a microscopical examination of the wound, but it's certainly the right size,' Cameron said. 'The angle of the blow appears to be slightly upwards. You can imagine the perpetrator reaching down, picking it up, and striking all in the same movement.' He demonstrated, looking like a tennis player returning a dolly ball. 'He'd have got up a good momentum that way.'

'That would suggest it was unpremeditated,' Atherton said.

Freddie shrugged. 'Don't put words into my mouth.'

'Time?' Slider asked.

'From the nasal temperature I'd say he's been dead less than four hours,' Freddie said. 'Rigor only just beginning in the jaw. So you're looking at some time after noon – with all the usual caveats.'

It was a smallish slot, Slider thought. Lavender and the burglar could almost have passed each other.

'Anything else?' Freddie asked. 'Or can we take him away?'

'Take him away,' Slider said. 'I'd like to bring Mr Lavender up to see if he can spot if anything else is missing.'

'Give us half an hour,' said Bailey, 'to do the doors and light switches and so on. All these knick-knacks'll take for ever. Then you can bring him. I'll cover the bloody bit with a tarpaulin. And make sure he keeps inside the tapes and doesn't touch anything.'

Slider sighed, but he didn't say, 'Tell your grandmother,' as he might have.

Outside it had got dark, and even colder, with what country people called a 'lazy wind' – too lazy to go round you, went straight through you instead. Slider's troops huddled, banged their hands together, hopped from foot to foot.

Lavender had looked at the drawing room and said he could not see that anything else was missing, and Atherton had taken him back to the station to make a start.

Mr Porson came for a look-in, but didn't stay long. 'Can't stand around here or I'll end up like Goebbels.' He pronounced it 'Go-balls', to rhyme with the ditty. 'What's it looking like?'

'Not sure yet, sir,' Slider said. 'We know of one thing that's missing. It could be a theft to order. No apparent break-in, so either someone had a key or they talked their way in, then panicked and whacked him. Of course, we can't be a hundred per cent sure nothing else is missing. It's Aladdin's Cave in there.'

'Burglar alarm? Cameras?'

'There's a burglar alarm, but it was switched off, as you'd expect with the householder at home. No cameras.'

Porson nodded. 'All right. I'll go and stall the press. "Treating the death as suspicious." That's all I'll give 'em today. But they already know who he is – it's been on the TV news. Not hard to find out, once they see which house it is. Bloody electoral rolls!' he complained.

'They'll always latch on to anyone who's anything to do with television,' Slider said. 'What are they saying?'

'So far just "found dead at his home in West London".' Porson beat his arms with his hands. His face was purple and grey, his eyes reddened by the wind. 'Bloody Nora, it's cold,' he said. He looked about a hundred and ten, but he strode off to do battle with the Hydra with purposeful tread.

Slider turned away. 'There's someone here wanting to see you, boss,' said Connolly, one of his DCs. In contrast to Porson she looked both warm and perky in a sheepskin-lined coat and a cap with long lappets. Ah, the blessing of youthful circulation!

'Who is it?'

'Little old mammy. 'Bout a hundred and ten, hundred and eleven. You'd hang her on a charm bracelet. Says she's the cleaner.'

'Name of Mrs Bean?' Slider asked.

'That's what she said. I thought she was making it up. I don't know if she just wants attention, or if she knows something. Will I send her back to the station?'

It occurred to Slider that someone who regularly dusted all that stuff in the drawing room might be the person to spot if anything was missing. 'No, I'll talk to her. Wheel her over,' he said.

Molly Bean was not quite in the lucky charm category but she was diminutive – about five foot two – and elderly. Though she had a certain look of whippy strength about her, it was hard to see her stabbing a man six or seven inches taller than her. Anyway, her clear, brown face and sharp eyes filled Slider with confidence.

'Mrs Bean?' he asked. 'What brings you here?'

She was wearing a thick black wool coat, worn grey at the seams. Her home-knitted hat was in red and green vertical stripes with a pompom on the top. She only needed a spout sticking out of one ear and a handle out of the other. Her nose was red and moist from the wind, but she seemed more stimulated than grief-stricken. 'It was on the news,' she said, her eyes scanning Slider alertly. 'They said Mr Egerton had been found dead, so I came to see if it was true. Then I saw all this carry-on –' she waved a hand to encompass the police presence – 'so I thought maybe I could help. Is it something bad? You wouldn't be doing all this if he'd died of a heart attack, would you?'

'I think you can help us,' Slider said, avoiding the question. 'Let's just get out of this wind, shall we?'

The SOC team had erected a tent over the entrance, which at least gave a bit of shelter. Mrs Bean followed him in, talking. 'Some of them lot back there were saying he's been murdered. Is that right?'

'First things first,' Slider said. 'When did you last see Mr Egerton?'

'Monday. Monday and Friday are my days, cause they mostly do their entertaining over the weekend. He was still in bed when I got here. He got up late and padded around a bit, then he got ready and went out to lunch. Something to do with his show, I think. He didn't get back before I left – half past four – and that was the last I saw of him.' Her excited eyes were impatient for more. She looked as if she might peck him. 'What was it, a burglar? Some lowlife robbin' his stuff?'

'You have a key, I understand.'

'Of course I do! How'd I get in otherwise, when they're not there? I've been with Mr Egerton nearly twenty years, so if he doesn't trust me by now, I don't know what!'

'Does anyone else have a key?'

'Not that I know of. Just me, Mr Egerton, and Mr Lavender.'

'Mr Lavender doesn't live there all the time?' Slider suggested.

'He comes and goes,' she admitted. 'Got his own place, but he's here as often as not.'

'I'd like to have a chat with you later about the gentlemen, but there's something you can do for me now, if you wouldn't mind.'

'Anything to oblige.'

'I'd like to know if anything is missing, and I'm guessing you must know Mr Egerton's things pretty well.'

She rolled her eyes. 'I ought to, seeing it's me has the dusting of 'em. And if I was to break anything! Not that I ever have, in all these years, bar the odd wine glass washing up, but you can't help that. Their little treasures I've never so much as chipped. But everything has to be put back in the same place or there's ructions. Fussy's not the word! And Mr Lavender's worse than Mr Egerton, if that's possible.'

Slider and Connolly escorted her along the passage to the drawing room, and she paused at the door almost on tiptoe and with her eyes on stalks, prepared to see God knew what evidence of mayhem. But without the body there was nothing to see, just the tarpaulin over the place where the body had been. She gave that a good, long look, sucking what juice out of it she could for when the neighbours asked.

'Was that him?' she asked. 'How did they do it?'

'Tell me if anything's missing. Take your time,' Slider said.

She scanned the room and said at once, 'The paintings are wrong.'

'What do you mean, wrong?'

'Over there.' She pointed at the wall beside the fireplace, which was opposite the door. 'The picture of the girl's gone. *And* the bottles have been moved up to fill the gap,' she said with an air of triumph.

The section of wall between the fireplace and a bookcase was paved with paintings, hung almost frame to frame, in three rows, but the bottom row had only three paintings in it, spaced further apart. Mrs Bean indicated a still life hanging in the middle of the middle row. 'These old bottles used to be there,' she said, pointing to the end of the bottom row. 'Someone's taken the Maurice O.'

'Maurice O?'

'That was the name of the painter. I don't know what the O stood for. It was a picture of a girl in her undies doing her hair in front of the mirror. "Girl at the toilet" it was called. Fancy using that word in a title! Coarse, I call it. But what can you expect from the French? You've never seen the like o' their plumbing. I went to France on a coach once, and the toilet in the caff where we stopped – well! I wouldn't want to put you off your dinner describing it. But then I didn't think much of it meself, the painting. Kind of messy and streaky, like a kid painted it. I've seen better,' she concluded with a sniff.

'Was it there when you cleaned on Monday?'

'Of course it was. Didn't I notice straight away it was gone?'

'Right. Anything else?'

She scanned the paintings, then turned on the spot, surveying the room at large. 'The green box is gone,' she said, pointing to the console table. 'It sat right there, in front of the clock.' She did another scan of the room. 'I don't see it anywhere else. Unless maybe he'd took it upstairs.'

'We'll check. Can you describe it?'

'It's about so big and so deep.' She gestured with her hands, making an oblong about five inches by three, and two inches deep. 'Dark green, some kind of stone – you know, like that oinks.'

'Oinks?' Slider was puzzled.

'They make coffee tables out of it sometimes. Me sister had one.'

'Ah, onyx,' he fathomed.

'However you say it. Like that, only dark green. With a gold frame and little white beads on the lid. It was made by that man, what d'y'call 'im? You know who I mean!' She pressed a frustrated finger to her brow. 'Famous. What's his name? The egg man.'

'Egg man?' What with eggs and pigs, he felt he'd fallen into a nursery rhyme.

She looked exasperated by his slowness. 'You know, the Russian bloke, the egg man!'

Connolly came to the rescue. 'Do you mean Fabergé?'

'That's the one,' Mrs Bean exclaimed, relieved. 'Them Fabergé eggs cost a fortune, don't they? So this box could be worth a bit.'

'It's possible,' Slider said. He glanced at his watch. 'Connolly, can I leave Mrs Bean with you, to go through the rest? And then I'd like a statement of anything that's missing, with as detailed a description as possible.'

'If it's descriptions you want,' Mrs Bean told him, 'all this stuff, the pictures and knick-knacks and so on, it's all on his computer. For the insurance, d'ye see? There's photos of everything, as well.'

'That's very helpful,' said Slider, though he wondered why Lavender hadn't mentioned it.

'Oh yes,' she said, pleased, 'he was very thorough. All his little treasures, all written down and photographed. You'll find it all in there.'

John Lavender was in what Atherton called the 'soft room', the interview suite for witnesses rather than suspects. Despite this, he was anxious and on the brink of being indignant.

'Am I being suspected of something?' he demanded when Slider came in.

'Why should you think that?' Slider responded.

'Because they took my clothes, and now they're asking for fingerprints and a DNA sample. What's that all about?'

'I've explained to you about your clothes,' Slider said. 'And we need your fingerprints so that we can eliminate them from all those we've found around the house. The same with the

DNA. Once we eliminate your traces, and Mr Egerton's and Mrs Bean's, we can see who else came into the house.'

Lavender looked unconvinced, drawing himself up and clasping and unclasping his big, knuckly hands.

'You haven't been arrested,' Slider said in his most soothing manner. 'You're just helping us with our enquiries.'

'When I've heard that phrase before, I've always thought it was a euphemism.'

'It's just a fact. Won't you sit down, Mr Lavender? I'd like to talk to you. You're the person who can help us most at this stage.'

Lavender stared a moment longer, then subsided like a long, slow puncture on to the sofa.

'Have you had something to eat and drink?'

'They brought me tea and a sandwich. Thank you,' he added belatedly. 'I would like some water, though.'

Atherton fetched a fresh bottle and a glass and put them in front of him on the coffee table. Slider sat down opposite him. The mention of the sandwich had reminded him that he had eaten nothing since the bacon roll. That might account for the feeling of weirdness and unreality he was experiencing – or it might be the hideous decor of the soft room that was to blame. Coming straight from Egerton's drawing room, the contrast with the cheap-'n'-nasty furnishings and carpet was eye-defying.

Lavender poured and drank some water, and Slider began. 'First, can you go through your movements, and Mr Egerton's as far as you know them, say, from Monday?'

'I was in my own flat on Sunday night, so I didn't see him during the day on Monday, but I know he had lunch with Gavin – that's Gavin Ehlie, the producer of *Antiques Galore!* I suppose that was to discuss the upcoming programme. I was in the shop all day. I went over to the house at about six, and we drove down to Winchester together. That's where the next show was being recorded, on Wednesday.'

'But you went down on Monday?'

'Monday night. There's always a set-up day, before the day of the shoot. You don't have to be there for the whole of it, but Rowland always likes to get the feel of the place where we're shooting, meet the owners, walk around the town, meet some of the people. He's very thorough.' He sipped water. 'Also find out the lie of the land as far as dealers go. You can make some good contacts that way, sometimes pick up some bargains.'

'Was that why you went with him?'

He looked up to see if the question was loaded and seemed to decide it wasn't. 'Partly. Of course, it was me who took care of the shop side of things. But he liked me to be there anyway.' He frowned. 'We were friends. Is that so hard to understand?'

'Not at all,' Slider said. 'Where did you stay in Winchester?'

'At the Royal. We ate there on Monday night – they were very good to us. People always are with Rowland – they think it's an honour to have him. On Tuesday we went over to Wykeham Hall – that's where the show was being recorded. Met the owners – a charming couple. They invited us to dinner on the Tuesday night. Looked round the place – mostly eighteenth-century, but a massive seventeenth-century great hall, which was where we were filming, of course. Walked about the town, popped into a few shops, chatted to a few locals. Wednesday was the recording. We went for a meal with Gavin and some of the others afterwards. Rowland needs time to "come down" after a show. Then he's exhausted, completely drained. I drove back, and he slept all the way. I dropped him off, picked up my own car and drove home. That was last night. I was in the shop this morning, catching up, then this afternoon I popped into Waitrose to get the things for supper and drove over to the house, and – you know the rest.'

The energy seemed to drain out of him as he came to the end of the narrative. He stared down at his hands. 'I can't believe it. It doesn't seem real. I keep thinking I'll wake up.'

Slider knew the feeling. 'What time did you leave your shop today?' he asked instead.

'When Georgia came back from lunch. About one thirty.' He met the enquiring look and added, 'Georgia's my assistant – Georgia Hedley-Somerton. She's a treasure – runs everything when I'm not there.'

Slider nodded. 'So you left at one thirty, drove to Waitrose – which one?'

'Kensington High Street. It's not the nearest, but I like it better, and sometimes I do other bits of shopping at the same time.'

'Did you today?'

'No, just the food shopping at Waitrose.'

'And you got to Mr Egerton's house at—?'

'I told you,' he said. 'At two twenty-five.' He gave Slider a frowning look. 'You aren't going to make me go through the rest again, are you?'

'No, that's not necessary now,' Slider said.

Lavender got in a question of his own before he could go on. 'Have you spoken to Dale yet?'

'His daughter?' Slider looked at Atherton.

Atherton said, 'We're trying to get in touch with her – without success so far.'

'Please offer her my sympathy – if she needs it. They weren't close, you know.'

Slider made no comment, and moved on. 'Did a lot of people come to the house?'

Lavender looked as though he didn't understand the question. 'Rowland had a lot of friends. He was handsome, talented, enormously successful – the sort of man every woman wants and every man wants to be. He was tremendously popular everywhere he went, always in great demand. He needn't have spent a single night at home if he didn't want to.'

'And were these friends the sort to drop in casually?'

Lavender still looked puzzled.

'I'm trying to get a sense, you see, of who might have called today. There was no sign of a break-in, so it looks as though Mr Egerton may have let the person in.'

'Well, he wouldn't have let a stranger in. He was too careful for that. And why on earth would a friend kill him like that? Everyone loved and admired him.'

'Evidently, someone didn't,' Atherton said.

Lavender raised hurt eyes. 'I don't know of anyone who wished him harm.'

'What about business rivals?' Slider asked.

'The antiques business isn't like that. Of course, it's competitive, but not to the point of violence.'

'Did he perhaps have debts?' Atherton asked.

'Of course not. He made a handsome living from his television appearances.'

'Did he take drugs?'

Lavender looked shocked. 'Certainly not! And he would never have mixed with people like that, if that's what you're suggesting. The idea is preposterous. He was very careful of his image, because of his large following.'

Slider sighed inwardly. This was getting them nowhere. Lavender was looking worn – and they still had to get his prints and buccal sample, and his statement. 'I won't keep you much longer, Mr Lavender. I'd just like to ask you about the box you said was missing.'

'What do you want to know about it? A gilt and malachite trinket box. It was by Fabergé.'

'Wouldn't that make it valuable?'

'Fabergé had a huge output. Practically industrial. There's a lot of the stuff out there. The eggs are very much in demand, of course, and anything with a Romanov connection, but anything else . . . The lid was set with diamonds, but they were unpolished, so they looked like irregular crystal beads. That would bring the price down, too. I don't suppose you'd get more than a couple of thousand for it – five at the absolute best.'

'Where did he get it from, do you know?'

'I don't know. He didn't say, and I didn't ask.' He looked slightly uncomfortable, his eyes shifting away. 'I don't quite know why he kept it. It wasn't particularly handsome, in my view. Often he acquired things that he changed his mind about. He could be a bit of a magpie – not discriminating enough. After a few days or weeks he'd pass them to me to sell in the shop. But he's had that box – oh, over a year. Perhaps he'd forgotten about it.'

Slider pondered. Five thousand was a good enough incentive for some people, but hardly enough to warrant stealing-to-order. It might have been opportunism: it was there to hand and could be slipped into a pocket. But there were other

pocketable things in the room. Why that? Did it mean something, or nothing? 'Did he keep something in it, perhaps?' he
asked.

'I've no idea. I never looked.'

'And you said you didn't notice that anything else was
missing from the house.'

He looked wary, perhaps sensing a trap. 'Well, I wasn't
really looking, of course. And I only went into the drawing
room.'

'Quite so. Are there valuable things in the other rooms?'

'Some paintings in the dining room, some silver and
ceramics. None of it particularly valuable. The nice stuff was
all in the drawing room.'

'There was a painting, I believe, by someone called
Maurice O.'

Lavender looked stonily blank.

'A painting of a girl doing her hair.'

His eyes remained stationary for a moment longer, then he
raised his eyebrows and said, 'Oh, the Morisot.' He pronounced
it very French, with a good glottal roll of the 'r'. 'Berthe
Morisot. *La Fille au Toilette* – the girl at her toilette,' he
translated kindly. 'What about it?'

'It's missing,' Slider said.

He frowned. 'Are you sure?'

'Yes, quite sure. Was it valuable?'

'Oh,' he said. 'Well.' He paused. 'It was quite an early one.
Not terribly accomplished. Not really an important painting.
Morisot was in any case only in the second rank of Impressionists. Women painters never really achieve the prominence
of their male colleagues.'

'What would it be worth, in your estimation?'

'It's hard to say. At auction, on a good day, perhaps ten to
fifteen thousand.'

'Worth stealing, then.'

Lavender made no response. His carved face gave nothing
away.

'Is it possible Mr Egerton sold it himself?'

Lavender shook his head slowly. 'I doubt it. Not without
telling me. In fact, if he'd wanted to sell it, I would have

handled the sale.' He searched Slider's face. 'It must have been stolen by whoever killed him.'

The painting, on the other hand, Slider thought, couldn't have been slipped into a pocket. Was it possible the intruder was stealing it to order, and killed Egerton when he got in the way, pocketing the box on impulse? But unless he had acquired a key, Egerton would have had to have let him in. And would anyone steal a fifteen-thousand-pound painting to order? Hardly worth getting out of bed for.

Lavender seemed to have been waiting for an answer to his last comment. Now he asked, rather as if it was being forced out of him, 'How do you know the painting is missing, anyway?'

'Mrs Bean heard about the death on the news and came to see if she could help. We had her look round the room, and she spotted it at once.'

He looked uncomfortable. 'Mrs Bean!' he muttered.

'Do you trust her?' Slider asked.

'Oh – she's been with us for years. And there's never been any trouble.'

'But?'

He shrugged it away. 'She can be a bit nosy, that's all. I'm sure she's honest – I mean, she wouldn't steal things.'

'What might she do, then?'

A pause. 'Well, she was the only other person with a key. And one doesn't know who her friends are.' He seemed to think better of it. 'But I don't know anything against her character,' he said briskly. 'Forget what I said, please. I'm sure Mrs Bean is a hundred per cent trustworthy. I don't mean to suggest there's anything wrong about her.'

Which, thought Slider, meeting Atherton's eye, was exactly what he *had* done.

THREE
Men Behaving Baldly

Hollis came to Slider as he entered and said, 'Bob Bailey rang, guv. There's no green and gold box or painting like you described in any of the other rooms. Also, deceased's wallet is in his bedside drawer, with cash and credit cards in it.'

That accorded with the watch and ring not being taken – it was not a simple burglary.

'And the old lady, Mrs Bean, says there's nothing else missing as far as she can tell.'

'Well, that's a start,' said Slider. 'But we'll have to check everything against the computer record anyway. That's a nice job for someone.'

Hollis nodded. 'Swilley's bringing the computer in when she's done there,' he said. It was standard practice these days.

'Anything on the next of kin?' Slider asked.

'The Henley police have been on,' Hollis said. 'They went round the Sholtos' house but there was no-one in. A neighbour reckoned they were away on holiday. She didn't know where, but she thinks they're coming back tomorrow or Saturday.'

'Right. Ask them to let us know as soon as they're back,' Slider said. He looked round. 'What's going on over there?'

Mackay was at the site overseeing the canvass, and Swilley was going through Egerton's office, but the rest were grouped round Connolly's desk, watching her monitor. She looked up and said, 'I pulled up one of your man's old shows. It's a total gas.'

He went over and joined them. He recognized the look of *Antiques Galore!* though he had never consciously watched it. But it was one of those Sunday afternoon shows you had always known about, and passed through when channel-hopping for something to beguile the long dark teatime of the soul. The format was familiar from numerous forerunners and comedy skits: members of the public bringing their antiques or other treasures for experts to identify and value.

Any amusement the show offered came from the potato-faced couple being told the vase they'd bought for a pound at a jumble sale and used as a door stop was a rare piece of Ming worth fifty thousand pounds. Occasionally, there was a *Schadenfreude* bit where some eager smart-arse was told his Sheraton side-table was a repro from Heal's. Otherwise the show proceeded at a gentlemanly, not to say soporific, adagio, with the public-treasures-experts theme interspersed by a bit of history of the venue and the area, presented by a wafer-thin ex-newsreader in dangly earrings.

Connolly said, 'Wait'll I run it on a bit till your man comes on.'

And there he was, Rowland Egerton, still alive; exquisite in a pale grey suit, with a yellow tie with cranberry spots and a crimson-streaked yellow carnation in his buttonhole. His lean, handsome, lightly tanned face looked the epitome of the aristocrat, his silver hair was swept back in a leonine mane that gave him a look of thrilling power, and his hands, when the camera panned in to see him handling the treasures, were elegant, long-fingered, and beautifully manicured. Slider recognized the gold and emerald ring. He didn't approve of men wearing jewellery, but he had to admit the hand was worthy of decoration, and the ring looked venerable and innocent of bling.

The hands were examining a miniature, lifting it from the green baize that covered the table and tilting it expertly for the camera. And the voice making the commentary was a pleasing tenor, musical but manly, the accent cultured, the tone firm with expert assurance, yet hinting at a warm friendliness that transcended class. Slider noted that he talked to the owners with no hint of *de haut en bas*, his manner suggesting they knew all this as well as he did and that he was only repeating it for the sake of the viewers at home. And when the camera showed their faces, it was clear they were entranced by him, smiling and flattered by his attention, pleased with themselves as partners in this benign conspiracy.

'He's good,' Slider commented.

'It's queer seeing him there in the whole of his health,' Connolly said, 'when you've only seen him dead.' She came originally from Contarf, and ten years of living in London had barely touched her Dublin accent. 'You can see now he was attractive. Fierce posh, but still a bit of a Bob. And look at all them eejits in the background. He's not even talking to them, and they've grins on them like Labradors at the dinner table!'

Slider was amused – the smiles of the onlookers had just that wholesome, ingratiating quality. 'He seems to have a big following,' he said.

'He's got brains, too,' said McLaren, his voice clotted with chocolate. He was eating a Crunchie bar, and he liked to suck the chocolate off first before biting down with a sound like splintering teeth. 'He did that "Royal Palaces" programme. Blimey, the things he knew! Not just about the pictures and the furniture, but all the history, going right back.'

'Have you had the results back on that dog that bit you?' Connolly enquired witheringly. 'It was a script, you plank! Did you really think your man knew all that stuff himself?'

McLaren swallowed a lump whole. 'Why not?' he defended himself, irritated. 'You don't know he didn't.'

Connolly addressed herself to Slider. 'I've looked him up on Wiki,' she said, clicking away and bringing up the page. 'Seems he's written books, as well. There's a kind of art-for-idiots yoke, one about how to go collecting antiques, and one about the Pre-Raphaelites. That one might be serious – the others are coffee-table books.' She looked up. 'Kind o' thing you buy someone for Christmas when you don't like 'em much but want to impress 'em.'

'I get the picture,' Slider said.

'But there's virtually nothing about his personal history,' she said. 'That's quite unusual. He must have been careful all his life, because once something's out there, it's out there, and the Wiki compilers'll pick it up.'

Slider's phone rang at that moment, and he went through to his office to answer it.

It was Freddie Cameron. 'Thought you'd like to know as soon as possible,' he said. 'It looks as though the paperknife *was* the weapon. The dimensions match the wound, and we recovered traces of blood and tissue from it. I'll send them off to the lab to compare with the victim's, but I think you can take it as read.'

'Thanks, Freddie. Anything else?'

'I haven't done the post-mortem yet. I just thought you'd like to be reassured about the weapon. I'll do the full PM tomorrow, but from superficial examination there's nothing to add. No other wounds, no sign of drug use. He was pretty fit for his age. And exquisitely clean. For which mercy, much thanks.'

'Right. Thanks, Freddie.'

Slider went back through, to see Swilley arriving carrying a box of papers brought from the house, followed by a uniform with his arms full of computer.

'There doesn't seem to be anything out of the ordinary,' she said, seeing Slider's look of query, 'but I've brought some stuff so I can go through his finances and his correspondence. There's another box coming – fan mail. Might be something interesting there.'

Connolly looked excited. 'I was thinking the same thing,' she exclaimed. 'With him being so famous, what's the bet it was one of the window-lickers whacked him?'

'Why would any of his fans kill him?' Gascoyne objected.

'Have you never heard of stalkers?' Swilley said.

'Sure, they're all mad as cats in a blender,' said Connolly. 'They start feeling he knows them like they know him. Suppose some header found out where he lived, talked their way in, declared true love, and, when he wouldn't shimmy, lost it?'

'Anything's possible,' Slider said, 'but his partner says he would never let a stranger in.'

'Sayin' it doesn't make it true. And wouldn't it make sense of the green box going missing? Grabbed for a souvenir before doing a legger.'

'But that doesn't explain the painting being missing as well.'

'It was Lavender, for my money,' McLaren said. 'Never mind all this toss about fans.'

'Toss, you call it?' Connolly said dangerously.

'Toss,' he repeated defiantly. He was much more confident

with his female colleagues since he'd started going out with Natalie. 'Lavender's got a key, we know he was there at the right time, he found the body, and it's always the nearest and dearest that done it.'

On cue, Atherton walked in. 'All done,' he said. 'Prints, swab and statement. And his clothes are packed up and sent off. Uniform's taking him home in a car – unless you want him for anything else?'

'Not at the moment,' Slider said.

'Anything new?' Atherton asked.

Slider told him about the paperknife.

'I wonder why chummy didn't take it away with him.'

'Maybe he wanted to make everything look normal,' said Swilley.

'Normal – with a dead body on the floor?' Connolly said.

'You know what I mean.'

'It's not that big. You could just about put it in your pocket and walk out,' said Gascoyne.

'What if he didn't walk out?' said McLaren. 'If it was Lavender, he can't put it in his pocket. Can't leave it where it is – got his fingermarks on it. Can't hide it anywhere – even more suspicious when it gets found. What's he going to do? Wipe it and put it back.'

Swilley looked at him. 'Maurice, take it easy. You know talking sensible gives you a headache.'

'Putting it back on the table and thinking we'll never examine it – that's just stupid,' said Connolly.

'He'd wiped it clean – so he thought,' Atherton said. 'If he'd put a few new fingermarks back on it the ruse might even have worked. But you can't expect them to think of everything.'

'I think putting it back makes it look more like Lavender,' Swilley said. 'Sort of instinctive, when it's your own home. An intruder wouldn't care.'

'And Mrs Bean did say he was fussy,' Connolly admitted.

'But Lavender doesn't explain the missing objects,' said Atherton. 'The painting and the Fabergé box. It's *got* to be a burglary.'

'But there was no break-in,' Swilley pointed out.

'Well,' said Atherton, 'there's always Mrs Bean. Even if she's honest, you don't know who else she knows. Anyone who knew where she worked might take her key and get it copied.'

Slider nodded. 'We'll have to look into her, of course. Check her background. And find out where she kept the key and who knew where it was. I don't think she would steal anything herself, after all this time, but she may have a son or neighbour who's suddenly fallen on hard times. And yet,' he pondered, 'how would someone like that know what to take? And why those things? It still doesn't make sense.'

'Lavender knows what everything is and what it's worth,' McLaren pointed out.

'He didn't have to kill your man to steal those things,' Connolly objected. 'He could have taken them any time. And why would he want to? They're there for him to enjoy anyway.'

'I must say, I hope it wasn't him,' said Atherton. 'I rather like the old duck. So old-school, and Egerton was such a mayfly. Talk about the odd couple. Eternally playing Watson to Egerton's Holmes would try the patience of a saint.'

'Let's not get too far ahead of ourselves,' Slider said. 'If someone came out of the house, with a bit of luck someone passing will have seen them. Let's see what the canvass brings up.'

'What now, boss?' Swilley asked.

'There's plenty to do. We'll have to check the house contents against the computer file, see if anything else is missing. Get an independent valuation of the box and the painting. Find out if anyone's trying to sell them. Look into their finances. Find who their friends were.' He sighed. With no obvious leads, there was nothing to guide the investigation one way or another. They were all looking at him. He glanced at the clock – it was late. 'Finish your reports and go home,' he said. 'Nothing more we can do tonight. Tomorrow there'll be plenty for everyone.

'Let's hope to God there are some eye witnesses,' he added to Atherton, who followed him to his room.

'Or some good spatter on Lavender's clothing. It would make it all so much easier if it *were* him. Are you going home?'

'Just some things to finish up. Half an hour,' said Slider, sitting behind his desk. He looked up. 'Want to come and have supper with us?'

Atherton hesitated.

'It'd do Joanna good to have company.'

'Are you sure?'

'Not seeing people can get to be a bad habit.'

'All right, then. Thanks.'

She met them in the hall. 'Nice to see you, Jim,' she said, lifting her face for his kiss. He thought, with a pang, it looked thinner, and there were shadows under the eyes. 'What would you say to a drink before supper?'

'I'd say, "Don't get too comfortable in that glass."'

She smiled. 'Gin and tonic?'

'I'll get it,' said Slider.

'Make yourself at home,' said Joanna to Atherton. 'I've just got to check how we're doing.'

But he followed her into the kitchen, where she pulled a big dish out of the oven. He recognized one of her staples – chicken pieces cooked over rice, with onions, peppers, olives and chunks of lemon. All those good juices soaked into the rice. It was simple but tasty. His stomach gurgled like a retort in a mad scientist movie. 'That smells good,' he said.

She tested the chicken with a skewer and put the dish back in. 'Half an hour,' she said.

He blocked her way as she turned and said, 'How are you?'

'I'm OK,' she said neutrally.

'Really? You look like hell.'

'Thanks.' She shrugged. 'I don't say it wasn't upsetting, but these things happen. I wasn't the first and I won't be the last. You have to get over it and get on with your life, don't you?' He looked at her steadily, but she didn't shift. He could see how such stoicism could be hard for a fond husband to cope with. As if she read his thought she went on, 'I'm worried about Bill. He seems really down.'

'He's worried about you.'

'I know. But he seems stuck in phase one.' She met his eyes. 'Is it the Job?'

Atherton shrugged. 'It's always the Job. None of us is really normal.'

She changed the subject. 'Heard anything from Emily?' she asked, too casually.

He moved to let her pass. 'Not since the Christmas card. I didn't expect to. It was all over between us, you know.' Emily had found out about one of his extra-curricular activities, and after a flaming row followed by a period of chilly anatomizing, they had split up. She had taken a post in New York – supposed to be for two years, but he didn't expect her to come back.

'It's a shame,' she said.

'I'm not the settling-down kind,' he said.

'You just haven't met the right person,' she said.

'Oh, I've met her,' he said lightly. 'But she wanted someone else.'

She looked at him sharply for a moment, but did not follow it up. 'Just time for that drink,' she said and led the way out.

Over drinks and over supper, they told her about the case. She knew who Egerton was, of course.

'I'm sorry it was him,' she said. 'I always rather liked him. I thought he had a nice manner – friendly enough but not too friendly. You want your expert to seem a bit above you, or why should you take their word? But not so much as to make you feel foolish. Was it his nearest and dearest did it?'

'Too early to tell,' said Slider. 'There are so many possibilities. Theft, lover's quarrel, blackmail, business rivalry. Even Connolly's idea of a mad fan.'

'And the old *cui bono* – the Will,' said Atherton.

'And jealousy,' Joanna suggested. 'Show-business is riddled with it. On a show like that, with all those experts competing for airtime and prominence . . . You only have to look at the quarrels and side and bitcheries in orchestra life – and we don't even have much contact with the public. Our faces aren't known. But this chap Egerton – he'd done pretty well out of it, hadn't he? Not just *Antiques Galore*—'

Atherton interrupted. 'No, you mean *Antiques Galore!* You missed out the exclamation mark.'

He was rewarded with a small smile. 'Silly title, anyway. But he's on that other antiques programme—'

'*Going, Going, Gone,*' Atherton supplied.

'And he seems to pop up all over the place, commenting on things, giving his opinion. He's practically the Beeb's resident expert. What do they call it? The "go-to man". The David Attenborough of antiques. Don't tell me all that didn't make someone jealous.'

'You could well be right,' Slider said. 'That's one of the things to do – find out about the show.'

'But it's most likely to be his friend, Mr Lavender – isn't it?' Joanna said, coming full circle. 'Just the fact that he put the murder weapon back. An intruder would have taken it away, wouldn't he?'

'That's what McLaren said,' Atherton remarked.

Joanna put her hands to her head in mock horror. 'Oh my God! I've agreed with McLaren! I've got "baby brain"! If I don't get back to work soon I'll be a drooling idiot.'

'There's no hurry,' Slider said. 'Take your time. Don't try to go back before you're ready.'

As soon as he said it he wished he hadn't. He saw the minute glance between Joanna and Atherton and felt annoyed – with himself for having betrayed his anxiety, and with them for colluding against him.

But Joanna said only, 'Can't work until I get offers, and I haven't had any so far. Anyone like any more of this? I haven't got any pudding, I'm afraid, except fruit.'

The wind had dropped by the next morning, and the world was locked in a bright, bitter stillness. Despite the wind dropping, it was even colder. There was a film of ice on the inside of the bedroom window where their breath had condensed and then frozen.

Joanna got up with him and cooked him bacon and eggs.

'What's the occasion?' he asked.

'You need a proper breakfast before you go out in this cold,' she said. 'You don't eat enough. I bet you missed meals yesterday.'

'I'm all right,' he said. 'You don't need to worry about me.'

She put the plate in front of him, then sat down between him and George and helped their son with his boiled egg and soldiers. He looked sleepy, but rosy – cold never seemed to bother him.

'Aren't you having anything?' Slider demanded.

'I'll have mine later, when I've got you two sorted out,' she said. He wanted to argue, but remembered The Look last night and held his tongue. Going off to work was almost a relief. At least the extreme emotions bound up in a murder weren't his emotions.

'I've had Mr Wetherspoon on this morning,' said Porson, surging restlessly back and forth between his desk and the window like a trapped tide. Wetherspoon was their boss, the Borough Commander. 'Celebrity murders. I hate 'em!' he complained. 'What's the partner like? Another Publicity Percy? Used to having everyone fawnicating over him?'

'I don't think so, sir. He's not a celebrity himself – seems quiet and retiring enough.'

'Thank God for small murphles. Bad enough with everyone else on our backs without him chasing us for answers day and night. What lines are you following?'

'I've got Swilley on the money. We've printed out the computer list, and McLaren and Mackay are going to check it against the stuff in the house, make sure nothing else is missing.'

'You've put out an enquiry about the painting and the box?'

'We're doing that, sir. All the usual dealers and galleries, plus my own sources. We're going to look into the antiques business and the shop, see what the financial state was, whether there was anything dodgy going on. And I'm going to talk to the television people, find out about the show and who else was on it and what his relations were with them.'

'I suppose that about covers it for now,' Porson said grudgingly. 'Nothing from the canvass?'

'Not yet, sir. But it's early days.'

'Early days it may be,' Porson barked, 'but that's all you get on a celebrity case. Procrastination is the thief of crime.'

'Yes, sir,' Slider said, the meek ass between two burdens.

Porson softened. 'There's a lot to do. You can have all the uniform you want to help you out.'

'Thank you, sir,' Slider said. Uniform was all right for the door-to-door stuff, but it didn't replace trained troops. Still, Porson knew that as well as he did, so there was no point in saying it and risking another mangled aphorism. Fair words never buttered fat parsnip.

The production company, First Forward Television, had its office in Soho Square, and Gavin Ehlie was there and only too eager to be interviewed. He was a good-looking man with an enviable head of hair, sculpted by the same firm that designed the Sydney Opera House, a seamless tan and rather disconcerting frameless glasses. He wore a white shirt open at the neck, a black waistcoat, skintight black leather trousers and state-of the-art trainers. Slider guessed his age at mid-forties, about a decade up on his clothes, hairstyle and manner. Probably, in television, he thought, you had to stay young or be overtaken on the inside.

The office was large and dazzlingly modern. The walls and carpet were black, but the wall between it and the outer office was made of glass bricks, and there was a vast window, so it still managed to seem light and bright. There was a desk big enough to sleep on, a cream suede sofa and two chairs grouped around a coffee table that seemed to be a single enormous slab of glass, and an entire wall covered with television screens and electronic equipment. There were framed pictures of celeb-rities everywhere, and a huge open bookcase all made of glass, given over to the display of awards. It was positioned so that when Slider sat on the sofa, to which he was directed, he found himself staring straight at them. He wondered briefly whether it was accidental.

'Can I get you something to drink?' Ehlie asked. 'Coffee? Tea? Mineral water?'

Slider didn't want anything, but he calculated Ehlie would talk better with the props of a social beverage, so he said, 'Coffee, thank you.'

Ehlie put his head out of the door to order coffee, came back and perched on one of the chairs opposite Slider, well forward, his hands clasped between his knees. All his move-ments were swift and energetic, his expression eager and enquiring. He looked as though his brain was so seething with ideas that he could hardly sit still. Television is a fickle mistress, Slider thought. The idea of having to keep up this level of youthfulness into your forties made him feel tired.

'This is so terrible,' Ehlie said. 'Poor Rowland! I can't believe it. And so soon after we lost Bunny – I'm starting to wonder if there's a jinx on us.'

'Bunny?' Slider queried.

'Julia Rabbet – everyone called her Bunny, of course,' he said, and then looked puzzled that Slider was not immediately enlightened. 'Don't you watch *Antiques Galore*?' Unlike Atherton, he said it without the exclamation mark.

'I don't get to see much television,' Slider said, though on reflection that was not the most tactful thing to say to a man in Ehlie's position.

'She was one of our resident experts. Jewellery and miscellaneous. Wonderful woman – very knowledgeable and a real trooper. Everyone adored her. She died about a month ago.'

'Oh?' Slider raised an eyebrow.

Ehlie caught on. 'Natural causes. She had a brain haemorrhage, poor darling. Lay in a coma for eight days and then . . .' He shrugged rather than say it. 'An awful loss to the show. And now Rowland too! And we're right in the middle of recording the next season. Fortunately, a couple of our old stalwarts have agreed to come back for the rest of the run, bless them, but it's devastating all the same.'

'You've already replaced Mr Egerton?'

Ehlie looked offended. 'I had to get straight on it. I have to have someone by Tuesday afternoon at the latest. These things run to a format and we couldn't possibly manage with a man short.'

The door opened and a smart, mini-skirted young woman came in with a tray. She placed mugs of coffee along with milk and sugar and a plate of biscuits on the table and retreated again. 'Thank you, Tara!' Ehlie called after her belatedly. 'Please, help yourself.' He took one of the mugs and sipped. 'Well,' he said, 'I'm sure you're a busy man too. What did you want to know?'

'You had a meeting with Mr Egerton on Monday, I believe.'

'Oh. Yes,' Ehlie said with the hint of a sigh. 'I took him to lunch. They all need their egos rubbed from time to time, bless them, and I'm afraid Rowland was one of the needier ones.'

'So this was a regular event?'

'Not exactly regular. Lunch a couple of times a year, coffee meetings in between. When I signed him up for another series, or if he had something particular on his mind.'

'What did he have on his mind on Monday?'

'He wasn't keen on Bunny's replacement. That's old Arnold Needham. He said that for jewellery I ought to have got another female. He thought Arnold was too old and not glamorous enough. He had a point, in a way, but . . .'

'You didn't like being told how to do your job,' Slider suggested.

'Believe me, you get used to it,' said Ehlie sourly, letting the youthfulness drop for a moment. 'That's the problem with dealing with people who know all about their own subject. They think they know all about everyone else's too. And they're such prima donnas – give them a spot of exposure on television and suddenly it goes to their heads. Well, most of them, anyway – not dear old Arnold, which is why he's going to be such a relief to work with.'

'Was Rowland Egerton a prima donna?'

'He's trouble. But he's so popular with the viewers and the punters, he's worth the trouble – he *was*, I mean. Although I don't know how long that would have gone on being true. One loses patience in the end.'

'In what way was he trouble?'

'Being demanding, you know. Everything had to be done just so, and done his way. Had to have the best pitch, the most camera time; had the production assistants running around doing errands. As far as he was concerned, he was the star of the show, and no-one else mattered.'

'I expect that got on people's nerves. The other experts . . .'

'Oh, well, they got used to him grabbing the limelight – they'd do the same themselves. And he was very charming, you know – always managed to smooth down the feathers after he'd ruffled them.'

'Ruffled them how?'

'Like I said, grabbing the limelight. Specifically? Well, snagging things on the trawl before anyone else could get them.'

'What's the trawl?'

'On recording day,' Ehlie explained, 'the punters start lining up early with their bits and bobs, and the experts trawl them to see what they've got and pick out the stuff that's especially interesting. Sometimes a real treasure comes up, something rare or quirky or valuable. All the experts want something like that to show in the recording.'

'I see.'

'They all do it, but there are unwritten rules about it. If you come up with something that's definitely someone else's speciality, you're supposed to let them have it. I mean, if you're ceramics and there's an exciting oil painting, you're supposed to let the oils man have first dibs. Obviously, there are things that don't fall into any particular category, and they can all do "miscellaneous" items, but it causes bad feeling when it's a case of blatant poaching.'

'And Rowland was a poacher, was he?'

'Well,' said Ehlie reluctantly, 'I don't want to speak ill of the dead. Let's just say there have been times when he's been less than scrupulous, and there's been a bit of ill-feeling. But, as I say, he's very good at smoothing people down.' He hesitated, and Slider read more information that he was unsure about sharing.

'Was there an incident recently?' he asked.

Ehlie met his eyes and sighed again. 'That was the other thing he wanted to talk to me about on Monday. There was a row between him and Rupert Melling at the previous recording – the one two weeks ago. Rupert is miscellaneous, but he has a particular passion for snuffboxes, and everyone knows it. Well, someone showed up with a very rare old snuffbox, and Rowland nabbed it. Rupert made a big fuss and demanded he let him have it, but Rowland refused. He said the panels were painted by some famous miniaturist, and paintings are his speciality. Rupert was particularly pissed off because he'd sent a nice oil Rowland's way in the previous show.'

'How serious was it, this quarrel?'

'It was nasty at the time,' Ehlie said. 'I had to go over and shut them up, because they were making such a row, some of the punters were starting to notice. I mean, you can't have the experts throwing insults at each other. Word would soon get around. We like to project a nice, friendly atmosphere, everybody getting on together and respecting each other. It's a family show, you know.'

'What sort of insults?'

'He called Rowland a thief and a fraud, among other things. He accused him of sending John round behind everyone's backs to get the juiciest items for him. Then said a few unpleasant things about their relationship, too, at which point Rowland really lost it. He couldn't bear anyone suggesting he and John were that way involved.'

'And were they?'

Ehlie looked at him. 'He's always said they were just friends and business partners, and I've no reason to think otherwise. I mean, nobody cares these days, anyway, nobody would have thought anything if they were. But I suppose Rowland comes from a different generation. Anyway, it was always something that got him riled – and Rupert knew that, which was why he said it, to get under his skin. Rupert's openly gay, and thinks everyone else should be as well. Out and proud – you know the sort of thing.'

'So this bad blood between Rupert and Rowland – how long has that been going on?'

Ehlie drew back a little, belatedly cautious. 'Oh, I wouldn't put it as strongly as that. They had a bit of a row, but it was soon forgotten. Everyone gets a bit worked up ahead of the recording – they're like actors, you see. Stage nerves. But it doesn't mean anything. We go out for a meal afterwards to wind down, and everyone's friends again.'

'How were things at the recording this week?' Slider asked. 'Any tensions?'

'No, not really, not that I noticed,' Ehlie said.

Slider read his face. 'No tensions between Rowland and Rupert Melling?'

'Oh – well – there was a bit of teasing, I suppose, but it didn't mean anything. Just friendly joshing, you know the sort of thing.'

'About?'

Ehlie squirmed, not wanting to say. But in the face of Slider's steady silence he had to give. 'Well, Rowland and John got invited to dinner by the owners of Wykeham Hall, and Rupert made a bit of a joke about it. He suggested they were trying to rook a poor old couple out of their treasures. Of course, he didn't mean it,' he added hastily. 'It was just a joke. As a matter of fact, John got more upset than Rowland.'

'What do you think of John?'

Ehlie shrugged. 'Not much *to* think. He's Rowland's right hand. Protects him like a bodyguard.'

'Protects him from whom?'

'Oh, everyone. If he thinks Rowland's not getting his rightful dues, or someone criticizes him, or the fans don't treat him with enough respect . . . Loyal, dogged, and a bit dull. He never says much in company, so I can't say I know him very well. He's just – an extension of Rowland, that's all. One hardly notices him as an individual.'

Walking away afterwards, Slider wondered whether John Lavender knew that was how he was regarded – a pseudo-podium of the star. Outclassed and outshone. Some people were simply proud to be useful to the person they admired; others might harbour a slow-growing tumour of grudge. He supposed it would depend on how the star treated the tentacle.

And it must be hard for a man with hair like Lavender's not to feel jealous of a man with hair like Egerton's.

FOUR

Escape from Alky Trash

Like the majority of the population, Mrs Bean didn't appear in records at all, nor did any Bean with the same address. Armed with this assurance, Connolly went round to her home, a ground-floor maisonette in Dunraven Road. The house, part of a two-storeyed terrace, was tiny, designed in Edwardian times for a smaller race of people. It was neat and perfect outside, red-brick with white trim and a minuscule front garden, with the original tiled front path and front door with stained glass panels. Connolly reflected, somewhat glumly, that this two-bedroom doll's house, built in 1910 to be rented to a railway clerk or a shop assistant, would probably fetch half a mill in today's bloated London market.

Mrs Bean opened the door, looking bright-eyed and bushy-tailed. Connolly held up her warrant card. 'Detective Constable Connolly,' she said.

'I remember you, dear,' said Mrs Bean. 'I thought you was the press. I've had one of them on the phone this morning already.'

'I'm afraid you may get more of that.'

'My back's broad. I didn't tell 'em nothing. Come in, dear. You look too young to be a policeman.'

'I'm ageing as fast as I can,' Connolly said, following her in. The passage was so narrow that a fat person would have got wedged. It passed on the left a sitting room and a bedroom, both about ten by twelve; dog-legged round a tiny bathroom, passed an even smaller bedroom, and led into a kitchen which, while small, about twelve foot square, was at least bright, with a window at the end on to the garden and a glazed back door on the left. It was immaculate and smelled of lemon Flash, but the kitchen cabinets and the table and chairs looked as though they dated from the fifties. The mystery of how Mrs

Bean could afford a place like this was solved – the Beans had been here all along. Probably protected tenants.

'I've got the kettle on. Sit down dear,' Mrs Bean said.

Connolly sat at the table. She'd have been seriously in the way if she hadn't. Even the table was tiny, about three feet long and two feet wide, just big enough to accommodate the plates of four people, a cruet set and two sauce bottles. She felt quite at home. She'd had school friends in Dublin who'd invited her back to 'tea' in kitchens like this. There were even the same round raffia table mats.

'So,' said Mrs Bean, with her back to her at the stove, 'you've come to give me a going over?'

'Just routine. Ask you a few questions.'

'Oh, I know. I'm not daft, dear. You're bound to wonder. I was the only other one with a key.' The kettle began a mournful whistle and was cut off as Mrs Bean poured water into the teapot. She turned her head to smile at Connolly. 'Stands to reason, you got to suspect me.'

Connolly grinned. 'I don't really. What'd *you* kill him for?'

'You're right, love. I'd've done meself out of a job,' Mrs Bean said, the smile fading. 'I'm at a bit of a loss, if truth be told. This should have been one of my days. Don't know what to do with meself. Ken's gone down the old people's centre – he helps out there on my working days, so as not to be on his own here. I told him to go – can't let the old folk down.'

'He's retired?'

'Ten years ago, with his back. He was on the railway – track maintenance. Forty years. Our son, our Billy, he went on the railway too. Men and their trains!' She tossed her head in affectionate contempt, putting the teapot down on the table, and reaching for mugs from the dresser beside it. Distances were so small in this room that she could reach them without moving. She also reached down a large tin of mixed fancy biscuits, pulled off the lid and placed it on the table. 'Help yourself,' she said. 'I always get a tin at Christmas, lasts us for weeks.'

Connolly could see the chocolate ones were mostly gone. She selected a Highland shortcake and nibbled on it.

'So is it just the two of you here, now?'

'Oh yes. Billy's married, lives in Swindon, got two kids. Nice girl he married, Linda. Always keeps the children lovely. We only had the one, Ken and me.'

Probably for the best, Connolly thought. Where the hell would you put a second child? 'So, I have to ask you this,' she said. 'Where d'you keep the key to Mr Egerton's house?'

Silently, Mrs Bean half stood and pulled open a door in the top half of the dresser, exposing neatly stacked crockery. On the inside of the door were lines of hooks on which hung keys. She pointed to a bunch from which dangled a furry object like a shrunken rabbit's foot. 'That's them. Front door – Yale and deadlock – and them two are the doors in the kitchen on to the garden. I s'pose you'll be taking 'em away?' she concluded a little wistfully. Then she braced herself. 'Still, even if he'd gone natural, they'd've had to be given back.'

'So they're always kept here?' Connolly asked.

'Except when I'm using 'em.'

'And does anyone else know about them?'

She looked doubtful. 'Well, Ken, of course. And I s'pose friends who pop in probably know that's where we keep the keys, though they wouldn't know which was which. I mean, that bunch there is to Billy's house, and that's my friend Gwen down the road that I go and feed her cat when she's away, and that's the spare set to the church hall – Ken's a sidesman, he often opens up or closes up when they have a do. But none of 'em's labelled. Anyway,' she finished with a clear look, 'they've never gone missing, so if you're thinking someone might've nicked 'em to make a copy, you're far wrong.'

Connolly smiled. 'If you keep getting ahead of me like that, you'll do me out of a job.'

'Oh, I may be old, but I'm not daft,' Mrs Bean said, pleased. 'I know what's what all right. Anyway, nobody that comes to this house is the sort to do such a thing, even if they could have. And if I wanted to steal from Mr Egerton I could have done it years ago, without harming the poor soul. Have another biscuit. Is your tea all right for you? Drop more milk?'

'No, thanks, I like it strong. Tell me about Mr Egerton and Mr Lavender. What did you make of them?'

'Very nice gentlemen,' she said firmly. 'Lovely manners. Mr Egerton, he could speak sharp now and then, if something wasn't done just the way he liked, but my back's broad. Mr Lavender, he was the quiet one. More the brooding type. He'd store it up, like, and then, out it would all come, with him looking at you like you'd killed his rabbit. I'd sooner be told off by Mr Egerton any day, if truth be told.'

'What was their relationship like with each other?'

'They were friends ever since I knew them. Some people thought they were *more* than friends, if you get my drift.' She surveyed Connolly to see if she did. 'I suppose that was with Mr Lavender never being married. But I never thought they were, not for a minute. Not that I'd mind. I'm broad-minded,' she went on. 'People can do what they like, so long as they don't do it in *my* front room. But no, they were just friends. And of course they had the business between them.'

'Did they get on all right?'

'Oh, they had rows now and then, like anyone else. I'd hear them sometimes in another room – they'd never argue in front of me. But it was just disagreements. They were devoted to each other, really.'

'Disagreements about what?'

'I couldn't say, dear. Business, I expect.' She sipped her tea firmly to put an end to this line of questioning.

'Apart from Mr Lavender, did anyone else come to the house regularly?'

'Well, I'm not the one to ask that, dear. I was just the cleaner. I did see visitors coming and going, but I couldn't tell you who they were. And they liked to entertain at the weekends – dinner parties and such like. I'd hear them planning them, and talking about them afterwards. Quite sociable, I'd call them. More tea? Shall I top you up?'

'No, this is grand, thanks,' said Connolly. 'That little box, now, that you said was missing. The green Fabergé box – what can you tell me about that?'

'Well, he'd not had it that long. About a year or so? It was a present from somebody. He set a lot of store by it. I remember

Mr Lavender said once it didn't look right on that table and he wanted to move it, but Mr Egerton said, quite sharp, that's where it was to stay. Pride of place, you see.'

'Did he use those words? Pride of place.'

'Not as such, I don't think, but that was the upshot. It didn't look like much, to my mind, with those dingy white beads on the top, but it might have been worth a bit. Or it might just have been the sentimental value.'

'Do you know who gave it him?'

Shake of head.

'Can you make a guess at who it might be?'

'No, dear. No idea – except it wasn't Mr Lavender.'

Connolly thought for a moment. 'Was there anything in it?' she asked.

'In the box?' Mrs Bean temporized.

Connolly's heart lifted. The sidelong answer was always a giveaway. She kept her expression neutral. 'Didn't Mr Egerton keep something in it?'

Mrs Bean hesitated a revealing second, then said, 'He wouldn't tell me if he did.'

Connolly, very casually, looking into the middle distance, said, 'Maybe it came open by accident one time, when you were dusting.'

'I'm not one for snooping,' said Mrs Bean, offended.

'Of course you're not,' Connolly said. 'But you have to pick it up to dust it, don't you, and you couldn't help seeing there was something inside, if it did happen to come open.'

Mrs Bean seemed torn, eyeing Connolly as if it might be a trick question – but which way? 'Well,' she said at last, doubtfully, 'there might have been a bit of paper in it.'

'What sort of paper?'

'Just a folded up bit of paper. Like it might be a letter, or something.'

'Like a love letter? Or a business letter?'

She met Connolly's eyes now. 'I couldn't say, dear. I never took it out and opened it. I wouldn't snoop about his private things,' she said firmly. 'Just a folded piece of paper, that's all I know.'

Connolly saw she would not budge from that – and it might

have been the truth, after all. She said, 'Did Mr Egerton have any relatives, do you know?'

'None that I know of, bar his daughter.'

'Have you met her?'

'I only saw her the once, when she came to the house. That would be – oh, five years ago, easy. Maybe more. Big, tall woman. Very smartly dressed. Didn't look like him at all – I suppose she took after her mother. I don't think they were close. I never heard him mention her. Mind you, he wasn't much of a one for chatting, except about himself. He liked to tell me when he'd done something clever or he'd been somewhere important. He'd stand watching me while I dusted his little treasures and talk about things he'd bought and sold and the programmes he'd been on and important people he'd been to dinner with. I tuned out a lot of the time, if truth be told. When you've heard one of them stories, you've heard the lot.'

'Did he have lady friends?'

'That I couldn't tell you,' Mrs Bean said firmly. 'But I'd be surprised if he didn't.'

Fulham Road had its fair share of antique shops, and those down the Kensington end were in the posh range of the spectrum. Egerton Antiques had a very elegant fascia – dark blue with curly gold letters – and a window display of an artfully-lit Sheraton desk, dressed with a mahogany letter rack, a silver ink pot and a rather splendid alabaster bust of what Atherton took to be Julius Caesar. It was the sort of antiques shop where you had to ring the bell to be admitted, which of course always suggested to the potential customer that if they had to ask the price, they'd better not bother.

He was buzzed in, and was met by an elderly Dandie Dinmont which tracked across the carpet from the back of the shop to greet him. After the brightness of the day outside it took a moment for his eyes to adjust to the dimness within. On a moss-green carpet, covered in the centre by an ancient Persian rug, a few choice items of furniture were displayed, lit with soft spotlights. It left the rest of the room in a level of semi-gloom similar to candlelight; very good for displaying eighteenth-century wares that would have been seen that way in their own time, he thought. Around the walls, among tables and bookcases, were some glass-fronted cabinets with ceramics and other small objects displayed, and on the walls were paintings, oils and watercolours, mostly in their original elaborate gold frames. It was everything he would have expected from a high-end antiques shop – and that also went for the woman who now rose from behind a table at the back and came towards him with a, 'Can I help you?'

'Georgia Hedley-Somerton?' he enquired, though he had no doubt of it. If anyone ever looked like a Georgia Hedley-Somerton it was this tall, elegant blonde, apparently in her late but exquisitely-preserved thirties, in a beige skirt and caramel-and-white angora sweater, with a double string of pearls round her neck and neat pearl earrings. It hardly mattered, with everything else she had going for her, but she was also attractive, with a nice smile and welcoming grey-green eyes. Despite the friendly mien there was about her – not only in her height and cut-glass accent – a certain something of authority and firmness that hinted that you wouldn't come in here to waste her time; or, at least, that you wouldn't do it twice. Atherton was glad of his own height and (he'd always been assured) good looks. Better for police work not to start off intimidated.

'I'm Detective Sergeant Atherton,' he began.

She anticipated. 'Oh, dear, yes. What a terrible thing about poor Mr Egerton. I expect you want to talk to Mr Lavender.'

'Is he here?' Atherton asked.

'He's in the flat, upstairs. He hasn't come down yet. He rang me last night and told me about it, and said he might not come down at all this morning. But I can ring upstairs for you, if you want.'

'No, don't disturb him. I'd like to talk to you first.'

A faintly doubtful look came over her face, but after a consideration she squared her shoulders to do her duty and said, 'Please, won't you sit down?'

There was a chair on this side of the desk – for people to sit while they made out enormous cheques, Atherton thought – and he sat, while she went back to her side, and the Dandie flopped down in a basket by her side.

'Have you worked here long?' he asked.

'Ten years,' she said. 'I was with Sotheby's before that. I started in post-sales services and went on to valuations. It was interesting,' she said reflectively, and perhaps a little wistfully. 'But once I started a family I needed less pressure and more flexible hours. Mr Lavender's been wonderful that way. We work very well together.'

'I believe the business is owned by him *and* Mr Egerton, jointly?'

'Yes, it's a partnership.'

'Did you have much to do with Mr Egerton?'

She gave a small smile. 'Oh, he popped in and out quite frequently.'

'Did you like him?'

She hesitated.

Atherton spread his hands. 'You can be frank with me. I need to understand as much as possible about the protagonists. And nothing you say can hurt him now.'

She regarded him steadily, but seemed reassured – perhaps by his use of the word protagonists. Ah, the power of vocabulary! Was there a country in the world where you made more judgements about a person from the way they talked?

'Well, since you ask – no. I didn't like him very much. He was too – showy.'

'You must be an unusual person. I understood women generally fawned over him.'

'A certain sort of woman,' she said, a touch scornfully. 'He was very obvious, you know, bowing over them and kissing their hands and complimenting them.'

'Like an obsequious dog?' Atherton suggested.

She laughed, and stopped herself at once, giving him a stern look. 'That's not appropriate.'

'But still true?'

She didn't respond.

'Did he ever make a play for you?'

He had guessed right. She coloured a little, looking away. 'When I first came here. I rebuffed him, but—'

'He didn't *stay* rebuffed?'

'He was rather persistent.' She met his eyes. 'I told him I

was married and he – he said he preferred married women. I didn't like that,' she concluded.

'I expect he had a lot of lady friends.' She didn't respond, so he made it a question. 'Did you know about any of them?'

She chewed her lip a moment. 'I can't tell you anything for certain, but I was aware from time to time of certain undercurrents with certain customers, or wives of customers. I wouldn't be surprised if he had had affairs with some of them.'

'Most recently?'

'Oh, nothing recently. This was when I first came here, when he was equally engaged in this side of the business. Since he's been doing the television shows, he's gradually spent less time in the shop. He leaves it mostly to Mr Lavender, so of course he doesn't have much to do with the customers now.'

'I'd have thought his television fame would be good for business,' Atherton said.

'Not *our* sort of business,' she said, a touch loftily. 'We do get people coming to gawp, but they never buy anything – most of them couldn't afford it. They find out about the shop and come dawdling by, hoping to see Mr Egerton. That's why we had the buzzer put on the door – it deters some of the less determined. But Mr Lavender's afraid our real clients will be put off by the autograph-hunters. He's said several times that we ought to change the name of the shop to keep them away.'

'How did Mr Egerton respond to that?'

She turned her mouth down. 'He didn't like it. He refused to allow it. He put the capital in, you see, to set it up. It was a bone of contention between them.'

'How long has this been going on?'

'He's been doing *Antiques Galore!* for about seven years now, but it took a while for his celebrity to build up. I'd say it's only in the last three or four that he's been really famous, and we've had the fan-trouble.'

'And *has* it affected business?'

She hesitated.

'We will have to examine the books at some point,' he went on, 'so you won't be giving away any secrets.'

'Why would you have to do that?'

'It's routine, to look into the financial background of a murder victim. I'm afraid very often money is the motive behind it.'

She looked troubled. 'You *surely* can't be suspecting Mr Lavender of anything? He's the kindest, gentlest man!' The Dandie caught something in her voice and looked up at her. 'And theirs has been such a strong, successful partnership. It wouldn't have lasted all these years unless they were really fond of each other, would it? You really *mustn't* think Mr Lavender could ever in the world have done anything to harm him.'

'We don't think anything at the moment,' he said reassuringly. 'We're just at the stage of collecting information. How did the partnership work, between them?'

'They balance each other,' she said, then paused, thinking it out. 'Mr Lavender is a real expert, with huge experience and knowledge about the business and about artefacts of all kinds. I've never known him to be stumped. But he's not very good with people. He's rather awkward, and comes across as cold and unfriendly. Before the television thing, Mr Egerton dealt with the customers, charmed them, made them feel comfortable. He was always the one who closed the deals. But he didn't have Mr Lavender's eye, or his depth of expertise.' She tried a small smile. 'Mr Egerton's made some mistakes over the years, sometimes rather comical ones. It was a joke between them that he shouldn't be allowed to go to a sale on his own, because he was too impulsive, too likely to bring back something gaudy but worthless. Mr Lavender generally did the buying, and Mr Egerton the selling.'

'It sounds as if that worked very well.'

She shrugged agreement.

'And now?'

'Now what?'

'If Mr Egerton's not around so much to do the selling, is the business suffering?'

'The antiques business is bad anyway,' she said, 'because of the recession. Everyone's suffering. But Mr Egerton's not always busy with TV. We do a bit at fairs, but most of our sales come from bespoke – hunting down specific items that our wealthier clients want. Mr Lavender does that. And we're having to do more restoration work as well, to stay afloat.'

'Mr Lavender does restoration?'

'No,' she said impatiently, 'we send things off to different expert restorers. We're the middlemen.'

'I see. So the shop is more of a front than anything.'

'Well, there's very little passing trade any more,' she admitted, reluctantly. 'But one has to have a showcase, and somewhere to meet the clients.'

'So how bad is the business?' Atherton pressed her.

She looked away, then back. 'We're ticking over.' Then in a burst of frankness, 'I don't know how Mr Egerton's death will affect us. The notoriety might bring in more trade, but whether it will be the right sort . . . I'm afraid the shop may have to shut, and then I don't know what will happen to my job.'

'You could go back to Sotheby's, perhaps.'

She braced up. 'I can always find something, I assure you. But I've been happy here. And Mr Lavender will be lost, with no shop and no Mr Egerton.'

He let her mourn for a beat, then said, 'Tell me about yesterday. What time did you get here?'

'About half past nine. I didn't check the clock, but that was my time and I'm not usually late. The shop opens at ten.'

'And where was Mr Lavender?'

'He came down just as I got in. That's what usually happened.'

'What then?'

'We got on with our usual routines. He opened the post in the back office.' She gestured through the door behind her. 'I did some dusting. We discussed rearranging some of the items. Had a chat about sales coming up. It was just a normal day.'

'Was Mr Lavender there all morning?'

'Yes. He was in the office some of the time, doing paper-work, and he went upstairs a few times and came back down. He usually pottered around like that when he was here.'

'And when did he go out?'

'When I got back from lunch at one o'clock. He said he was going shopping and then to Mr Egerton's house.' Her lips trembled and her voice faltered. Atherton encouraged her with a look. 'I can't help thinking what a terrible shock it must have been for him, finding Mr Egerton dead like that. He didn't say much about it last night, but I could hear from his voice he was terribly shocked and upset.'

'I'm sure he was,' said Atherton.

'It was a burglary, wasn't it?' she asked. 'Was there much taken?'

Atherton avoided a direct answer and asked her about the malachite box.

She looked blank. 'I don't think I've ever seen it. It certainly didn't pass through this shop.'

The Morisot drew a better response. 'Oh, yes, I know about that. Mr Lavender found it at a country house sale. Nobody else knew what it was, and he got it for a song. He was very pleased with himself. He had it cleaned and gave it to Mr Egerton as a birthday present.'

'Is it very valuable?'

She frowned. 'It's hard to say,' she said. 'Morisot isn't very well known and not the most collectible, but it's a pretty subject, and the Impressionists are very popular at the moment. And of course as the prices of the better-known artists go beyond reach, the second rank become more desirable. I'd say you might realize a hundred thousand for it at auction, on a good day. Why are you asking about it? Is it something to do with Mr Egerton's death?'

'I can't say at the moment,' said Atherton.

'And this malachite box?'

'I'm afraid I can't tell you any more. Do you know who Mr Egerton's next of kin is?' he asked, to distract her.

She frowned. 'I'm afraid not. I think he had a daughter – he was married once. Would it be her? Mr Lavender would know more than I do about that. Would you like me to call him?'

'No, don't trouble him at present. We'll catch up with him later. I'm sure he needs his sleep after such a shock.'

'Yes, he really was dreadfully upset,' she said. 'They'd been together such a long time.'

He asked her for the name of the shop's accountant, thanked her, and took his leave.

An interesting discrepancy, he thought, between Lavender's estimation of the painting's value, and Georgia Hedley-Somerton's. Was that because he was the real expert and she was not? But she had been in the valuation department at Sotheby's – although it was a long time ago. Or was it so much a matter of opinion and the temporary state of the market, plus who happened to be at the auction, that they could both be right?

He got to the door and stayed his hand on the doorknob. There were some shapes lurking outside, like wolves at the limit of the firelight. Their blood would be up, fuelled no doubt by the sort of liquid lunch he could only dream of. Policemen drank whenever they could, but journos drank whenever they couldn't as well.

He looked over his shoulder. 'I'd be careful who you open the door to,' he said. 'In fact, if I were you, I'd pull the blinds down and turn the sign over to "closed".'

She looked alarmed. 'What is it?'

'The press have found you.' He surveyed her expression. 'Look, you're not the sort of person to relish having your face in the paper. The best way to deal with them is to say absolutely nothing. Once you let a single word pass your lips, they think you're a seam and never give up trying to mine you.'

'I have no intention of talking to the press,' she said coolly.

'Well, they'll have every intention of talking to you, so rather than test your resolve, best to keep away from them. If they see me come out, it'll give them ideas – most of them know who I am. Is there a back way out?'

'There's a door into the yard, and a gate on the far side of that leads to the garages. You can get out on to the side road that way.'

'Good. Let me out that way, and lock everything behind me. They'll come barging in if they find an unlocked door.'

'Surely they wouldn't do that?'

'They're not above it, in the same way that the sea is not above the sky.'

She managed a smile. 'How can you joke?'

'Requirement of the job,' he said. 'Otherwise you'd go mad.'

FIVE

Bolshoi Artist

S lider rang the office, and got Swilley.
'I'm going to grab a sandwich and go and see one of the other *Antiques Galore!* people.' He told her about his interview with Gavin Ehlie and the row with Rupert Melling. 'Anything happening?'

'Nothing apart from the canvass, boss. McLaren and Mackay are still at the house checking the goodies. Connolly's back from Mrs Bean. She doesn't think there's anything there – says the old bird seems twenty-four carat. Now she's trawling the Internet for recent guff on Egerton. Atherton's given me the name of the accountants for the antique shop, so I'm going to get them to send over the accounts.'

'Have you found a will?'

'No, boss. Not so far. I've still got some things to sift through.'

'If you don't find one, look for the name of his solicitor. They'll have a copy.'

'You think it's an inheritance thing?'

'I don't think anything yet.'

'Oh – Atherton said the press turned up outside the shop while he was there.'

'That's inevitable,' said Slider.

'And Connolly said Mrs Bean told her she'd had them on the phone.'

'Damnit! That's not inevitable. How did they find out about her?'

'I don't know, boss. Maybe one of her friends or neighbours. You know what people are like about wanting to get in on the act.'

Slider knew. To be the next-door neighbour of the person who cleaned the house of a famous person was exciting enough, but if the famous person got murdered and was all over the papers, the appeal of being associated with the news story would be irresistible.

I danced with a man who danced with a girl who danced with the Prince of Wales.

Or someone might have leaked.

Soho was, of course, the perfect place to be for grabbing a sandwich. He found a sandwich bar he liked the look of – small and cheerful with an impressive queue for takeaways – and secured a seat on a tall stool by the shelf along the window, so he could look out. He treated himself to a hot salt beef on rye and a cup of tea, and while he was waiting for it he rang Pauline Smithers.

'Hello, Bill. How's it going? I heard about Joanna losing the baby. I'm so sorry.'

'How did you hear that?'

'Oh, grapevine. News travels. People know I'm interested in your fate, and things get passed along.'

'That makes me feel nervous.' He watched the people hurrying along outside, huddled against the cold, and enjoyed the steamy warmth of the café all the more by contrast.

'It shouldn't. Isn't it nice to know your Aunty Pauline is keeping an eye on you?'

'You were never aunt material. Certainly not where I'm concerned.'

'Flattery will get you everywhere. How's she holding up?'

'Stoically,' Slider said, not wanting to go into it. Not that Pauline was ever a rival to Joanna – their flinglet had happened many years ago – but he never liked talking about one woman to another. It seemed like bad manners, somehow.

'I know you, Bill Slider,' Pauline said sternly. 'You're blaming yourself. You think you should have stopped her doing that tour.'

'It wasn't for me to stop her or not stop her. She makes up her own mind,' he said. But she was right – of course he *did* blame himself. He had been uneasy about the strain of the tour in her condition even beforehand. But he had always believed partners in a marriage should be equal and autonomous, and Joanna had her own career and made her own choices about it. Still, that didn't let him off the hook. When it came to the baby, it was his as well as hers. And the loss was his as well as hers. 'The doctor said the tour had nothing to do with it, anyway,' he went on. 'It was just one of those things.'

'Then you'd better start trying to believe it,' Pauline said. 'Punishing yourself won't help her.'

He tried to change the subject. 'How are things in SCD1?'

She accepted the redirection. 'Fairly busy at the moment.' She was in the Homicide Unit at the Yard, but in the less frenetic missing persons section. 'The usual teenagers gone AWOL, plus two children snatched by their father and taken to Pakistan. They always give me the child abductions because I was in SO5,' she sighed. Two years working in child pornography had almost broken her. 'I thought I'd got away from all that.'

'You're doing essential work,' he comforted her.

'So are you. I gather you've got the Egerton case?'

The waitress placed his plate and mug in front of him, and he mouthed thanks. 'That's right, and I've got a couple of missing artefacts – a painting and a Fabergé box. I was wondering if Bernard knew anyone in the Art and Antiques Unit.'

Bernard Eason was in cheque and plastic crime, but they both came under the SCD6 aegis.

'Bernard knows everyone,' Pauline said. 'But if this is part of the investigation, won't you be making a formal request?'

'Oh, yes, but you know how these things go. Without a bit of leaning, I'll get put in a queue. I'd rather like someone to talk to personally. If Bernard could give me a name, I'd be grateful.'

'I'll ask him. I'm sure he knows someone. And, listen, you and Joanna must come and have dinner with us. When this case is out of the way.'

'I'd like that. If Joanna feels up to it. We haven't been going anywhere.'

'I understand. But she's got to climb back on the horse sometime. Don't mollycoddle her.'

'OK. Thanks, Pauly. I'm glad Bernard's working out all right for you,' he added, to distract her from more Joanna-advice.

'He's a perfect pet. He's a bit like you, in some ways.'

Oh hell! Slider thought. 'Don't say that.'

'Got to go,' she said briskly. 'My landline's ringing. Speak soon.' And she was gone.

Slider tackled his sandwich, which should have been glorious, but between dismay that Pauline might have chosen a man because he was like him, and annoyance that everyone had an opinion about how to cope with the miscarriage, some of the shine was off it.

Rupert Melling lived in a slim Georgian house in one of Hampstead's narrow and precipitous streets, where parking was a nightmare. Slider had to cram himself somewhat illegally into a space on a corner, put a ON POLICE BUSINESS card in his windscreen and hope for the best. Rumour had it that Hampstead parking wardens were trained by ex-Stasi enforcement officers who had been sacked for gratuitous brutality.

The sky was beginning to cloud over with high, fine streaks of cirrus, sure sign that a front was coming. It had grown even colder since this morning, with a doomed, iron feeling to the air that Slider knew presaged snow. It hardly mattered in London, but he had grown up in the country, where snow was something to be dreaded. He hunched into his coat, feeling the cold strike through the inadequate cloth, and stumped back down the narrow road to the house. The cobbles already felt slippery underfoot.

He had called ahead, and Melling answered the door himself – a well-preserved forty-something with a perma-tan. He was wearing black Turkish trousers, a white muslin buccaneer shirt and a red velvet cummerbund marrying the two. It was an outfit so flamboyant as to be theatrical. His hair was dark, curly and shoulder length, and the blue of his eyes was so intense Slider suspected tinted contacts. And all off duty. This, he thought wisely, was a vain man.

'Hello!' Melling cried, as if he had only been waiting for

Slider to arrive for the fun to start. 'Come in! Have you had lunch yet? We're just going to have something.'

Slider was still in the process of proffering his warrant card. 'I haven't introduced myself,' he said, slightly minatory. 'You should check my ID.'

'Oh, but I was expecting you,' Melling said gaily. 'And I'm sure nobody could look more like a detective inspector than you do! But if it will make you happy . . .' He took the card and studied it with pantomime thoroughness. 'Mmm – mmm – mmm! That seems to be in order, Inspector – though the picture doesn't do you justice.' He handed it back. 'Doesn't show off your marvellous blue eyes. Your best feature – you should make the most of them. Don't you agree, Alex?'

A lean and sulky young man had lounged up behind him: thick, tousled blonde hair, pale gold skin, high cheekbones, pouting mouth, like a young Rudolf Nureyev. The column of his neck disappeared into an open-necked blue shirt with the sleeves rolled up to display long, rather veiny forearms. Below were baggy fawn cut-offs, strong brown legs and bare nubbly feet. He looked as though he ought to be doing languid acrobatics on Santa Monica beach, not hanging about Hampstead on a bitter winter's day.

'This is my friend and house-mate, Alex Anton. Detective Inspector Slider, Alex. Take his coat. Come in, come in. It's a beastly day, isn't it? We've got the fire lit.'

Alex took Slider's coat with reluctant obedience and hung it on the newel post of the stairs, and they followed Melling through the narrow hall into a room which, though small, had such beautiful Georgian proportions and original features that it felt spacious. A fire was glowing under a marble fireplace, and big red-plush armchairs and a massive leather chesterfield were drawn up to it. The rest of the room was furnished in an eclectic mix of antique and designer-modern, and everything in it had the air of being placed there to be a conversation piece. Slider had never been in a room in which so many objects clamoured, 'Look at me, look at me!' all at the same time. It was enough to give you a headache.

'Come and sit down, you must be frozen,' Melling said, urging him towards one of the chairs. It was the sort you wallow in, and Slider felt tiredly that he wished he was here on a social visit so he could enjoy it. 'Let me get you a drink. Scotch, gin, vodka? Wine? Shall I open a bottle of champagne?'

'Nothing for me, thank you,' Slider said.

'Oh, don't say that! You'll have some wine with lunch, at least? I'm sure even your ferocious bosses must allow you to eat and drink like a human being.'

'I'm afraid I've already had lunch,' Slider said firmly. He was aware that all this was an act, but what it was supposed to be telling him he wasn't sure. Or even if it was aimed at him. Alex seemed to be getting grumpier by the syllable. 'But don't let me stop you. We can talk while you eat.'

'Oh, all right, but you've taken the fun out of it,' Melling said. 'Alex, bring in the tray. Are you sure I can't get you *anything*? A cup of coffee? A glass of water?'

'I'm fine, thanks,' Slider said. Between the sofa and the fire was a large coffee table, wooden, with a glass top under which was a deep recess lined with green baize, on which was displayed a collection of snuffboxes of various shapes and sizes, every one an exquisite artefact. 'Your collection?' he said, leaning forward to look. 'I was told you were especially interested in snuffboxes.'

'They have everything,' he said. 'The art of the miniaturist, without all those tedious faces of other people's relations. I always think they are like a form of jewellery. I'd like to wear them on a charm bracelet.'

Slider smiled at the enthusiasm. 'They are very lovely,' he said.

Alex came back in and thumped a laden tray down on the table, skimming it past both Slider's and Melling's noses and making them jerk back inelegantly.

'Ah, lunch,' said Melling lightly, with a hint of threat. Alex went back out. 'Excuse him, he's in rather a paddy today. Mislaid his teddy bear, or something. Are you sure I can't tempt you? Look, it's all finger food, easy to manage, no mess. We just couldn't bear to leave this lovely fire, so we thought we'd have a mini-buffet in front of it.'

As a rule, Slider loathed buffets. Atherton said he suffered from Smorgasphobia. But this one was a masterpiece. There were all sorts of cold delicacies laid out with garnishes of salad – prawns, smoked salmon, and slivers of ham and different cheeses all arranged on bite-sized crackers, along with small pieces of sausage, olives, and what looked like tiny squares of cheese flan. Slider was glad his sandwich was recent enough to help him withstand temptation. 'No, thanks, I'm fine.'

Alex came back in with a bottle of wine and glasses.

'Ah well, let the feasting begin!' Melling said, took a plate and helped himself. He sat on the sofa. Alex filled the glasses and slumped like a puppet with its strings cut into the other chair. His arms were so long, he could reach the food without moving. 'So, what do you want to talk to me about, Inspector?' Melling asked, having inhaled a couple of hors d'oeuvres and washed them down with a gulp of wine. 'Oh, I say, I can't keep calling you that! Too terribly *Sleuth* circa 1972. Haven't you got a first name?'

'I think we should keep things on a formal footing,' Slider said. He'd never been very good about people using his first name. He liked to keep it for friends and family. In a brief flash of irrelevant memory he remembered he had never heard his parents call each other by their first names in all the time he'd known them.

'Oops. All right, can I call you Mr Slider?' Slider nodded to that, and before he could ask a question, Melling went on, 'If you've been talking to our Gavin, he'll have given you the usual line about how we're all one big happy family on *Antiques Galore!*'

'Is that what it is – a line?' said Slider.

'Gavin's got PR in his blood. No, his blood *is* PR. Stab him and it wouldn't be red that poured out, it'd be black and white – liquid press notices. And that programme is his baby. It's his *raison d'être*. It's what he has instead of a life, poor poppet.'

'So you're *not* one happy family?' Slider persisted.

Melling opened his eyes wide. 'Well, we're definitely a family: quarrels, bitchiness, rivalry, spite, shifting loyalties, doing each other down. Like all families up and down the land.' He emptied his glass. It was a large glass and left little red ticks at his mouth corners, like the Joker's.

Slider wished he'd caught Melling in a suit and without his Rudy for an audience. 'Was Mr Egerton generally liked?' he asked, hoping the 'Mr' would steady him.

'I don't think Rowland cared about being liked. He just wanted to be worshipped. And of course the punters obliged. They adored him. They took him at his own evaluation, which is what all of us really want, isn't it?'

'What about among the other cast members?' Slider asked stolidly.

Melling eyed him sidelong. 'You're not going to let me have a *bit* of fun, are you? Oh well!' He refilled his plate and dropped the flamboyance a notch. 'No, Rowland wasn't entirely liked, but nobody hated him enough to kill him, if that's what you're after. He was a poseur. He was full of it.'

What Mr Porson called a bit of a bolshoi artist, Slider thought.

Melling went on, thoroughly warmed up now. 'He was selfish, and he was grubby, and not above bending the truth to his own advantage.'

'Specifically?'

'Oh, he always wanted the best pieces for himself, and he'd elbow anyone out of the way to get them.'

'The trawl?' Slider suggested.

'You know about that, do you? Well, Rowland was mustard during the trawl – mustard, pepper and a good dash of Tabasco as well. And it wasn't only for the programme. You see, if the punter wants to sell afterwards – and a lot of them do: it's not all fun when a painting you bought for a fiver turns out to be worth fifty k. I mean, you're living in a suburban semi in Shinfield, how are you going to keep it safe? How can you afford the insurance? How can you be sure your neighbour's teenage son isn't going to jemmy open your window one night? You can't trust your friends any more. You can't get a wink of sleep. So of course they want to get rid of it, realize the cash, go on a Mediterranean cruise. And they naturally offer it to the specialist who presented it. They don't have to, but they don't know anyone in the business, and they feel a sort of gratitude, bless their woolly little hearts.'

'And I suppose that can be lucrative to the specialist?'

'Oh yes. Especially if they cream a bit more off the top to take account of the punter's ignorance.'

'Did Mr Egerton do that?'

Melling looked away, pursed his lips. 'I don't want to speak ill of the dead. But there were suspicions. And then there was the poaching.'

'I heard about the snuffbox.'

He looked back. 'Oh, did you? Well, I could have got the punters a better price, if he'd let them come to me. I know everybody in that field. I asked him to send them to me. He *should* have sent them to me, by the unwritten rules. In fact, I should have presented it in the first place. But he was too busy playing the great star and having them lick his boots.'

'So you were angry with him.'

Melling shrugged. He was fashionably thin, and his shoulders looked dangerously pointed as they shot up towards his ears. He could have given himself a double trepanning. 'We had a fair old ding dong, but you mustn't take that sort of thing too seriously. Any business has a bit of dog-eat-dog about it. And show business is full of edgy characters trying to grab the limelight. But it's all superficial. Most of the time we all just get on together. We always go out for drinks together after the recording, and all these little issues are put aside.'

Slider felt Melling was trying to have it both ways. 'But I understand the row you had with Mr Egerton two weeks ago was more personal than that. You said things about his relationship with Mr Lavender.'

Melling stared a moment, then laughed, largely and showily, as if he was on stage. 'Oh, *that*! No, you mustn't mind that. I was just teasing him. I like to pull old Rowland's tail from time to time. You see, the man's a raging queen, but he can't bear to have it pointed out. It makes him as mad as a wet cat, so of course I can't resist poking him from time to time, just to see the fireworks.'

'You mean he's homosexual?' Slider asked.

'No, no, I don't mean that. He's a queen in the theatrical sense – loves the display and the make-up and the clothes and the adoration of the audience. He's a hairdresser. An interior designer. A natural Barbra Streisand fan. Camp as a row of tents and gay as a striped parrot. But not in a sexual way. No, he only has eyes for women. In fact, I understand, from some *very* reliable loose gossip I heard, that back in the day he was always bedding the female punters and the locals – even one of the TV presenters once. Quite a cocksman. So naturally when I egg him on to come out and make John an honest man it drives him nuts.' He smiled. '*Most* enjoyable.'

'You say "back in the day" – do you mean he wasn't pursuing women any more?'

'"Pursuing women" – what a lovely phrase! Well, he seems to have settled down a lot recently. I don't know what he gets up to in his private life, of course, and I'd be surprised if there wasn't someone in tow, but he's been much more patriarchal with the punters lately. No more winks and pinches and sly assignations. I think it's part of his new image, now he's doing so much more for the Beeb, as the Last Word on Antiquity. He has to have a bit of gravitas. But—' He hesitated.

'Yes?' Slider said. 'Please don't hold back anything. You never know what might be helpful.'

'Oh,' said Melling, 'I'd tell you anything I know for sure, don't worry. I wouldn't scruple. I'm not a deep well, I'm a babbling brook.'

Alex made a sound at that moment, and both of them looked at him. But his face was calm, his eyes blank. He put another *hors d'oeuvre* whole into his mouth and chewed, staring into space.

'You were saying?' Slider prompted.

Melling looked at him. 'Well – and I don't know this for sure, you understand – but I think he was involved in a rather more serious way for the past couple of years. That could be another reason for his change of behaviour. And I suspect it was someone on the show.'

'Why do you suspect that?'

He looked uneasy. 'I don't know, really. I can't put my finger on it. It was just an undercurrent of feeling.' He thought for a moment. 'There was the Fabergé box.'

Slider's attention pricked like a dog smelling liver sausage. 'A green malachite box?'

'Yes – is it important?'

'It might be. Go on.'

'Well, it was on the show – quite a while ago. Rowland discovered it on the trawl. It wasn't wildly valuable, but it was interesting because everyone thinks of Fabergé as nothing but the eggs. Also it was decorated with unpolished diamonds, which is unusual. I happened to be standing nearby when he was talking about it to the owners – I remember he made some joke about diamonds in the rough. He was quite taken with it, and in the end it went forward for the recording. And after the show, when I went into his dressing room to see if he was ready to come to the pub, there he was, standing there, unwrapping the tissue-paper from around it. When he saw me he tried to cover it up again, but I said, "Is that the Fabergé box? Did they sell it in the end?" and he said, "No, it's a present."'

'From the owners?'

'I asked him that. He said, no, from someone else, and that's all he would say. When I pressed him he changed the subject. Well, I suspected at the time that he'd chased the punters and bullied them into selling it cheap. He's done *that* before, I can tell you. Very persuasive, our Rowland, when there's a profit to be made. But afterwards I thought he might have been telling the truth. Someone else from the show could have caught them before they left and bought it for him. And who would do that but a woman? A woman he was having an affair with.'

'But you've no idea who?'

He shook his head. 'Not a clue. There've been some cute production assistants, and there's Sylvia Thornton who does old clothes – she's not on every show, and I don't remember if she was there that week. And there's Felicity Marsh, the presenter – she's quite tasty, and I've seen them hugger-mugger once or twice. Though of course that could just be him trying to get the best spots. He's always hanging around Gavin, too. But I do know he kept the box, rather than sold it on, because he had a Christmas party every year for the *Antiques Galore!* cast, and other TV people who might be useful to him, and I've seen the box there in his drawing room, in pride of place.'

That expression again, Slider thought. He pondered a

moment, while Melling and Alex ate and drank, watching him brightly like cats for his next movement.

'You say Mr Egerton wasn't homosexual,' he said at last. 'What about Mr Lavender?'

Melling did his large and lovely laugh again. 'Oh, *John*! Good heavens, no! The straightest of the straight. He's like a lovely old headmaster, or the colonel of the regiment, upholding the old standards, ever so slightly dismayed at the things that go on nowadays. But lovely old-fashioned manners. Very pains-taking, too. He'd be the one you'd go to if you wanted a difficult, boring job done, and wanted it done properly. His powerful sense of duty would carry him through. "No slacking in the ranks, there!" No sense of humour, bless him. Just the tiniest bit grim, if you ask my opinion. You wouldn't cross him.'

'So what was his relationship with Mr Egerton?'

Melling thought a moment, selecting the words. 'He was like a big, fierce, loyal guard dog. Nothing would shake his devotion to his master. Whatever Rowland needed, Rowland would get. He did a trawl of his own, you know, before any of us got out there. That's how Rowland got so many of the plums. And he really knew his stuff. I've often thought the show should have hired him to do research and pre-select the best objects – you know, visit the area beforehand. But he was a one-man dog. He wouldn't have obeyed commands from anyone else.'

'How did he feel about your teasing?'

Melling looked uncomfortable for the first time. 'To be honest, he didn't like it. Not because he cares what I say about him – he has hide like a rhino wearing Kevlar – but because he could see it upset Rowland. I sometimes wondered if I'd get a stiletto between the ribs as I walked back to the hotel.' Slider raised an eyebrow, and he smiled apologetically and said, 'Sorry, I shouldn't say things like that to a policeman. It was a metaphor. I can't see him doing anything violent. He could have punched me many a time if his leanings were that way. I think he was too polite for retaliation – he'd have thought it bad manners. But inside that dour exterior there's a raging cauldron, you mark my words. Passion of an uncommon order.'

'What makes you think that?' Slider asked.

'Well, nobody could be that dull all the way through, could they?' Melling said lightly. 'And there's his devotion to Rowland, who often treated him in a very offhand way. That suggests some well of . . . I don't know. Something. Love, or something.' He reflected a moment, frowning. 'Of course, Rowland had terrific charisma. And a man like John with no charisma couldn't help admiring him. He must have felt grateful that a star like Rowland even bothered with him. And I'm sure his shop reaped the benefits from Rowland being famous. So all in all, there's nothing surprising about old John's devotion.'

The wine was all gone, and Alex stood up abruptly and said, 'Coffee?' It was the first word Slider had heard him utter. It didn't give much scope for analysis, but Slider would have bet it was said with a foreign accent.

'Yes,' said Melling, coming back from his thoughts. He looked at Slider. 'Will you have some?'

'No, thanks all the same. I must be going,' said Slider, standing up. Melling stood too, and he said, 'By the way, when was the last time you went to Mr Rowland's house?'

Melling did the laugh again. 'You aren't thinking I did the old boy in, just because we had a row a fortnight ago?'

Slider gave him a steady look. 'It's just routine, sir. If your fingermarks are likely to be in the house, we have to eliminate them.'

'Oh, good one! Most unthreatening,' Melling said jocularly. 'Well, as a matter of fact I haven't been there since the Christmas party. Rowland and I weren't best buddies. I only got the invitation as part of a job lot. And if the place hasn't been cleaned since then . . .! I assume he has a cleaner. Unless John dons the pinny and dusts all his little treasures for him.' He roared with laughter at his own wit. 'I can just see it! What an image!'

'And if you wouldn't mind just telling me,' Slider went on, unmoved, 'what you were doing yesterday?'

'I was at an auction at the Guildhall in Northampton nearly all day, and Alex was rehearsing. He's with the Royal Ballet. I went to meet him when he'd finished, and we went for a meal with friends at the Café des Amis.' He gave Slider an amused look. 'Do you want their names and addresses?'

'Not necessary at this stage, thank you,' Slider said. 'It's just a routine question.'

Melling seemed to feel he was being encouraged. 'It really wasn't me that killed poor Rowland, you know,' he said, grinning. 'How did they do it, by the way? Candlestick, lead pipe, dagger in the library?'

'I'm not at liberty to tell you that, sir,' Slider said stiffly, hoping to quell the merriment.

'Of course you're not!' Melling cried, unquelled. 'Well, thank you for coming, inspector. I've really enjoyed your visit.'

That's what we're here for, to entertain the public, Slider said as he was ushered back out into the cold. But he didn't say it aloud.

SIX

The Woes of the Name

The phone rang on Saturday as Slider was having breakfast. Joanna had been too long a policeman's wife even to look up as he went to answer it.

It was O'Flaherty, the sergeant on morning relief in the shop – a vast man of large appetites, whose inherent frenzy had been tamed by his wife's magnificent cooking until he had become almost a father figure among the uniforms. He was, to Slider, a living example of the importance of feeding the beast.

'Ah, there y'are, Billy, darlin'.'

'Where would you expect me to be at this time of day?'

'Out sleuthin' o' course. I've news for ye. Henley police have been on to say that the Sholtos are back home, and did you want them to do the Knock?'

It was what they called the visit to inform a relative of a death.

Slider thought rapidly. He swallowed toast. 'No, thanks, Fergus,' he said. 'I'd like to do it myself.' First expressions could be valuable.

'Are you still on your breakfast, you lazy article?' Fergus wondered. 'I can smell the eggs from here. No reliefs, no weekends. Sure, you CID boyos have the easy life.'

'Ah, but you see our brains are working all the time.'

Fergus snorted, but not unsympathetically. 'I hope ye hadn't a grand family day planned.'

'As a matter of fact, Matthew and Kate are coming for the weekend,' he said. They were his children from his first marriage. 'I'll have to organize something else for them.'

'I doubt they'll be surprised that Daddy has to work,' Fergus said. 'Right y'are, darlin', I'll let Henley know.'

*   *   *

Dad said he and Lydia were more than happy to stand in. 'I'll come up and talk to Joanna about it in a bit,' he said when Slider rang him. 'We're still in our didies.'

'It's not the weather for anything outdoors,' Slider worried.

'We'll find something, don't you fret. Go on, off with you. Put us out of your mind.'

He half managed. He rang Connolly – she was nearer than Swilley, and he wanted a woman along with him – then took a tender farewell of his sad-eyed wife. She smiled as she sent him on his way, and returned his kiss, but he was aware of the absence in her. A part of her was always absent, these days. The miscarriage was, for her, a bereavement, and mourning took time. But missing her left a hollowness in him that a good egg breakfast couldn't fill.

He and Connolly met up at a lay-by on the A40. She parked down the nearest side road and hopped nimbly in beside him, pulling off her lappet hat with one hand and buckling up with the other. She had the eager air of going on an outing.

'Swear to God, it's cold enough to freeze a dog to a tree out there,' she exclaimed.

'Very graphic,' said Slider, pulling out into the traffic. It was light at this hour on a Saturday. The weekenders all lemminged out on Friday night. 'Hope I didn't catch you in the middle of anyone,' he said lightly. Connolly's private life was a mystery, which made her an object of seething curiosity to every man in the department. Like Swilley before her, she would not date anyone in the Job, claiming that they were all headers with their brains in their mickeys; but she was attractive in a sharp, policewomanly way so it didn't stop them trying.

'Ah no,' she said. 'I was just painting the cat and brushing me nails.'

She was a good companion, able to sit quietly without chattering, which Slider appreciated at this time of day. After the Polish War Memorial, the speed limit came off and the road widened invitingly towards the motorway. He put his foot down. Connolly's lips parted as though she were drinking the wind of their passage, and for a moment he wished he had a summer day and a convertible for her.

Instead he said, 'Look at that sky.' It was grey and curdled like scum in a washing-up bowl. 'It's going to snow.'

'I don't mind,' she said cheerily.

'You think this is a nice day out, don't you?' he said, glancing at her curiously.

'Anything that gets me away from our flat is grand by me,' she said.

'Not nice?' he hazarded.

'It'd be gank enough without three girls sharing, but you'd want to see the state of it after a Friday night in. It'd give you mares. I'm well out of it.'

'Perhaps they'll tidy up while you're gone,' he suggested, and she snorted derisively in reply.

'Still, on the plus side, there's always someone around, so you don't have to go out for the mighty craic of a weekend. Saves a stack o' jingle.'

Craic? Slider's mind vaguely offered him a range of ceiling and other plaster-related domestic disasters, but it was mostly occupied with getting past a knot of ditherers and a lorry with a flapping canvas, so he didn't pursue it.

He drove on in silence, westwards towards the darkening clouds, distantly pleased that at least he knew one more fact about his companion – that she shared a flat. Though, given London property prices, he might have guessed that.

Henley approached. After much rain, the fields all around lay under wide pools of water, reflecting the sky in the stillness before the on-creeping weather. He could see skims of ice on them here and there, and on one shallow lakelet, which had obviously frozen solid, some disconsolate ducks were waddling and skidding, out of their element. The bare trees stood still, awaiting whatever was coming to them; rooks flapped about nervously, loose and erratic as cinder-paper, sensing the change. The countryside in winter was not a place for cissies.

But the Sholtos lived on an estate just outside the town, a place of tight brick, tarmac, concrete, and human control, which gave the impression that there was no such thing as weather – indeed, hardly any such thing as outdoors. As long as the electricity didn't fail, you had everything you needed

within your four walls. Outdoors was something you drove
through in your car to get to another indoors.

There was no movement anywhere. In commuter-land they
didn't need to get up and about early on a Saturday. The houses
were modern and detached, each with an unfenced oblong of
front lawn innocent of garden design. The Sholtos' house was
number twenty-one. On the hardstanding before the garage
stood a dark-blue BMW and the inevitable Range Rover, both
exquisitely clean.

'Yeah,' Connolly said disparagingly, with a glance about
the recreated urban environment. 'You really need a four by
four, living in a place like this. Eejits.'

'You're a car fascist,' Slider said. 'Why shouldn't they have
what they like?'

'First time they back over their own kid in the driveway
. . .' she muttered warningly.

They got out. She had left her hat in the car. Slider looked
with concern at her near-naked head. 'You ought to grow your
hair a bit longer in the winter,' he said. 'Give you a bit of
protection.'

'I could say the same thing to you, sir.' She grinned at him,
then composed her face into solemnity for the task at hand.

The door was opened by a very tall woman, fully dressed
in beige slacks and a cream cashmere jumper. She had short
brown hair, waved and carefully arranged, and a plain face,
lightly made-up. She looked worn, but that might have been
the effects of travel – Henley said they had arrived back in the
early hours of that morning. Or was it bereavement?

What Slider noticed most of all was the look of lightless
patience in her face, as though she had long ago accepted that
the brightly coloured, more pleasant things in life were not
meant for her. It made him sad, and he didn't want any more
sadness in his life.

'Mrs Sholto?' he said, showing his brief. 'I'm Detective
Inspector Slider from Shepherd's Bush, and this is Detective
Constable Connolly.'

'If you've come to tell me about the murder, I already know,'
she said.

Slider looked the question.

'We picked up the newspaper at the airport. I suppose you know we've just flown in this morning?'

'I'm sorry to disturb you so early,' Slider said.

'It's all right. We didn't go to bed. Didn't seem worth it. Do you want to come in?'

'If you don't mind. I'd like to talk to you.'

She nodded indifferently, stood back for them, closed the door behind them. The house seemed utterly still. There was no sound at all, and no discernible smell, as though it was brand new out of its wrapping. The floors were polished wood, the walls white, the spaces well-lit. They were ushered into a large sitting-room with a beige rug and a taupe-coloured three piece suite, and windows on to a featureless garden of lawn and bare shrubs. Slider had never seen a room so utterly devoid of personality. He could feel the will to live being sucked out of him into its vacuum.

'Please sit down,' said Mrs Sholto in her neutral voice.

Slider sat on the spotless sofa. Connolly and Mrs Sholto took the chairs. There was nothing on the coffee table. Nothing at all.

He had been in rooms of clashing carpets, cabbage-rose wallpaper and orange-and-purple upholstery; rooms cluttered with hideous china ornaments, weighted with horse-brass collections, manic with Toby jugs, and one with a model train layout all the way round the walls at dado level with little swing bridges to allow you to open the doors. There had been rooms that smelt of dog, rooms that smelt of chips, rooms that smelt of cigarettes, and rooms where you didn't let yourself wonder what the smell was, and tried not to have to sit down. They had all been places where people lived, redolent with their characters, good and bad. This room defeated him. It was like a terribly tasteful tomb. He longed for a bag of knitting on a chair, a cat tiptoeing in, tail erect, a browning apple core forgotten on the mantelpiece – anything to show warm-blooded creatures lived here. You couldn't imagine anyone actually *choosing* this place; just as you couldn't imagine anyone actually choosing Mrs Sholto. How could you do anything so positive as to choose such an absence of a person?

'Is your husband in?' he asked.

'No, Jeremy had to go in to work. He's with an investment bank. Things pile up. But he insists we're out of communication while we're away. Otherwise it's no holiday at all.'

Slider nodded. 'I see. Well, as you say you already know about your father's death, may I first of all offer my condolences for your loss.'

'It's all right,' she said. 'Phil and I weren't close.'

'Phil?' Slider queried.

She raised an eyebrow. 'He left us when I was five years old. You can't expect me to call him "Dad" at this stage of my life.'

'No,' said Slider, 'I was wondering why you call him "Phil".'

'Because that's his name. Phil Harris.' She surveyed them both. 'You didn't know that? You didn't really think he was called "Rowland Egerton", did you? That was something he made up because he thought it would appeal to his upper class clients. The Pont Street set, my mother used to call them. He so longed to be one of them. It was rather pathetic, in a way, how hard he tried. But of course he never was. They'd invite him to their houses, but he could never really be accepted.' She spoke without heat, without resentment, just narrating, as she might read aloud from a book that didn't really interest her.

It was good, Slider thought, that at least she seemed inclined to talk. 'I'd like to ask you a bit about him, if I may,' he said, with a friendly, encouraging smile.

It slipped off her impermeable facade and lay withered on the carpet. 'Why would you want to do that? It can't make any difference now, surely.'

'We don't know who did this,' Slider said. 'The more we know about him, the more chance we'll have of working it out.'

'What do you want to know?' she asked indifferently.

He was going to have to prime her. He tried, 'How did he meet your mother?' That was always a good one.

'It was at university,' she said.

'They were at university together?'

'No, he was at Nottingham, doing history of textiles. She was doing a BDS at UCH.'

He untangled the initials. 'She was a dentist?'

'Yes,' said Mrs Sholto. 'She came over here to study because the course was shorter than in the States. And because there was still something of "swinging London" about it back then. She thought it would be more fun.'

'She was American?'

She nodded.

'So how did they meet?'

'Phil had a school friend who was at UCL. He gave a big party one Christmas and Phil came down for it. The friend's girlfriend had invited her brother Bob, and he brought my mother along as his date. There was nothing serious going on between them – they were just doing the same course, they were friends. During the evening Bob got off with someone else and Mom got off with Phil.' She paused a moment, reflectively. 'Apparently, he was very handsome. Mom always said girls couldn't resist him. Charming, too. He had all the chat-up lines.'

'So they got together?'

'Not right away. He had to go back to Nottingham. But he wrote to her – they kept in touch. He finished his degree the next summer and came down to London to get a job. Mom still had two years to go, but I think she liked having a boyfriend with money in his pocket, especially one who seemed to know how to have fun, so she hooked up with him. I gathered it was a bit on and off for the two years. But when she graduated, he proposed, and she accepted, and that was that.'

'What sort of work was he doing?'

'Interior design. He'd wanted to work in textiles restoration for one of the museums, or maybe the National Trust or one of the royal palaces, but his qualifications weren't good enough. Also those jobs tend to go to people with connections – the old school-tie – and Phil didn't have any. He was just a nobody from Nottingham. He got himself a job with Marino & Page in King's Road instead. At least that way he had an income, and he met the right people. And when Mom graduated and started working, he set up on his own and tried freelancing.'

'That must have been tough,' Slider suggested.

She gave him a blank look. 'It was. And it didn't help

matters when I came along. In the end, Phil decided we were holding him back, and he skipped.'

'That must have been hard for you,' Slider said.

She shook her head. 'It's a long time ago, now. I don't remember minding too much. Mom and I were all right. She built up a private practice and made a good income. I think she'd realized Phil wasn't the real deal, and that she was better off without him. He wasn't faithful to her, you know,' she added, looking into the distance, as if the subject was distasteful to her, but the revelation necessary. 'He could never resist any woman. Mom said it was like a sickness with him. She didn't really blame him – he was so good-looking, women threw themselves at him – but after a while that sort of thing gets tiresome. So she was relieved more than anything when he split. They remained on friendly terms. He always remembered my birthday and Christmas presents, and I saw him once in a while. I can't say we were ever close, but I bore him no ill-will. He gave me away at my wedding.'

She stopped, her eyes distant, remembering, perhaps. Slider studied her old-young face. He had worked out that she must be around thirty-three, but she could have been ten or fifteen years older. Her calm dissection of her parents' marriage was almost chilling. It must be hard anyway to be very tall when you were a woman, but then to be plain on top of that, and have your father abandon you so young. But to have no spleen – not even any passion – about the hand life had dealt you . . . He glanced round the characterless room and saw how she fitted in to it. Had she early become too afraid to have emotions, because of what they might cost? She had put off youth untasted for the safety of middle age.

'Did your mother remarry?' he asked.

'No. She wasn't really interested in that sort of thing. Her career was everything. And she was only forty-seven when she died.' Her eyes came back to him. 'Pancreatic cancer,' she said briskly.

'I'm sorry,' Slider said.

'At least it was quick,' said Dale Sholto. 'She was gone literally in days.'

'Did your father have any other relatives?'

'No. He was an only child. Mom had a sister – Aunt Jean. She lives in Rhode Island. All the grandparents are dead now. And now he's gone too. So there's just me.' The words were heartbreaking, but she said them without emphasis. 'Jeremy and I never had any children,' she added.

Stop, I may cry, Slider thought desperately. He struck off on a new path. 'How much do you know about John Lavender?' he asked.

'He and Phil have known each other for years. They're business partners. He's an antique dealer, he has a shop in South Kensington. I think they met at an antiques fair or something like that. Phil was pretty well set up in his interior design business by then, and one of the things he had to do from time to time was to source antique furniture or *objets d'art* for his clients.' She seemed to think some explanation was necessary. 'He only took on the really wealthy ones, preferably English nobility, if he could get them. That was why he assumed the name. Thought they'd trust him more if he sounded like one of them. Though he wasn't averse to an oil sheikh, as long as he had good taste. He didn't like the recent influx of Russian oligarchs. He says all they want is bling.' The modern word sounded odd on her lips – but of course was Egerton's word, merely reported.

'So he and Mr Lavender got together – how?' Slider asked.

'Oh, at first it was just John helping him source things on a casual basis. Then bit by bit he started using John's shop to meet clients and show them his ideas – and John's ideas.' She met Slider's eyes. 'You see, Phil really didn't know anything about antiques. He had an eye for colour and fabric, and he was good with people. John was the real expert. So after a bit they went into partnership with the shop, and ran the interior design as a sideline. It was through the shop that Phil got asked to do the television programme – one of John's regular customers was an investor in the television company, and recommended him. And of course everything took off from then.'

'How did he manage on TV if he didn't know anything about antiques?' Slider asked.

'Bluff,' Mrs Sholto said, with as close to a critical tone as she had yet come. 'Oh, I suppose he'd picked up a bit by then. But of course, he always had John at his elbow. The shows aren't live, they're recorded. He couldn't have managed if he'd had to give instant opinions about the things they brought him. But there was always time for John to brief him. John was the one with the real knowledge – Phil just coasted along on the back of it.'

This was a new and interesting slant, Slider thought. He wondered how Mrs Sholto had come by that opinion.

'Didn't Mr Lavender mind that?' Connolly was asking. 'I mean, there was he, the one who knew all that stuff, and there was Mr Egerton taking all the glory.'

'You'd have to ask him that,' said Mrs Sholto. 'He didn't seem to mind, to judge by the times I saw them together. And the partnership lasted all this time, so he couldn't have, could he?'

'How well do you know him?' Slider asked.

'John? Oh, not at all, really. I've met him with Phil, that's all. I don't think,' she added thoughtfully, 'he'd be an easy person to get to know. He doesn't say much when Phil's around.'

'When did you last see them?' Slider asked.

'At Christmas. They both came over for lunch. I don't think John has any family.'

'Your husband got on all right with them?'

'Jeremy doesn't mind them. And he thinks family is important.'

'Did your father say anything about any troubles, or worries he may have had? Did he seem different in any way?'

'No,' she said, leaving him nothing to get hold of.

The thought of the four of them sitting round the dining table gave him the willies. Of course, he didn't know what Mr Sholto was like, but anyone who could choose Dale for a wife must have very low expectations of social merriment. He imagined the leaden lunch, wallowing along like a waterlogged ship, only kept afloat by the sparkling flow of Egerton's self-regard. An invitation to avoid.

And what of the ineffable John Lavender? He was no closer to fathoming him.

'I'm sorry to have to ask, but do you know how your father's estate was left on his death?'

She didn't seem to mind the question. 'You mean, who inherited? I believe he left everything to me.' She shrugged. 'I was his only relative. I've never seen a will, but he told me a few years back he'd had one made. He'd had a bit of a heart scare – it turned out to be nothing serious, but he said it was a wake-up call, he ought to set things in order just in case. He told me he was making me his beneficiary. I've no idea what he had to leave,' she said indifferently.

Slider tried fishing. 'The house is full of things, probably many of them valuable.'

'Some of them might be John's,' she said. 'Anyway, I wouldn't want them. I don't like clutter.'

You can say that again, Slider thought, with a glance round the bare room. And Egerton might have been a magpie, but it was rather dispiriting to hear his lifetime collection of treasured objects dismissed as 'clutter'.

'I expect he did rather well out of his television appearances,' he suggested. 'There may be money to leave.'

But she didn't stir. 'Perhaps. But Jeremy and I both have good salaries. We have everything we want.'

'What's your line of work, might I ask?' said Slider.

'I'm a dental surgeon,' she said. 'Like my mother.'

'And she never even offered us a cuppa tea, the meaner,' Connolly said as they climbed back into the car. The grey had settled heavily into the sky now, like hypostasis, and the cold was numbing. 'Jesus, Mary an' Joseph, I wouldn't want to go to the dentist and find her hangin' over me with a pointy bit o' metal. Did you not find her scary, boss?'

'I found her sad,' Slider said, backing out into the empty street.

'Creepy,' Connolly amended firmly. 'All that calling her dad by his first name. That's never right, even if he did bale out on them. And he seems to have hung around enough to give her presents. I wonder –' she distracted herself – 'what the hell he found to give her?'

'*I* wonder,' Slider said, 'what she and her husband spend their good salaries on.'

'Wild hedonistic debauches,' Connolly suggested drily. 'Sure, they'd come expensive.'

'Still, no-one has so much that they wouldn't like a bit more,' Slider said, following his own stream. 'I've seen so many fatal resentments build up over inheritances.'

'Yeah, but she and her hubby were out of the country, weren't they?' Connolly said, a little sadly – she'd have liked to put robot woman into the frame, just for not putting the kettle on like any civilized person.

'We only have her word for that,' Slider said. 'And we only have her word that they're well off enough not to need Egerton's money.'

'I'll check it out,' Connolly said eagerly. 'Wouldn't that be a grand alibi, though? They could book the flights, tell the neighbours, get a taxi to the airport for extra corroboration, then sneak back and do the deed . . . Or, wait, they could *go* on the holiday and hire someone to whack the old geezer!'

'Hmm,' said Slider, and the excitement drained out of her.

'Yeah,' she said. 'Can I quite see your woman as a murderer? I can't see her wanting anything that much. She's a seething cauldron of indifference.'

'Or a very good actress,' said Slider.

'Talking of seething cauldron, though,' Connolly went on, 'it does make you wonder about Lavender.'

'Yes. He seems to have got the fuzzy end of the lollipop all along.'

'And if your man left everything to Robot Woman, what about him, and his business, and the house, and all those antiquey yokes? How does it leave him?'

'That's also something we'll have to find out,' said Slider.

They drove in silence for a while, then Connolly said in discontented tones, 'I can't get over that gobshite Egerton, though. Swanking about pretending to be the big expert, and all the time he was Nobby Nobody and knew nothing. It's no wonder somebody lamped him. He was a complete phoney.'

'That's one way of looking at it,' Slider said. 'You could also say that, coming from nothing, he worked hard, improved himself, and found a way to make his particular skills pay handsomely. Isn't that something to be admired?'

Connolly didn't want her opinion shaved. 'What about changing his name, and all that sucking up to the nobs?'

'Well, that's harder to admire, I admit. But he probably gave a lot of pleasure to a lot of people.'

'Huh?' said Connolly.

'Most people love to be sucked up to.'

Something round and wet smacked into the windscreen. 'Rain?' said Connolly.

'Snow,' said Slider. More followed, and soon it was snowing quite fast. They had left the flooded fields behind, and it settled quickly on the drier lands, turning the everyday greens and browns to sophisticated black-and-white. Slider felt triumph. He'd said it would snow, and it had.

No, not triumph – relief. The relief of having the problem you'd worried about finally arrive, out in the open, so you could get on with tackling it. Something solid to be dealt with – unlike the nebulous veil of other people's loss, bereavement, and sadness.

SEVEN

They Caecum Here, They Caecum There

The office was quiet, with most people out supervising or taking part in the various canvasses. Swilley had received the shop's accounts from Lavender's accountants and was going over them, along with various bank accounts, business and private. And Hollis was there, drooping as sadly as a heron, looking thinner than ever with a grey sweater over his shirt that had a hole in one elbow. Such hair as he had ever had seemed to be abandoning his head in despair.

'Message for you, guv,' he greeted Slider. 'A Peter de Wett rang, and would you ring him back.'

'I don't know any Peter de Wett,' Slider said.

'SCD6,' Hollis further elucidated. 'Art and Antiques crime.'

That must be Pauline's work, Slider thought. 'Get me a cup of tea, will you,' he said, heading for his desk. Outside, the greyness had turned whirling white.

De Wett answered at once, in the kind of accent that only the English upper classes ever master – anyone else trying it always sounds false. 'Ah yes,' he said, 'Bernard Eason asked me to call you. He's a good chap and I owe him a favour – an investigation we cooperated on. So you're looking for a Berthe Morisot?'

'Do you know about her?' Slider asked.

'About her, yes. I've never had one through my hands. Frankly, we tend to deal with rather more important works. Morisot is one of the minor Impressionists. But I'll be happy to put through the usual enquiries for you. Art appraisers, auction houses, galleries, various agents. I'll also leave a marker with shipping companies and air and maritime insurance agents in case there's an attempt to get it out of the country. And HM customs will be asked to be on the lookout for suspicious cardboard tubes.'

'That sounds comprehensive. Thank you.'

'But the greatest likelihood is that it will go underground,' de Wett continued. 'Either straight to the end customer, if it was stolen to order, or to one of a number of specialist fences. I have my informants on the inside, and I'll ask them to keep an eye out for me. Something may come up.'

'You don't sound as though you hold out a great deal of hope,' Slider said.

'It's not a very memorable painting, and there are so many routes it could go. Now a more valuable piece, or one by a better known artist, tends to get funnelled into certain channels. There aren't so many fences who will handle it. But smaller stuff slips under the radar all the time.'

'I understand. When you say "smaller stuff" – what would you say it was worth?' Slider asked.

'Oh, very hard to say. Put to auction by its owner, it would depend on who was there on the day. I'd say anything from eighty to a hundred and fifty thousand. Stolen and fenced, half that – depending whether the fence had an end buyer ready.'

'I see. Well, thanks – do your best for me.'

'Of course. As it's part of your case, I'll make sure it's to the forefront,' said de Wett with curiosity sticking out all over his voice. 'As I said, I owe Bernard a favour.'

And now I owe Pauline one, Slider thought as he put the phone down. *Not for the first time.*

His tea hadn't arrived, and he went out into the main office, where he found Hollis with it in his hand as he talked to Connolly. 'Oh, sorry, guv, I was just bringing it in.'

'That's all right,' Slider said, taking it from him. 'What were you two talking about?'

'I was telling Colin what your woman said about Egerton being a phoney.'

'In her opinion,' Slider warned.

'I believe it. Sure, I've seen him on TV. He looks like a big shaggin' fake, with the carry-on of him!'

'It gives a bit more motive to Lavender as the murderer,' Hollis said. 'I mean, it must have griped his tripes, playing second fiddle to the bloke, if all the time he was the real brains behind the operation. He didn't even have his name on the shop.'

'But everyone so far has said he was devoted to Egerton,' Slider said. 'There doesn't seem to have been two opinions about that.'

'You can *act* devoted,' Connolly said. 'When it's in your interests.'

Swilley looked up from her books. 'There *is* the discrepancy about the painting, guv. Lavender saying it was worth about ten thousand and that Georgia woman saying it was worth a hundred thousand.'

'The SCD6 man I've just been speaking to says between eighty and a hundred and fifty,' said Slider.

'Well, still more than ten,' Swilley said.

'But why should he want us to think it was worth less?' Hollis objected.

'And why didn't he say that he'd bought it as a present for Egerton?' Swilley went on.

'I don't know,' Slider said. 'But equally, why would he steal it? And if he wanted to steal it, why would he kill Egerton to do so?'

'Like Everest,' Hollis said laconically. 'Because he was there.'

'He didn't have to do it while Egerton was at home. He had the key,' Slider pointed out. He sighed. 'I'm going to have to have another word with him, I know that. But I can't make sense of those two missing items, among a houseful. Why them? Why not anything else? And why then? And we don't know,' he added robustly, 'that Egerton hadn't sold them himself, or otherwise disposed of them.'

'Why'd he do that?' Connolly demanded.

'Why indeed. But they were his to dispose of, and maybe they had nothing to do with his murder. After all, the other painting was moved to fill the gap. Who would do that but Egerton?'

'Lavender,' said Hollis and Connolly together.

Slider shook his head.

'All the same, boss,' said Swilley, 'Lavender is the obvious suspect. I mean, his alibi is no alibi at all. He was there at the right time, and we know he was there, and he can't hide he was there, so what's to say he didn't do it? If it *was* someone else, they must have missed each other by minutes. Much the most likely it was him.'

'But if it was him, why wouldn't he skip off and set up an alibi,' Connolly said, changing sides, 'instead of calling the peelers and establishing the time o' death to his own disadvantage?'

'Because he had blood on his clothes,' Slider said. 'And maybe he's clever enough to know that that's what an innocent man would do.'

'Double bluff?' Connolly said. 'I like it!'

'By the same token,' Slider said, 'if it was him, it will be almost impossible to prove. Unless we can establish a motive strong enough to shake him into confessing.'

'Which is where we came in,' said Hollis.

'If he's got a motive,' Connolly said, 'it can't just be living in Egerton's shadow all this time. Because if it was that, why now all of a sudden? Why not any other time?'

'Accumulation,' said Slider.

'No, my bet is it's something new, something recent that's come up,' Connolly said.

'Well, this isn't a branch of Paddy Power, so we're not taking bets,' Slider said. 'We want evidence.'

'What of, boss?' Connolly asked pertly.

'Anything,' Slider said, frustrated. 'Why don't you get on the Internet and find out what Egerton's been doing lately – any recent sightings or chat about him.'

She nodded and drifted away towards her desk.

'Where's Atherton?' Slider asked Hollis.

'I don't know, guv,' said Hollis. 'He went out with the others. I suppose he's canvassing, or following something up.'

Slider nodded. He fidgeted a bit on the spot, putting his hands in his pockets and taking them out again, staring at the window. The snow had stopped whirling and was now falling quietly and thinly. There was a little on the roofs opposite, but his window sill was only wet, and he could hear the traffic swishing down in the street, sure sign it was not settling. He felt restless with unresolved thoughts. He had to get out.

'I'm going to see a man about a dog,' he said, heading for the door.

'Any particular dog, guv?' asked the patient Hollis, whose duty it was to tell people where he was and when he'd be back, unless instructed otherwise.

'I'm going to talk to some of my snouts,' said Slider.

It being Saturday afternoon, Lenny Picket was camped out in a bookies shop in Shepherd's Bush Road, folded newspaper in hand, skinny roll-up clamped in his lips, eyes screwed up against the fitfully rising smoke. It was in the nature of roll-ups to go out every few minutes and to need to be relit, which meant the owner spent as much time ministering to the thing as consuming it. It had led Slider over the years to the conclusion that smoking them was less a need for nicotine and more a form of occupational therapy.

Appropriately to his name, Lenny Picket had followed a lucrative career as a fence until, after a second stretch inside in the space of three years, his wife had put her foot down and he had retired from the profession. Despite his initial reservations about swapping sides, he had placed his wide experience at the disposal of the Met, did a little unofficial probation work turning youngsters back to the path of rectitude, and occasionally took a fee for sourcing a piece of kit, if it was unusual enough to tempt his vanity. He was now a respectable member of the community.

Also appropriately to his name, he was a small, sharp, narrow man, neat as a pin and quick as a squirrel.

'Hullo, Lenny. Had any luck?' Slider greeted him.

Lenny did a quick glance round before answering, but that was old habit. 'Hullo, Mr Slider. Nah, nothing so far. Three-legged ponies. Did a nice bit yesterday at Haydock, but that was luck really. Trouble with National Hunt – too variable. Roll on the flat season!'

'Too early for a pint?' Slider said.

'Is it ever?' Lenny answered.

'Shall we pop next door, then? I'd like a word.'

'Figured you did. Just a mo.' He stared at the muted television screen on which tiny horses strove their hearts out. The reaching legs dashed past the little white lollipop and the result came up. 'Gah!' said Lenny in disgust. 'I don't know why I bother.'

In the interests of tact, Slider forbore to agree.

They settled in next door with a pint of Pride each, and Lenny, starting another roll-up, said, 'Well then, Mr S, what's on your mind?'

Slider told him about the missing artefacts. 'I've got official sources looking for them, but often the unofficial is more effective. That's you, in case you wondered.'

'This something to do with that antiques bloke on the telly that got whacked?' Lenny asked sharply.

'You don't need to know that,' said Slider.

'Which means yes,' Lenny concluded. 'Well, as you know, I've never been keen on that sort of kit. Never handle nothing that there's only one of, that's always been my motto. I got my fingers burnt with that Gainsborough, all them years ago, as you'll no doubt remember.'

'It was a Constable,' Slider said. 'Yes, I know, Lenny. I just want you to put me in touch with Ginger Bill. I've been trying to track him down, but no dice. The numbers I had for him have come up blank. No-one seems to have seen him.'

'They wouldn't,' said Lenny. 'He's dead.' He nodded to Slider's expression of surprise. 'S'fact. Dead as a herring, oh – year before last, back end. You ain't rung him recently, that's obvious.'

'What happened?'

'Appendicitis.'

'People don't die of that much these days.'

'His own stupid fault. He was always terrified of doctors and hospitals, was Ginger. Do anything rather than go. He'd had a grumbling appendix for weeks but he wouldn't get it seen to. Even when it bust, so I heard, he just lay there groaning and wouldn't call the ambulance. When they finally got to him, it was too late. Peritonitis and I don't know what else. His whole belly was full of pus. Puffed up like a toad with it, he was.'

Slider looked down at his pint with less enthusiasm than a few minutes ago. 'I see,' he said, and to forestall any further medical details hurried on with, 'Do you know anyone else in that field? Fine art and antiques fencing?'

Lenny took a long suck at his fag, managed to extinguish it in the process, and fumbled out his lighter again. 'At a matter of fact,' he said between renewing puffs, 'I got a new bloke now, much better than old Bill ever was. He was lazy, was Ginger Bill, and you got to apply yourself to get anywhere in this world. Crafty Harris, that's your man. Used to fence, now he's gone legit, does antiques fairs, knows every dealer from here to Aberdeen.'

'Is he willing to help us?' Slider asked.

'For a finder's fee.' Lenny shrugged. 'We all got to make a living.'

'Fair enough. Let me have his number.'

Lenny blew out thin, acrid smoke. 'Better let me talk to him. You got pictures?'

Slider handed over the pictures of the painting and the malachite box they had taken from Egerton's computer. Lenny studied them a moment. 'Funny pair. Why them?'

'If I knew that, I'd be halfway home,' Slider said.

Lenny nodded and put the pictures away. 'I'll talk to Crafty, get him to give you a bell if he gets a sniff.'

'Why Crafty?' Slider had to ask.

'Craft fairs and such like. He's a decent bloke – straight as I am. Jim's his real name. Lives in Northampton, nice and near the M1 for travelling. Got pitches in shops up and down the country. You can rely on him. Got your card handy?'

Slider gave him one.

'I'll get him to bell you,' said Lenny.

There was half a pint left in Slider's glass. Time for a little gossip. 'So, tell me,' he said, 'who else is still around?'

'Did you hear Scruffy Barnet snuffed it?' Lenny said, settling down with relish. 'Heart. He had a ton on some outsider at Market Rasen and the bugger come in. Fifty to one. He dropped down dead with excitement. His missus was in to collect the winnings the same day. Came straight from the hospital, soon as they confirmed he was gorn. S'fact. Oh, and you remember old Calvert, the dog breeder? Well, he came a cropper . . .'

It started to snow again, but they were cosy with beer and Schadenfreude.

When he got back, Atherton was there, sitting on Swilley's desk, annoying her by looking at pages she was trying to work on. He glanced up as Slider came in. 'They said you were seeing a man about a dog,' he said. 'Surely not? This is no time to go greyhound racing.'

'I was trying to track down Ginger Bill Hanratty. Had trouble contacting him. Turns out he's dead.'

'That'd do it,' Atherton said.

'Where were you, by the way?' Slider countered.

'I was spending my time fruitfully in social intercourse with a solicitor,' Atherton said with the smile of the cat that had got into the cream-pot.

For a moment Slider misgave. He was aware that Atherton had been seeing a solicitor called Jane Kellock, of Kintie and Abrams – in fact, she was the fatal element in the ending of his relationship with Emily. Surely, surely he wouldn't have been off hobnobbing with her when he should have been working? Of course, doinking on the firm's time was a well-known failing of CID officers up and down the land – what could you expect when you gave red-blooded males large amounts of freedom and unaccountability? The orchestra world was rife with it, too, as Joanna had often confirmed – but he wouldn't have expected it of Atherton, his right-hand man.

Then he saw Atherton was watching him closely for his reaction and realized it was a tease. 'Any solicitor in particular?' he asked lightly.

'Arbuthnot, Yorke and Cornish,' Atherton replied, 'which despite its schizophrenic name takes the corporeal form of a sweet young woman, Eva Tavistock, who just couldn't do enough for me.'

Slider wasn't biting any more. 'Who,' he said firmly, 'are—?'

'Egerton's executors,' Swilley answered before Atherton could. 'You got his will, Jim?'

'I got his will,' Atherton confirmed.

'And God knows what else besides,' Swilley muttered, not quite inaudibly.

Atherton produced it, Swilley unfolded it across her desk, and they crowded round, joined by Connolly and Hollis.

It was relatively simple. The house and its contents and any cash deposits at the time of death went to Dale Sholto. Egerton's share in the business and its assets went to John Lavender.

'I suppose that's fair enough,' Atherton said. 'Lavender couldn't have expected more.'

'Depending on what value there is in the business to leave to him,' Swilley said. She linked her hands behind her head and stretched, sensationally. 'From what I've seen so far, it isn't doing very well.'

'That's what Georgia said,' Atherton agreed. 'But she said it was the same all over the antiques business.'

'That doesn't make it any better for Lavender,' said Swilley.

'How close are you to understanding the state of it?' Slider asked.

'It's complicated, boss,' said Swilley. 'There's the value of the assets to be taken into account. But some of them have been on the books for a long time, and if they haven't sold yet, who's to say they have any value at all? I can tell you that Lavender has been drawing a reducing income for years. And it looks as though Egerton's been propping things up from his TV earnings. He gets a big cheque in every so often, and a lot of that goes straight out of his account and reappears in the shop's, for paying rent and electricity. And Hedley-Somerton's wages.' She looked at Atherton, deliberately using the surname. 'Luckily, they're pretty small. I'm guessing either she has private income, or she's hanging on out of loyalty, because she could surely earn more than that elsewhere.'

'So the business is in trouble?' Slider mused.

'Not exactly, not yet,' Swilley said, 'but I can tell you this: the lease on the shop falls in in six months' time, and if it's anything like property everywhere else in London, the rent will double when it's renewed. And we're talking about South Kensington. I'm not sure the business can survive that.'

'Well, that means the will's good for a motive for the Sholtos,' Connolly remarked, 'but it's a shit motive for Lavender.'

'Yeah,' said Hollis. 'His TV earnings'll dry up, and without them, the shop could fold.'

'If the motive was money,' said Atherton, 'and not passion.'

'Oh, you'll know all about passion, we realize that,' said Swilley.

'Well, it makes more sense as a *crime passionel* than a financial hit,' said Atherton.

Slider let them argue on for a bit longer, his mind coasting, out of gear. Then he roused himself to look at the clock. It was getting dark outside, though that was partly the heavy clouds, threatening more snow.

There was a sound of footsteps and voices, and the rest of his people came trooping in from a day's canvassing, a little disconsolate and very cold. Their reports were largely negative, though some grains of supposed information would have to be analysed and cross referenced before they could be dismissed. Suddenly, the room was full and noisy and the dismal day outside retreated a step or two. Talk bubbled up about pubs and pints, curries and pizzas, and other such warming topics.

'I'd better go and see Mr Porson,' said Slider.

He drove home along wet roads, shiny in the headlamp's light, windscreen wipers going hard against the still-falling wet snow and the filthy spray from the tyres in front. A border of grey slush was forming along each kerb, but so far the snow was only settling on well-insulated roofs and the wider patches of grass. He had forgotten to have lunch again, and the pint of Fuller's was moaning with loneliness in there, making acid as a frustrated child smashes toys.

Which reminded him – his children would be there, full of their day's business, talking, squabbling, complaining, demanding, making more noise and disruption than you would think possible from looking at them, unless you were a parent. It was life – real life. He hoped it would do Joanna good, help to ease her out of the cold dark place and back towards the light. Perhaps after supper he could persuade everyone to a family game of some sort – Monopoly or Cluedo or something like that. Better than slumping in front of the telly, with the consequent bickering over which programme to watch, and the inevitable complaints from Kate and Matthew about not having a television each in their bedrooms. They had them in their rooms at their mother's house, but Slider suspected that was more for Irene's and Ernie's benefit than theirs.

The house seemed too dark when he pulled on to the hard-standing, with light only downstairs, coming through the stained glass panels in the front door. He heard the music before he got the key in the lock, and it swelled towards him as he opened it and stepped in. Joanna was in the drawing room, practising. He hadn't heard her practise in a long while. It was Bach, he thought. He remembered her saying to him once that by all the rules, Bach really shouldn't work, in the same way that a bumblebee really shouldn't be able to fly. But in both cases it did work, miraculously and wonderfully. He shrugged off his coat and walked quietly towards the sound.

She was standing near the window, half turned away, the music stand up high, the music on it looking from where he stopped like an infestation of black caterpillars. He stood and listened, and watched, as the notes streamed out from nowhere, from the black oblivion of nothingness and into the light, the strands coming together and moving apart, overlapping and weaving, only her strong hands controlling the flood, creating a space in which the music could bloom in all its terrible beauty.

He moved carefully closer, not wanting to disturb her, but at the same time wanting her back. She was gone away, her eyes not looking at the pages, but through them. She didn't see those odd black marks; she was looking with the far gaze of an astronomer at the music itself, at the sounds that a man who had died a quarter of a millennium ago had heard in his head, and now came spinning through one woman's eyes and hands into the head of another man: ignorant, but humble and glad, ready to be transported beyond cold feet and hunger to a more lambent sphere where one might glimpse the face of God.

She became aware of him. Delicately, she let the shining strands falter and fall, so that there should be no crash. She lowered the fiddle and looked at him.

'It's beautiful,' he said.

'Getting better,' she said. 'I'm not as stiff as I was.'

'You're all alone? Where are the kids?'

'Your father has them. He took them to the Imperial War Museum, and when they got back, Lydia came up and collected George as well, so I could practise. They're having hot chocolate and watching *Doctor Who*.'

'Sounds like heaven.'

'Good day?' she asked.

He examined the tone of her voice from several angles. 'Do you want me to go down as well and leave you be?'

She looked grateful. 'Another half hour. Then we can all have supper together.'

He kissed her cheek. 'It's yours,' he said.

EIGHT
Happy as Kings

As soon as he woke, he was aware it wasn't just the ordinary quiet of Sunday. There was a quality to the silence that he knew of old. He got out of bed and crept shivering to the window, pulled aside the curtain, and found the world transformed. He stared at the all-enveloping white with the usual mixture of pleasure and dismay. Everyday things redecorated were just so *pretty* – the black-and-white theme so elegant, so classy – but with it came the knowledge of mess, delay, inconvenience and the atavistic memory of danger and death. But for now, he would allow himself to enjoy it. As he stared, a fox came over the fence from next door and trotted across the lawn, lifting its feet high at every step, clearly puzzled by the phenomenon. It went over the opposite fence, leaving neat footprints and a trail between them from its brush.

He let the curtain fall and hopped back to bed, shivering. He'd have liked to fold himself into Joanna, the way he always had in the past, in the time Before the Miscarriage, but she seemed to be sleeping quietly and he didn't want to wake her. He lay still until the bed-warmth unlocked his limbs, and then drifted back to sleep for a pleasant hour before the television went on downstairs and shortly afterwards the sound of bickering roused him to go and do his parental duty.

By the time he drove in to work the main roads had been worn clear by passing tyres, though the Sunday pavements were still unblemished, and the roofs and gardens were flaunting their make-over. The sky had cleared and the sun was doing its bit, sparkling on things that didn't usually sparkle, like car lots and light-industrial units, covering up man's careless unloveliness.

They had had a big family breakfast – Dad and Lydia had come upstairs for it – and he had talked to his children. He was well-fed and nurtured, and Joanna had been practising last night, so all was well – or at least better – with the world. He felt more cheerful this morning – more hopeful about the case. *Atmospheric pressure*, he told himself. It affected one's mood more than most people realized. But it didn't alter the basic fact that today he felt as though he might win.

Mackay had been coordinating the reports from the ground and the phone-ins. 'We got a few possibles so far,' he said. 'Two of a man coming out of the house. One says "some time after two" and the other says "about twenty past", so split the difference and they're probably the same sighting.'

The inexactitude of public witnesses was legendary. But Slider said, 'If Lavender wasn't the murderer, we may be talking about quite small time differences, so it doesn't do to assume.'

Mackay nodded. 'All right. But they both say a tall man in a dark overcoat came out of the house. The later one, the two twenty one, says he was wearing a hat, a trilby, either brown or black, and carrying a briefcase under his arm. Says he's gone to the boot of a car parked outside. Seemed to be unlocking the boot. Then the witness has gone past so he doesn't see any more. The other one, the earlier one, doesn't mention a hat or a briefcase, just got the impression of a tall man coming out of the house. But she wasn't really looking, and she's not even sure it was the same house.'

'Did she see him going to the car?'

'No, guv. She was texting as she walked so she didn't look over there again.'

'Either of them get a look at his face?'

'They say not,' said Mackay, aware these were sub-standard offerings.

'Anything else?'

'Well, we've got another man in a hat going *into* the house. That witness says about twenty *to* two. Middle height, dark overcoat, didn't get a look at his face.'

'What sort of hat?'

'He didn't know the name; he said the sort posh blokes wear at the races, so it sounds like a trilby. No briefcase. No mention of the car. Says when he turned into the street the bloke was walking ahead of him, then turned into the house. Which looks as though, if he had a car, he must have parked it some way off. Or come on the tube, or a bus – or a taxi, maybe, and got dropped at the end of the road.'

'All possibilities,' Slider said. But it was all frustratingly vague. All three could be Lavender; they could be two different, or three different people; or they could be nothing to do with it, and it was a different house altogether. 'All right,' he said, 'have another go at them. More description. And try and pin them down a bit more on time. Ask them to come in, if you like – it sometimes concentrates their minds when they realize it's important. And have the others keep going. If there are three witnesses there must be more.'

'Right, guv.'

'Nothing from the other residents?'

'Nothing so far. Most of them are out at work, weekdays. And people don't stand looking out of their windows much.'

Slider nodded. 'And there are no street cameras down there, more's the pity, so we can't check the cars in and out. But put out an enquiry to the taxi firms, for anyone dropped in or near the street between twelve thirty and two thirty.'

'Yeah, guv, I'm on it,' said Mackay.

He left, and Slider thought a moment, then called Swilley in. 'Have you an idea yet about the state of Lavender's personal finances?'

'It's hard to say, boss,' said Swilley. 'It's all so tangled up with the business. The lease is on the whole building, and the rent of the flat isn't calculated separately. Same with the electricity and the rates. I suppose that's because originally it was all in his name and he didn't bother. But it means effectively he lives rent-free. And then he charges expenses to the business – travel and hotels and food while he's on the road, which is all legit. As far as I can make out most of the furniture in the flat belongs to the shop as well. So what's left would be his day to day expenses – food and so on – and clothes, and from what you've said I don't suppose he spends a bundle on them. As to entertainment—' She shrugged. 'The parties are all at Egerton's place, and I suppose he pays for them. Ditto if they go out to eat.'

'So all in all, Lavender can live pretty cheaply.'

'As long as he's Egerton's lapdog,' Swilley agreed, with a dissatisfied look. That made it less likely that he would kill him, and he was their best suspect. 'He does draw a regular salary, but it's small. Year before last it was twenty-five thousand. Last year it was twenty.' She met Slider's eyes. 'Enough for a simple life, but practically pocket change in those circles.'

Well, he probably didn't need more than pocket change, in his life of service, Slider thought. All the same . . . 'I think I'd better go and have another word with him,' he said.

'Now?' said Swilley. 'Do you want me to come with you?'

'No, I'll take Atherton. You're better occupied here,' he said, and saw a quick look of relief cross her face.

'There's still a lot to sort out,' she said. 'I'd like to cross-match individual sales and purchases for the shop, see what sort of a profit they made on that stuff. And how long they were having to keep them before they could shift them.'

'Sounds like an accountant's nightmare,' Slider said.

'And a taxman's dream,' she said, heading back to her toils.

Atherton was humming softly as Slider drove. Something operatic, he thought, and from the jigginess of the tune he deduced his colleague was in cheerful mood. After a bit, the humming got on his nerves so he fished for conversation instead. 'Good evening last night?'

'Is that a bizarrely inappropriate salutation, or are you inquiring after my social life?' Atherton responded.

'Forget it,' Slider said. 'It was just chit-chat.'

'I had a very good evening, thank you.'

'Jane Kellock?' Slider hazarded.

'Actually, no – though it was a solicitor.'

'Don't tell me – not the Egerton one?'

'Dear little Eva. As different from the statuesque Jane as can be.'

'What if Jane finds out?'

Atherton made an amused sound. 'You're not getting the

picture. Jane and I have fun. That's what's so good about it. We enjoy each other instead of making demands. No expectations, no guilt.' He locked his hands behind his head with a feline smile. 'The world is so full of a number of things,' he said, 'and a good proportion of them are agreeable females. Why ration yourself? As long as everyone knows the rules of the game.'

'That sounds like an awful lot of justification,' Slider said.

'We're not the same, you and I. I've finally learned it the hard way. We don't want the same things.'

Slider ventured one step on to unstable ground. 'I thought you were happy with Emily.'

He saw Atherton's expression of pain out of the side of his eye.

'There always comes a point,' Atherton said, 'when they're not satisfied with things as they are, however good they may be. It's inbuilt in women – they need to feel a relationship is "going somewhere". And when they start looking broody, I start eyeing the exits. They feel that if it's not developing, it's dying. Whereas I am dedicated to the status quo. I don't want to "go somewhere", I want to stay right where I am.'

'That's very shallow,' Slider said pleasantly.

'Thank you,' Atherton said with a smirk. 'Now Jane, the magnificent Amazon, is just my sort of woman. Career first, with as much bonking as can be fitted into the schedule, and domesticity so far down the order you couldn't get odds on it.'

'I'm glad it's working out for you,' Slider said. 'But I must say, I wouldn't be in your trousers for a ton of fivers.'

'*Autres gens, autres moeurs*,' said Atherton.

John Lavender looked dreadful. He had gone downhill fast. Slider had called ahead, to check he was in and that he would open the door when the bell rang. The big man seemed somehow diminished. Hunching at the shoulders didn't help, and his face was noticeably thinner, but mostly it was that the appearance of solid granite had abandoned him, leaving him shrunken from the status of mountain to a pile of scree. He was haggard, his hair awry, and though he was wearing the trousers of a suit, his shirt was open at the neck and he was tieless. Slider guessed this was a wild departure from the norm, occasioned by desperation. If ever there was a man who dressed properly everywhere, he thought it would be John Lavender. The proverbial dinner-jacket-on-a-desert-island Englishman. Three-piece suit even at breakfast. The man probably didn't even own a pair of casual trousers.

He led them into the sitting room, which had a window on to the street. Lavender went straight to it, in what looked like a habitual movement, and tweaked the curtain aside an inch to look out. There were no press camped out there today. In the absence of any crumbs from the Department, they were concentrating their efforts on Egerton's house.

'Have they been bothering you?' Slider asked.

Lavender let the curtain drop. 'I haven't been outside, not since I came back here after – after I spoke with you.'

'How are you managing for food?' Atherton asked.

'I'm not interested in food,' he said. He wandered back, sat down opposite them, but sitting forward in the armchair, hands on his knees, as though he might soon get up again. That great impermeable stillness was gone.

The room was small and rather dim, with brownish wallpaper that might have been fifty years old or the latest retro fad. The furniture was either antique or just old, none of it particularly handsome. The Turkish carpet was definitely old, threadbare in places, the pattern merged into murk. The pictures on the walls were, even to Slider's untrained eye, pretty dismal, like the rejects from a shop at the junkier end of antiquery. There were the ashes of a long-dead fire in the grate, and a film of dust on every surface. Mrs Bean had said Lavender was even fussier than Egerton, but it didn't seem to stretch to his home environment. Unless, of course, he didn't regard this flat as home. Or was one of those people that Slider had always found rather creepy, who were smart in public and careless, even negligent, where no-one else could see it. The dingy underwear brigade.

'How are you coping?' Slider asked, to get him warmed up.

He blinked, drew a breath and let it out, seemed to be thinking what to say. 'I keep—' he began, and stopped.

'Yes?' Slider encouraged.

'I keep remembering. How he looked.'

'You're upset,' Slider said neutrally.

There was a little flash of anger. 'Of course I'm upset. My friend – my *friend* – has been horribly murdered. How would you feel?'

Good, Slider thought. As long as he could still be provoked . . . 'You spent a great deal of your time together,' he suggested.

'Of course we did. We went to sales together, saw customers together, I went to most of his recordings—'

'And you socialized together,' Atherton put in.

He seemed to object to the word. '*Socialized*? Yes, we spent much of our leisure time together.'

'I wonder you bothered to keep a separate place here,' Atherton said.

Lavender looked at him with dislike. 'We didn't live in each other's pockets. We had our separate lives. But we were good friends. And now he's—' He looked down at his hands, frowning.

Slider picked it up. 'You say you went to his recordings. I believe he was quite dependent on you, on your expertise. Without you, he wouldn't have been able to make much of a showing on those television programmes.'

Now he looked up – a touch warily? 'Who says so?'

'Oh, come on,' Atherton said. 'You were the real brains of the partnership. Mr Egerton was just the showman. It must have been hard for you, living in his shadow. Never getting the credit you deserved. Hearing him praised for his tremendous expertise when it was really *your* expertise, and he was simply coasting on it.'

There seemed to be some struggle going on under the rocky face. The big hands clenched into fists. But when he spoke, it was intensely, but calmly. 'You shouldn't listen to gossip. Television is full of it. As for being "just a showman" – you have no idea how much talent that takes. Rowland was wonderful, not just on camera, but with people. He charmed them, put them at their ease. Few people can do that – certainly not as well as he did. He earned his fame. I was just the background technician – like the camera men, if you will, or the producers. Necessary, and quite as much valued in our way. And, no, I wasn't jealous, if that's what you're trying to imply. I was proud to be his associate.'

'Indeed,' Slider said. 'I believe your association was quite lucrative for you, as well.'

Lavender looked pained, as though he had said something indelicate. 'He supported the business with his external earnings. That was the arrangement from the beginning.'

'The business hasn't been going very well lately, I understand.'

'It's the same everywhere. People don't buy antiques in a depression. We're all suffering.' He gave Slider a clear look. 'Rowland has been putting even more in lately. It was he who was keeping us afloat.' He took a breath, and added in a low voice, as though it was hard to say, 'So I had no incentive to kill him – quite the opposite.'

Slider gave him a reassuring smile. 'I never suggested you did.'

'But that's what all this is about,' Lavender said resentfully. 'You didn't come here to enquire after my health. You're regarding me as a suspect.'

'I'm sorry if you think so,' Slider said. 'A follow-up interview like this is perfectly normal, quite routine. Often people remember different things on different occasions.'

'So I presume you are no closer to determining who did kill him?'

'There is very little to go on,' said Slider. 'Apart from the missing objects. The painting and the Fabergé box.'

'Why didn't you mention that you bought the painting yourself as a present for Mr Egerton?' Atherton put in.

Lavender straightened a little in the chair. 'Why on earth should I?'

'It would just seem a natural thing to say when the subject came up.'

'It didn't occur to me,' Lavender said crossly. 'Who told you I bought it?'

'Miss Hedley-Somerton.'

He gave a faint shrug. 'I buy most things in the business.'

'Did you often buy things for Mr Egerton?' Atherton asked. 'As presents, I mean.'

He hesitated. 'He wasn't an easy man to buy for. The proverbial "man who has everything".'

'And the Fabergé box? What do you know about that?'

'I don't know anything about it. Somebody gave it to him as a present. He didn't say who. It was just there one day, when I went round, on the console table.' He looked away, as though tiring of the subject.

Slider tried another tack. 'What do you think of Dale Sholto?'

'I don't think of her at all,' Lavender said.

'You don't like her?'

'That's not what I said. I hardly know her. I've met her with Rowland a few times. They weren't close.'

'But you had Christmas with them, the Sholtos.'

A flicker crossed his face, which Slider took as annoyance. 'Rowland and I went over there on Christmas Day, for lunch. A duty visit.'

'Mr Egerton's will leaves everything bar the business to Mrs Sholto,' Slider tried, watching him for any reaction.

'I know,' he said, his face immovable again.

'He told you?'

'Who else would he leave it to? She's his daughter, his only family.'

'Do you have any other family?'

'No,' he said, and offered nothing more.

'So, I have to ask you again, have you any idea of who might want to harm Mr Egerton? Anyone who had reason to kill him?'

'Of course not,' he said. 'Why do you even ask? It was the burglar who did it, surely? Whoever stole the Fabergé box and the painting. Who else could it be? He must have walked in on them, and they killed him. Isn't that the way these things go nowadays? One reads about it all the time.'

Slider said nothing, watching him.

'Nobody hated him – put that out of your head. It must have been the burglar.'

'But there's no sign of a break-in,' Slider said, and waited. At this point, the guilty man hastens to offer explanations of how it could be done; but Lavender only looked at him, blank on the surface and exhausted underneath, like an animal run to its limits and turned at bay – not afraid, just finished.

He caught Atherton's eye, and they exchanged a mental shrug. Soon afterwards they made their adieux. In the tiny space at the top of the stairs, which did service as the hall, there was a row of coat hooks on the wall. Atherton nudged Slider and jerked his eyes towards them. A couple of overcoats were hanging, and a neatly-furled umbrella. And an elderly, dark trilby hat.

Outside, Slider said, 'Yes, I saw. But it doesn't necessarily mean anything. In that class and age group they're fairly common, and Blenheim Terrace is the sort of place where people of his age and class live.'

'That sounds like an awful lot of justification,' Atherton said. They walked back to the car.

'Just stating a fact,' said Slider.

'Still, we've got a sighting of a man in a hat going in and a man in a hat coming out,' said Atherton. 'That's also a fact.'

'But Lavender didn't come out,' said Slider. 'And the times weren't right for him. And one of the hats was walking, whereas we know Lavender came in his car. So it would suggest at least two hats.'

'People never get times right,' Atherton said.

'If Lavender really arrived at two twenty-five, none of the sightings was him.'

'But he could be lying.'

'Oh, quite. People lie in season and out. But why? What has he got to hide?'

'I'm sure there's something.'

'So am I. But I don't think he killed him. There's no reason for it.'

'Lovers quarrel.'

'They weren't—'

'Metaphorically speaking. It's odd about the box.'

'Specifically?'

'Well,' said Atherton, 'if he acquired it while doing the show, you'd think Lavender would have known about it. But he said he saw it first at Egerton's house. Which means that

Egerton was very careful to keep it out of his sight on the day he got it.'

'Easy enough to do – it would have fitted into a jacket pocket. A bit bulky, perhaps, but possible. Or – we don't know he didn't have some sort of bag with him.'

'But why would Egerton want to keep its origins so secret?' Atherton pursued.

'If it was a present from someone he was having an affair with,' Slider suggested.

Atherton snorted. 'The sort of toad Egerton was would relish everyone knowing about his conquest.'

'You don't really know what sort of a toad he was.'

'Everyone says he was a noted cocksman. Why the sudden reticence?'

'I don't know. The other possibility is—'

'That Lavender's lying and he did know where the box came from. And probably, then, where it's gone to. But *why*?'

'If we knew that, we'd know a lot. If the box has a significance and wasn't just stolen at random.'

Atherton shook his head. 'Maybe the person who gave it to him took it back. And I keep coming back to it: if not Lavender, who?'

'That,' said Slider patiently, 'is what we have to find out.'

'Touché,' said Atherton. They got in the car and drove off in thoughtful silence.

Connolly was tapping away at her keyboard and looked up as they came in. 'Boss,' she called.

'That's me,' said Slider.

'I've got something a bit interesting.'

'Only a bit?'

'Well, it's showing promise. It could be interesting when it grows up and leaves school.'

He went over to her desk.

'See, I was looking for recent sightings of your man, like you asked, and the most recent that's nothing to do with his TV shows is this, at the funeral of Julia Rabbet.'

'That was TV-show-related,' Atherton objected, joining them.

'Up to a point,' she said patiently. 'Thing is, the funeral was supposed to be private, family only. And I checked with Gavin Ehlie, and he said that was right, they were all told ever so politely it was off limits, no flowers, donations to some charity. He said nobody from the show went, even though she was Miss Popular with everybody. They all went for a drink one night instead to send her on her way.'

'But Egerton went to the funeral anyway?' Slider said. 'How do you know?'

'A photographer caught him,' Connolly said, pleased with herself. 'It's on the Internet. Look.' There were several shots of well-heeled, black clad folk coming down the steps of a church and gathering in solemnly-chatting groups in front. She scrolled through. 'Here. This one. See him in the background, creeping out after everyone's left, God love him? It's the height of hilarity! The big media star trying not to get noticed.'

Yes, in the photo concerned most people were in chatting groups in front of the steps, and just appearing in the church doorway, looking unexpectedly furtive, was the unmistakable figure of Rowland Egerton in a dark overcoat, just in the process of raising a hat to his head, perhaps to disguise his trademark hair.

'He'd to take the hat off inside, o' course,' Connolly said. 'He musta found a dark corner to sit in.'

'But why wouldn't he want to be seen?' Atherton said. 'When the whole of his life otherwise seems to have been dedicated to the opposite?'

'Because he wasn't invited,' Connolly said. 'Private. Family only. Sure, he's so desperate, the big eejit, he'll even crash a family funeral for publicity.'

'Publicity doesn't work if nobody knows you're there,' Atherton pointed out.

'He's biding his time,' Connolly said, undeterred. 'He'll not want to get burned too soon. Get the lie of the land and work out the best way to flaunt himself.'

'It's odd,' said Slider thoughtfully. 'Why him, of all the people on the show?'

'Perhaps he just couldn't stand being told what he could and couldn't do,' Atherton suggested.

'Wait'll I tell ya,' Connolly went on eagerly. 'There's more. This one's even better.'

She brought up another picture. It wasn't much changed, still the informal groups lingering and talking, though some were moving away and others had gone. But right behind them all, to the side of the church, was the figure of Egerton, now wearing the hat, holding it on with one hand as though it was going to get blown away. Another man, bareheaded, was facing him, standing very close as though they were having a confidential discussion.

'Who is that?' Atherton asked, peering over Connolly's shoulder. 'He looks familiar.'

'It's the Rabbet's husband. Philip Masterson. He's something to do with the government, apparently,' Connolly said.

'Philip Masterson! Yes, of course,' Atherton said. 'He was Minister for the Arts. One of the new Bright Boys. But he got downgraded in the last shuffle to Minister for Climate Change. Not so bright after all.'

'You mean he blotted his copybook?' Slider asked. He didn't keep up with politics the way Atherton did. Never seemed to have the time.

'Not necessarily,' said Atherton. 'Just didn't exactly shine in his previous job, one gathers. Climate Change is the dog's job. They always keep a few Cabinet posts for the seat-moisteners, the dim but loyal. Every government needs them.'

'I wonder what he's saying to your man Egerton,' Connolly said.

'Probably asking if his intentions are honourable,' Atherton said. 'I don't know, you plan a private, media-free funeral for your beloved spouse, and the biggest self-publicist in her circle turns up uninvited! I'd have thrown a brick at him.'

'They're just talking,' Slider said. 'Can't deduce any hostile intent from that. Still, we're looking for anyone with a beef against Egerton.'

'I can't see party-crashing as a hanging offence,' said Atherton. 'It's hardly even a beeflet.'

'Of course not. But perhaps there's more to it – a history between them.'

'Boss,' said Connolly, 'the photographer's the one at a

wedding or a funeral that sees everything. He's facing the other way from everybody else. I've got his name here, David Palgrave. Studio in Islington. Will I have a lash at him?'

'Why not?' said Slider. 'When you've got nothing, you've got nothing to lose.'

NINE

The Peasants are Revolting

David Palgrave didn't live above the studio. Connolly located him at home in Denham, but when she told him what she wanted he agreed to come in and meet her at the studio. She was sitting outside in her car when his drew up – a handsome grey Jaguar. She wasn't too surprised. His website had made him out as photographer to Society, and his boasting-list was heavy on the titled people, celebrities and the upper reaches of government. He wasn't your typical kids-parties-and-meringue-brides sort of snapper-merchant.

He was a compact young man – you can't call someone in that income bracket 'short', Connolly thought – and solid, though not at all fat. More sort of muscular and springy under that navy cashmere coat. He had thick dark hair worn *en brosse*, brown eyes and a number of charming brown moles, and teeth straightened and whitened to film-star standards. She supposed they were one of his professional tools. He flashed them at her in a smile that seemed more dutiful than warming, but could still have had an oncoming motorist swerving into a lamp-post. Not that there were many. This part of Islington was not a tourist haunt and was sunk in Sunday somnolence, just the occasional bored kid doodling along the pavements on a Christmas bike that hadn't yet lost its allure. She guessed his shop was not the important part of his business. Probably not much walk-in trade round here, except for passport photos. Duchesses were thin on the ground in N1.

'So you're interested in the Rabbet-Masterson funeral,' he said briskly, hoicking out a vast bunch of keys. He rolled up the metal shutters, let them in, turned on the lights and locked the door behind them. 'Can't be too careful round here,' he commented.

'Yeah,' she said. The peasants *are* revolting, she thought.

The shop which sprang into view was an oblong of white walls and wood-strip flooring, with a modern desk and chairs at the far end, and enormously-blown-up unframed portraits on the wall in black-and-white. Halfway down one side was a white back-screen with a tall stool in front of it – where the passport photos were taken, she supposed. He unlocked and led her through a further door, into a tiny lobby of filing cabinets, beyond which she caught a glimpse of what was obviously the dark room and processing lab.

He opened one filing cabinet drawer, flicked through the contents, and withdrew a ziplock bag with a memory stick in it and a white label on the outside. 'Rabbet-Masterson. This is it. Come through.'

He put on the lab lights and led her over to a computer on a bench on one side. He fired it up, inserted the memory stick, and drummed his fingers impatiently while it loaded. 'I suppose you're not going to tell me why this is important?' he said, frowning at the screen.

'You're dead right,' she said. 'I can't, anyway – nobody tells me anything. Lowest of the low, that's me. Just a drone.'

He flicked her a look that said he didn't believe her. 'It must be something to do with Rowland Egerton,' he said. 'He and Bunny were on the same show.'

'Did you know her?' Connolly asked, to deflect him.

'Bunny? Of course. I've known her family all my life. Her father was John Rabbet, the racehorse owner. Had a string of Derby winners. Whisky Zulu. Bright Morning. Arcturus. You remember them? Bright Morning won the triple crown. Photographing his horses was how I got started, as a matter of fact.'

She nodded to keep him happy. What she didn't know about racehorses could be written on the back of a football pitch. *So, he'd grown up among the nobs*, Connolly thought. Accounted for a lot.

The file was up on the screen, and he paused with his hands over the keys. 'Look,' he said, 'these people are my valued clients, a lot of them are my friends. You're not going to go and ask them a lot of rude and intrusive questions, are you?'

'Me? I'm not doing anything.'

'You know what I mean. I don't want to be the cause of them being put to a lot of trouble and upset. I have my business to consider.'

'Nobody wants to upset anyone. I'm just looking for information.'

'You think somebody at the funeral was involved in some way?' he pursued.

'Well, they're your friends – what do *you* think?'

'Nobody I know would do anything like that.'

'Then you've nothing to worry about, have you?' she said. 'Let's see the pictures, so.'

She watched as he brought them up one by one, until they came to the shot with Egerton coming out of the church door. She stopped him and asked him to enlarge that part of the photograph.

'Yes, I saw him,' Palgrave said. 'I didn't think anything of it, really – just assumed he was another guest. I mean, he's very well connected. But he didn't join any of the groups, or come up to pay his condolences to Philip. He just sort of crept round the back and seemed to be heading for the side gate when Philip spotted him.'

'How'd he do that?'

'I don't know. He was looking round for someone, I think, and when he saw him he hurried straight over. I've got quite a bit of the sequence in the background. Watch.'

He flicked through. In little jerky bites of memory, Connolly saw Masterson slip free of the crowd as Egerton was going down the side of the church, close in on him, saw them turn to face each other. A conversation was evidently had.

'Any idea what they were talking about?' Connolly asked.

'Of course not. I was too far away. But it didn't look very friendly.'

It didn't. Masterson seemed to lean forward and Egerton to lean backwards in compensation. At one point a Masterson hand was up and a finger seemed to be wagging, either sternly or aggressively.

'Look at your man giving out to him,' Connolly admired. 'It's a gas!'

'But it wasn't all one-sided,' said Palgrave. 'Watch.'

Egerton had stopped leaning backwards. He was standing straight, and Masterson seemed to be shrinking. His chin was down. He'd folded his arms – the classic defensive pose. Then Egerton was away, back view, heading for the gate, and Masterson was rejoining his guests.

'Has Mr Masterson seen these pictures?'

'I've no idea. He hasn't asked for any copies, but there are a couple on the Internet.'

'That's where I saw them. You didn't take them for him, then?'

'No, I did them freelance for a society magazine. He gave me permission to take some shots in the churchyard because I was an old family friend. No other photographers were allowed in. There were a couple of bouncers keeping the press back at the gate. It wasn't a big affair, though. A couple of local reporters, one photographer from the *Telegraph*. He put out a press release asking for privacy and saying there'd be a public memorial service. The big guns were holding back for that.'

'More celebrities,' Connolly suggested.

'You can bank on it,' Palgrave said with professional relish. 'Bunny knew everyone.'

'Can you make me some prints of one or two of these?' Connolly asked.

'Of course,' he said.

She pointed out what she wanted, and he printed them off efficiently and put them into an envelope for her.

'Is that it?' he asked.

'That's it,' she said. 'Keep that memory stick somewhere safe.'

'I keep them all safe,' he said huffily. 'It's my job. Can I go home, now?'

She looked at him steadily for a moment, then said, 'You don't like Philip Masterson very much.'

'Why do you think that?'

'You talked about protecting your friends and clients, but you didn't mind giving him up.'

'I didn't "give up" anything – you asked to see the shots, and I showed you them.'

'But you made a point of photographing that little tiff between him and Egerton,' she said.

He shrugged. 'Just photographer's instinct. You naturally look at anything that's out of the ordinary.'

'But you *don't* like him, do you?'

'I don't *dis*like him. He's just – not quite one of us. None of us really knew why Bunny married him.'

'A bit of a culchie, is he?'

'I have no idea what that means,' Palgrave said, a touch frostily.

'A bit of a bounder,' she said in her best English accent. 'A pleb.'

A spot of colour appeared on his cheeks. 'That's not a word I have ever used.'

Connolly grinned. 'But it's what you think, all the same.'

He was offended and didn't answer. She took her leave, pleased with the result. It was growing dusk, and freezing hard, and the snow on the pavement, worn to slush, had now turned to ice, bumpy, grey and unappetizing. She picked her way carefully to the car, clutching the envelope, and thinking longingly of a cup of tea.

McLaren, back with the others from canvassing, had gone down to Mike's and come back with a bag of cakes to go with the brew-up: a couple of rather tough Danish pastries (it was the end of the day, after all), some currant buns, and those strange jobs made of flaky pastry and jam, topped with icing and coconut strands, known confusingly in London as cheesecakes. There was a bit of a cult for them in the department just now (recently replacing the fad for Tunnock's Teacakes), and you had to be quick to nab one. Fortunately for Slider, Connolly went in hard and presented him with one on a plate.

Unfortunately, before he could put proprietary toothmarks in it, Mr Porson came in and appropriated it, by the simple method of taking the plate out of his hand with an: 'Ah, thanks! Rather partial to these. Very nice.' He settled on the edge of a desk and said, 'Right, fill me in. Let's hear what you've got.'

For everybody's sake, Slider went over everything from the

beginning, with Hollis from the back dutifully filling in details where necessary.

Porson listened attentively, munching his way through Slider's cheesecake, a stray strand of coconut wagging on his lips until a quick swipe of his tongue dealt with it, to Slider's relief. 'So,' he concluded, pressing the last flakes from the plate with a forefinger and licking them off, 'Lavender's still pretty much your best boy. Though I can see problems with him. Being the one to find the body cuts both ways, as the Chinaman said when he gave his father a two-edged knife. He's either got to be clever as a fox or a congenial idiot.'

Mackay said, 'About the sightings we've got so far, sir. I was thinking – that briefcase. You glance at a bloke, smartly dressed, with something square and flat under his arm, all right, you're going to assume it's a briefcase. But what if it isn't?'

'I've been thinking the same thing,' said Atherton. 'The malachite box could be slipped into a man's overcoat pocket. But how would you naturally carry a picture, to leave your hands free to get out your car key?'

'You'd tuck it under your oxter,' said Connolly.

'That *was* a rhetorical question,' Atherton said, pained.

'But the times are all wrong for Lavender, sir,' said Gascoyne. 'He says he got there at two twenty-five and the shout was at two thirty. All the sightings are earlier than that.'

'The sightings so far,' Mackay warned.

'Anyway, we don't want him coming out, we want him going in,' said Connolly.

'And that's a problem,' said Atherton. 'If he left the shop at one thirty he could hardly get to Waitrose for the shopping and still be the man seen going in at one forty.'

Hollis spoke up from the back. 'Guv, I've got the notes on Hedley-Somerton's interview. It says she got back from lunch at one. Lavender said one thirty.'

Atherton and Slider looked at each other. 'She did say one. How did we miss that?'

'Even if she came back at one, he might not have left until one thirty,' Slider said. 'What with pottering and chatting. But if he did leave at one, he could be the one forty man. We have to check up on his movements. Gascoyne: Waitrose. They can give you the time of the till transaction. If he paid by credit card it's straightforward enough, but even if he paid by cash you can check it by the purchases in the shopping bag. They were all logged by SOCO.'

'Yes, sir,' said Gascoyne.

'And Fathom – traffic cameras between the shop and Egerton's house.'

Porson waited for this to be concluded. 'If he *was* One Forty Man, what was he doing in there all that time?' he asked, and answered himself. 'Killing Egerton, then waiting to call the police to make it look as if he'd arrived later.' He shook his head. 'That's a risky saterjee. Far better to get right away and try and establish an alibi.'

'He had blood on his clothes,' Slider pointed out.

'Didn't you say he lived there? Then he'd have other clothes upstairs. He could have changed, taken the soiled clothes with him and dumped them. That's the way *they'd* think,' he added, *they* meaning *criminals*.

Slider nodded. Porson wasn't wrong. 'But on the other hand, he could have been paralysed with fright over what he'd done. Just stood around wondering what the hell to do next.'

And Porson nodded. *They* also did that, as often as not.

'Then who were the past two o'clock and two twenty geezers seen leaving?' McLaren asked.

'If they weren't false sightings,' Slider said, 'they bring us to hypothesis number two. That Lavender's telling the truth, and it was someone else going in at one forty, possibly the murderer.'

'Possibly?' Swilley queried.

'Death could have been earlier than that,' Slider said. 'Doc Cameron gives us from around twelve thirty.'

'Not much comfort there,' Porson grunted. 'All right, if not Lavender, who've you got? The daughter and her husband, I suppose? The old *cui bono*?'

'Dale and Jeremy Sholto,' Slider supplied. 'But they were out of the country.'

'I checked with the airline, boss,' Swilley affirmed. 'They were definitely on the plane.'

'They could've hired a hit man,' said Fathom excitedly. He was still young enough to confuse fiction with reality.

'You'd better hope they didn't,' Porson said quellingly, 'or we'll be here till Christmas. You can do a background check, see if they've got money troubles, find out exactly how much they stood to get from Egerton. Did they have a key?'

'She said not,' Connolly answered. 'But who knows?'

'Well,' Slider said, 'if the murderer didn't let himself in – and it's a wide field: there's no knowing who might have managed to make a copy of the key at some time – it looks as though Egerton let him in. And that's also a wide field. He knew a lot of people.'

'Any suspects?' Porson asked.

'Nobody leaps out,' Slider said. 'He had a rather public row with one of the bods on the TV show, Rupert Melling, but it doesn't look like grounds for murder, and he seems to have a solid alibi, though we've still to check all the details. Egerton apparently wasn't much liked on the show, but again, disliked enough for murder? It seems unlikely. And now there's this apparent quarrel between Egerton and Philip Masterson—'

'That name sounds familiar,' Porson said.

'Minister for Climate Change,' said Atherton.

Connolly explained about the photographs and her interview with Palgrave.

Porson grunted. 'And that was how long ago?'

'Two weeks, sir.'

'Well, I hate to throw a spanner in the ointment, but that's a bit long to hold a grudge over a gatecrashing incident. We're clutching at straws here. The fact of the matter is you've got nothing except Lavender, and Lavender's going to be the hardest one to prove. Unless he obliges us by having it away on his tiny toes so we can put pressure on him.' He sighed, putting down his cup. 'We can hope. It's always your first-timers who bolt. Run like cheap tights, your amateurs. Can't stand the strain.'

When he had gone, Slider said, 'None of which explains the painting and the box.'

'Maybe Mrs Bean took them,' Atherton said comfortingly.

Swilley said, 'Boss, how about talking to some other people

on the show? I was thinking, particularly the women. If he was a nuisance, the way we think, they might have some dirt on him.'

'Yes, that's a good idea,' Slider said. 'Find out if he really was having an affair with anyone. Women are generally more observant about that sort of thing.'

Atherton stretched and glanced at the clock. 'What now?' he asked.

'Home,' said Slider. 'I need to see my children before they disappear again.'

'Anyone for a pint?' Connolly asked around the rest. 'Me tongue's dragging.'

By Monday morning, the snow was reduced to a line of dirty ice along the edges of pavements and a white streak under garden hedges, and the day was sparkling, hard, bright and cold. Slider had an early call from Tufty Arceneaux, the bodily fluids expert, a man of huge appetites and mighty lung power.

'Bill, my old fruit bat,' he roared. '*Eto ti?*'

Slider moved the receiver a little further from his ear. 'What about tea?' he said hopefully.

'Just back from hols. Practising the lingo. Have to show some profit. Food was diabolical.'

'How was your flight?' Slider asked politely.

'Attractively crash-free. How are you?'

'I've never felt better,' said Slider. He sighed. 'Sometimes I wish that just once I had.'

'We must get together. I brought back a suitcase full of caviar and vodka. Left all my clothes out there. Who needs 'em?'

'You paint an attractive picture – naked and covered in fish eggs. Have you got my results for me?'

'Yes, and you'd have had them sooner if I'd been around. Found 'em lying on my desk. My young replacement has no work ethic. Thinks we don't work weekends.'

'So – what are they?'

'Weekends?' The roar took on a puzzled note.

'The results, oh Duke of Decibels.'

'Sorry, was I shouting? Force of habit. Can't get a word in

at home unless I break out of my usual restrained murmur. Your results: blood on the trouser knees and the coat cuff was the victim's. No other blood stains, and no spatter. I don't know if that was what you hoped for.'

'It just adds to the inconclusivity,' Slider said.

'Well, you don't want the game to be easy, or anyone could play it,' Tufty bellowed. 'Other traces – skin and hair – have been typed, for the record. They match the wearer – name of Lavender, I believe? – except for one sensational long blonde hair on the back of the right shoulder. No match to anything you've sent us.'

'He has a blonde assistant that he works with every day,' Slider said.

'Lucky bugger. Well, that's it. Let me know when you're ready to come and help me demolish the old spoils.'

'Does it have to be nude?'

'Just as you please. Liberty 'All in our house, as you very well know. Diana asks after Joanna – as do I, come to think of it. She well now?'

'Physically OK, according to the doctor.'

'It was a rotten show,' Tufty said with sympathy, reading between the lines. 'Caviar and vodka. Cheer her up. Show her life's still worth living.'

'Thanks. I'll bear it in mind,' Slider said.

Atherton telephoned Georgia Hedley-Somerton. She sounded relieved when he identified himself. 'Something wrong?' he asked. 'More trouble from the press?'

'No, they seem to have given up and left us now. It's just that – I know it's foolish, but I feel unsettled and nervous here in the shop on my own. As if it's haunted. Not that I believe in ghosts,' she added hastily, 'it's just an odd feeling of unease.'

'Quite natural,' he said. 'Your mental rhythms have been disrupted by a very out-of-the-usual occurrence. It's a sort of mild shell-shock, I suppose.'

'It can't be so out-of-the-usual to you,' she replied. 'How on earth do you cope?'

'It comes with the job,' Atherton said lightly. 'How's business?'

'There've been a lot of phone calls – most of them nothing but ghoulish curiosity dressed up as enquiries about opening times. Quite a few clients ringing with sympathies. And a couple of genuine enquiries from people who didn't seem to have heard about Mr Egerton, or didn't associate the news with the shop.'

'So you're keeping busy.'

'Not busy enough. I'm passing the time updating the inventory, in case the shop has to go. Was there something you wanted, or was it just a courtesy call?'

Atherton was charmed by the idea that they had time to ring round and see how everyone was doing. 'I was concerned for your welfare, of course,' he said – no harm in enhancing the Met's reputation – 'but I also had a small question. On Thursday, could you confirm what time you went to lunch and what time you returned?'

'I thought I'd told you,' she said. 'I went out at twelve thirty and came back at one. I just went down to the bank at South Kensington and had a quick sandwich at a café there.'

'And is that your usual time?' he asked.

'I don't have any fixed time,' she said. 'It depends on what we're doing. If Mr Lavender's away, for instance, I might stay in the shop and have a sandwich at the desk. But if there's something in particular I want to do, we arrange it so I have the time I need. It's all very flexible. Mr Lavender is very helpful like that.'

'Right,' said Atherton. So it wasn't that Thursday had been unusual and Lavender had absent-mindedly given the usual time. He had either misremembered or misspoken. 'How is he today?' he asked. 'Still keeping to his room?'

'Oh no,' she said with a touch of pride. 'He's back at work. Did you want to speak to him? Because he's not here. He's gone to a sale, won't be back until late.'

Atherton felt a stirring of unease. Had he skipped? 'What sale is that?'

'It's a big antiques fair at Banbury. They have one every year at this time. It runs all week, but the Monday and Tuesday are dealers only.'

'So – was it a last minute decision to go?' Atherton asked, trying to make it casual.

'Oh, no, it's been in the diary for weeks – months. He always goes.' Evidently, he hadn't sounded casual enough, because she said, anxiously, 'Why? You don't think—? He wouldn't do anything foolish, not Mr Lavender. He's naturally upset about Mr Egerton – they've been friends for so long – but he's not likely to *hurt* himself.'

'No, no, of course not,' Atherton said soothingly. 'He'll be back tonight, you said?'

'Probably,' she said. 'He does sometimes stay over, if there's anything else going on in the area, or if there's someone he wants to see. There are a lot of dealers in the Cotswolds, and they all know each other.'

'If he's not coming back, I expect he'll ring you,' Atherton suggested.

'Of course – so I'll know to take care of the shop tomorrow.'

'If he does ring you, will you let me know? Tell me where he's staying in case I need to get in touch with him?'

'Yes,' she said, 'I'll call you.' She sounded uneasy, and he guessed he hadn't managed to convince her that he wasn't.

'It's probably nothing,' said Slider. 'If it's been in the diary a long time, as she says. He probably just needs to get away and keep busy. Sitting up there in that flat would give anyone the willies.'

'Yes,' said Atherton, 'but . . .'

There was always the 'but'. 'Might be an idea to ask our brothers in Banbury if one of them will look in and see if he's there,' said Slider.

'They might even have someone there anyway, if it's a big event,' said Atherton. 'I know I would. In any case, they can't have anything else much to do, in the country. It's not sheep-rustling season.'

'You're so prejudiced,' Slider said. 'Anyway, Lavender's becoming less of a suspect by the hour.' He told him about the blood evidence.

'Lack of spatter isn't good,' Atherton admitted. 'But it's not conclusive. He could have had something else on – a different jacket or a raincoat or—'

'A smock? A pinny?' Slider mocked him. 'And where did

he put this bloodstained protective clothing? The house was searched by SOCO.'

'I was going to say "or he managed not to get spattered",' Atherton concluded. 'He has long arms, and if the angle was right—'

'Well, let's get his timings checked out, then we can think about it some more,' Slider said. 'And, just so that we clear as we go, check Melling's alibi. And Ehlie's.'

'Connolly's doing Melling. Hollis is on Ehlie,' Atherton confirmed. 'And Swilley's going to have a go at Sylvia Thornton and Felicity Marsh.'

Slider nodded. 'It's thin pickings, all the same,' he sighed. 'Meanwhile, I suppose I must go and have a word with Philip Masterson. You'd better come with me. You know more about the politician scene than I do.'

Atherton brightened. He was always game for an outing. 'I'll go and find out where he is. Probably sitting in a committee this morning. We ought to catch him when he comes out for lunch.'

'The things you know,' Slider said kindly.

TEN

Sex in a Cold Climate

An assistant in Philip Masterson's office set up a meeting for them at lunchtime in Interview Room One at Portcullis House, the new building across the road from the Palace of Westminster. When Slider and Atherton arrived, there was a queue of about fifty people stretching along the pavement, visitors waiting their turn to pass through the extremely thorough security checks.

'For once it pays to be a copper,' Atherton murmured as they used their warrant cards to jump to the head of the queue. Once through security they were let loose like butterflies into the giant hothouse that was the central atrium. It reached the whole height of the building to the glass roof, which was supported by strange, curved ribs of steel: a vast area containing full-grown trees and shallow stretches of water. With the bee-like murmur of voices, and the light filtering through leaves, Slider thought it was probably a bit like being inside the original Crystal Palace with its elms and fountains. What looked from the outside like a hefty, solid office building was in fact a hollow shell, with the accommodation around the empty centre like the rind of a coconut.

'What a colossal waste of space,' Slider commented. 'When you think they only built it because there wasn't enough room over the road for all the MPs.'

'Ah, the nineties!' Atherton said. 'When there was money to burn, and the golden age was never going to end. Stairs or lift?'

They had only been waiting in the interview room for ten minutes when the door opened and Philip Masterson appeared, looking flurried and a little damp about the collar as if he had been hurrying.

'I'm sorry to keep you waiting,' he said, a trifle perfunctorily, as though that was *their* problem. 'Committee for Overseas Development. Solar farms. I had to sit in. I have to be at the debate this afternoon and I've still got some papers to look at, so we'll have to make this quick. Mind if we go and get a coffee while we talk? It's just along there.'

He was out again before they could object, and they hurried to follow him along the passage to the coffee area which took up one of the curved corners of this floor. There was no-one else there, and Slider and Atherton settled into a group of chairs around a table in the corner and watched their man as he manipulated the coffee machine. 'You're welcome to a cup as well,' Masterson said over his shoulder.

'Thank you, we're fine,' Slider said patiently.

At last he came back towards them, coffee in hand. He was early-fifties, of middle height, not fat, but softening and spreading around the waist and chin in the manner of a man who spends too much time sitting down at his job.

They had looked him up. His father had died when he was a year old; his mother had remarried a solicitor, and he had grown up with his stepfather's name. He'd gone to Westminster, and Trinity Cambridge, and then straight into politics as a research assistant to an MP friend of his stepfather's, and was later put up for a safe seat, which he won at the same time as he married the well-connected Julia Rabbet. With so much going for him he ought to have shot to the stars, but somehow he hadn't managed to live up to his promise. There was something, Slider thought, looking at him now, too ordinary about him.

He had light-brown hair, artfully highlighted, styled in the floppy Hugh Grant fashion, and his face looked slightly greasy, as if he used a lot of moisturizer or – heaven help us – was wearing make-up. His suit looked expensive but hard-worn and a little crumpled, and his aftershave didn't quite mask the smell of warm body underneath. Not yet the smell of sweat, but not far off, as if he'd had a hard morning. He was neither handsome nor the opposite; a wide face with a round chin and a nose-shaped nose. Nothing to notice about him at all except for his rather full-cut mouth, which he had the habit of pursing when he was thinking, as though hoping for a kiss.

'So, what's all this about?' he said briskly, hitching his trouser legs and sitting opposite them. He drank from his coffee cup, licking foam from his upper lip as he lowered it. Slider felt an irrational suspicion of any man who drank cappuccinos. Men ought to drink coffee plain and black, and that was that. Masterson's fingernails looked as though he had them manicured, too. And he wore a gold signet ring and a plain wedding band on the same finger. 'I haven't got much time, as I mentioned,' he went on, 'so I'd be glad if you'd just get down to it.'

Slider's glance threw it to Atherton. He wanted to be free to observe.

Atherton took his cue. 'We're investigating the death of Rowland Egerton,' he began.

'Who?' Masterson asked, frowning. 'Oh, you mean that fellow on the television.'

Atherton thought this was going too far in the I'm-too-important-to-bother-with-little-things direction. 'I'm sure you know who I mean. Your wife was on the same show.'

'My *late* wife,' Masterson objected. 'I know you chaps have to do your job, but a little tact wouldn't go amiss. Feelings are still raw.'

'I'm very sorry for your loss,' Atherton said neutrally. 'Your late wife must have known him pretty well. They were on the same show together for many years.'

'Knew him as a work colleague, yes. But the show didn't take up much of her time, you know. One day's filming once a fortnight, thirteen shows a year. It hardly made the basis of a deep friendship.'

'I believe she was a dealer in her own right?' Atherton on. 'With a shop in Woburn.'

'She shared a shop with two other dealers,' Masterson said, reluctantly, as though admitting something not quite *quite*. The little woman had to go out to work? Shame on you. But this was the twenty-first century; and Woburn was a posh place to have an antique shop.

'And I expect she went to antiques fairs and country house sales,' Atherton suggested.

Masterson agreed warily.

'So I'm sure she met Mr Egerton on many occasions. All these dealers know each other, as I've been told several times recently.'

Masterson looked both wary and slightly annoyed now. 'Yes, I expect she did meet him from time to time. What of it? I wish you'd get on with whatever you want to ask me. Time is precious.' He looked ostentatiously at his watch – a Hugo Boss chronograph, all over dials and knobs. Expensive, but not discreet, Atherton decided. Masterson was a man who needed props to impress. It perhaps explained why he hadn't reached his potential.

'Very well, sir,' said Atherton – the sort of 'sir' that only a policeman can deploy, a 'sir' that lashes contempt and menace together with the cling film of politeness. 'If you insist – when did you last see Mr Egerton?'

Masterson coloured slightly. 'I don't like your tone,' he said. 'Why should I have seen him at all? He was Bunny's friend, not mine.'

'What about his Christmas party?' Slider put in. It was a punt; they didn't know Rabbet had been there, but Melling had said 'everyone' – and if Rabbet, then surely Masterson? He struck Slider as the sort of man who wouldn't miss the chance to hobnob with celebrities. 'I know partners were invited to that.'

The lips pursed, and behind them the front teeth chewed on something, as if he had finally dislodged a raspberry pip that had been bothering him. 'Yes,' he said at length, 'now you come to mention it, there was a Christmas party. But Bunny went on her own. I had family commitments.'

'So when *was* the last time you saw him?' Atherton pressed.

Masterson allowed himself annoyance. 'I really have no idea! What on earth is the point of these questions?'

'Well, sir,' said Atherton at his most silky, 'may I remind you that he was at your late wife's funeral?'

Masterson opened his mouth in fury, but no resentful bellow emerged. A cautious, politicianly look came into his eyes, and he closed it again, took a breath, and said more calmly, 'Ah, yes, as a matter of fact I had forgotten that. As you can imagine, I had other things on my mind that day.'

'Of course, sir,' Slider said soothingly. 'Please tell us how Mr Egerton came to be there.'

'How? He just came, that's how. Invited himself. I'd made it very clear it was close family only – told everyone – even went to the trouble of telling the producer of the show that we requested they stayed away. But that wasn't good enough for *him*.' He was growing annoyed again, with the memory. 'He had to come anyway – shove himself in where he wasn't wanted. Hoping to get his face in the papers, I suppose. Typical of him!'

'So you confronted him,' Atherton said. At Masterson's slight hesitation, he added, 'Your altercation was caught on camera, in the background of the authorized photographs.'

'Why on *earth* were you looking at those?' he asked, affronted.

'It's our job, I'm afraid, sir. Tell me about the altercation.'

'Oh, it wasn't anything like that,' Masterson said briskly. 'I told him he wasn't welcome, he apologized and went away. That was all.' He gave a little laugh. 'It was so insignificant, I'd forgotten all about it. As I said, I had other things on my mind.'

'And was that the last time you saw him?'

'I wish you wouldn't keep saying "last time", as if there were dozens of times. I tell you, I hardly knew the man.'

'But you said shoving himself in where he wasn't wanted was "typical of him",' Slider said.

'By reputation. I heard stories about him – from Bunny. And others. Many people disliked him for being so pushy, you know.' He looked again at his watch. 'Look, I really must go. I have to read those papers before the debate.'

'Just one last question, sir,' Atherton said, catching the ball from Slider. 'Would you mind telling us where you were on Thursday last. It's purely a matter of routine – to eliminate anyone who knew the deceased and had seen him recently.'

Masterson seemed to like the word 'eliminate'. 'Thursday? That's easy,' he said. 'Deregulation committee in the House from eleven until two, then I had lunch downstairs here and I worked alone in my office for the rest of the day. Went home

at around six. Did emails and read letters, then watched a
little television while I had supper. I have most of my meals
on my knees, now. I don't like eating alone,' he added pathetically. 'It helps to have the TV on. The house is so silent
otherwise.'

They emerged on to Bridge Street and breathed in the cold
air. Tourists were flocking everywhere, noisy and directionless,
blocking the way and bumping into each other, like black-
headed gulls on a rubbish tip. An intrepid – or possibly
demented – man in a kilt was playing the bagpipes on
Westminster Bridge. Simply the thought of it made the normal
man's assets shrivel. On the full, slow river a pair of barges
moved monumentally downstream and a white pleasure-boat
swung across the current to dock at Westminster Pier where
the next passenger load was waiting. In the background the
London Eye turned imperceptibly against the hard blue sky,
and in the foreground vermilion double-deckers inched past
the gothic tracery of the Houses of Parliament, like the establishing shot of all establishing shots. Being in this part of
London always made Slider feel as if he was in a movie.
    'Well?' Slider said.
    'Didn't like him,' said Atherton. 'Shallow and showy. And
it sounds as if he didn't like Egerton.'
    'But he's got the perfect alibi,' said Slider as they headed
off. 'House of Commons committee until two.'
    'He was on his own for the rest of the day. No-one to
corroborate that part of his alibi.'
    'Egerton was dead by then. He doesn't need an alibi for
the rest of the day.'
    'I'm wondering whether he knows he doesn't.'
    Slider glanced at him. 'You're getting way too clever,' he
said. 'He'd only know he didn't need an alibi for the rest of
the day if he was the murderer. And if he was in committee
until two he couldn't have been the murderer.'
    Atherton sighed. 'Oh well, at least we can cross him off.
But I still think he was evasive about the quarrel at the funeral.
It looked like a lot more than him saying, "Would you mind
leaving, old chap," and Egerton saying, "Certainly, old fellow."'

'He's a politician,' said Slider. 'They're paid to be evasive.'

'I'm starving. How about lunch before we head back?'

'Round here? It's all tourist traps,' Slider objected.

'There's the Albert, in Victoria Street. That's only five minutes away. Taylor Walker pub. And they do a decent fish, chips and mushy peas.'

'You've sold me,' said Slider. 'But we mustn't be long. Lot to do today.'

'You sound like Philip Masterson,' said Atherton.

Felicity Marsh, her agent told Swilley with a touch of importance, was in Paris, filming a documentary, and wouldn't be back until Thursday.

But Sylvia Thornton was at home and happy to be interviewed. 'Come to tea!' she cried gaily. 'One so loves company!'

She gave an address in a village in Hertfordshire, then gave copious directions on how to get there. 'Write it down!' she kept trilling. 'Write it down, you'll never find it otherwise! And don't pay any attention to anything your satnav tells you. It's all rot.'

Swilley looked at the address with grave misgivings. She hated the countryside with a deep and visceral loathing. She liked tarmac and concrete, streets and pavements, brick, steel, glass and lamp posts. Fields and cows filled her with horror. But the directions turned out to be immaculate and brought her via a web of narrow lanes to a gravel patch beside a small, square cottage, where she parked next to a dumpy red Renault Clio. *Old lady car*, she thought unkindly. The cottage was so sweetly pretty it made her teeth ache – and this was winter. In summer, covered in roses, she guessed it would make even Richard Curtis nauseous.

Sylvia Thornton had the door open to welcome her before she got anywhere near it. 'Come in, come in! How nice to see you! The kettle's just boiled, and I've got a lovely fire going. Horrible cold day, isn't it? So you found it all right?'

Swilley, following her in as she chuntered, said, 'Yes, your directions were very good.'

'Thank you! Long experience of losing visitors down the cracks. Let me take your coat. Now sit there, make yourself comfortable, and I'll get the tea. Unless you'd prefer coffee?' she added doubtfully.

'Tea is fine,' Swilley said.

The room was small and chintzy and beamy and china-ornamenty, but the fire was cheerful. An enormous tabby cat was curled in one of the flanking armchairs. It opened one eye to inspect Swilley, as she sat on the floral chintz sofa, and closed it again dismissively. Thornton returned with a tray, which she put on the coffee table, and took the other armchair. Swilley was horribly afraid she was going to say, 'Shall I be mother?'

In the flesh she looked older than last time Swilley had seen her on television. Her plump, softly creased face was like a gently expiring balloon, her carefully waved white hair appeared thin. But she wore full make-up, diamond-encircled pearls at her ears, diamond rings on her fingers, three strands of pearls around her neck, and the rest of her was covered in a pink velour jump suit and pink sequin slippers.

Catching Swilley looking, she put a ring-heavy hand up to pat her pearls and said, 'When you get to my age, you have to have a bit of bling about you. Look at Barbara Cartland! If she hadn't got herself up like a great big fluff of pink candyfloss, no-one would have noticed her at all. She'd have been just another little fat old lady. Like me.' The hand reached for the teapot, diamonds sparking in the firelight. 'Shall I be mother?'

Tea was poured and passed. 'Have a piece of cake,' said Thornton. 'It's lemon drizzle. Very good.'

'Did you make it yourself?' Swilley asked politely.

Thornton laughed. 'Oh my dear! Look at these.' She extended her hand, displaying the long, pink-painted nails. 'Are these the hands of a cook? No, there's a bakery in the village, run by such a lovely girl, Miranda, and her husband. They make everything on the premises. Gorgeous bread and cakes to die for! They're famous – people come from miles around. Now, have you got everything?'

Swilley took the plate with the cake on it, settled herself, stretched her legs. 'I wanted—' she began.

But Thornton was off again. 'You are a very lovely young

woman. Not at all what one thinks of as a policewoman. Or are detectives called policewomen? And so tall, too. It must be lovely to be tall. Women of my generation never are – poor feeding, you know, during the war and after. It wasn't until the sixties, really, that there was enough so that people grew to their full potential. All you young people are lovely and tall and healthy. It's very comforting. But I expect you want to talk to me about poor Rowland. Do you watch the show?'

'I've seen it, once or twice,' Swilley said cautiously.

'Of course, you young people have better things to do,' Thornton said comfortably. 'I was the same when I was your age. It's only old people who watch television these days. Well, Rowland was a stalwart of the show. I expect he thought of himself as the lynch-pin, though I'm not sure everyone else would agree. But he was the rookie once, of course. Seven years ago, when he first joined, he knew nothing about cameras. But he was good looking, of course, and he had that intangible thing, star quality, so I knew he'd make it all right. He and I had a little fling, you know.'

'No, I didn't know,' said Swilley.

'Oh yes. That was before he joined *Antiques Galore!* We used to meet on the dealers' circuit. And I was on *Treasure Trove*, *AG*'s predecessor – do you remember that? – and he used to come and watch me recording sometimes. I suppose that might be what gave him the idea of trying it himself. Not just lots of lovely exposure on the screen, but lots of lovely young women ready to be impressed. Celebrity is a tremendous aphrodisiac, you know. Where was I?'

'You had a fling.'

'Oh yes. Well, I don't claim great distinction for it, because he was very rampant, you know. Went through every female he could lay his hands on. But I had my turn, and very nice it was, too,' she added reminiscently. 'I was still on the HRT at the time, so I was horny as a hoot-owl, and it must be said that Rowland was a top-notch performer. At the drop of a hat. Mr Ever-Ready. A bit like the energizer bunny – he'd always have a bit more just when you thought he'd finished. Am I making you uncomfortable, talking like this?'

'Not at all,' Swilley said, privately thinking it was revolting. 'It's very refreshing. And helpful.'

Thornton nodded. 'So we had our fling, lots and lots of lovely sex, and no harm done. I miss it,' she said with a sigh. 'My doctor told me I had to come off the HRT because of health worries, and that was that. No more sex-drive. No more anything. Except weight-gain. I became what you see now,' she said, spreading her hands, 'and no man will ever look at me again. And I'm not on the show much any more. I'm a sort of reserve, on the bench in case of injuries. Well, little fat old ladies are not what television's about, even though that's mostly who watches it. Ironic, don't you think?'

Swilley didn't want to talk about that. 'Was that why Mr Egerton dropped you?'

'Don't call him that. Call him Rowland, as we're discussing his private life. And call me Sylvia, while you're about it. All right?'

Swilley nodded, managing not to say, 'Yes, ma'am.'

'So, why did Rowland drop me? It wasn't really like that. We weren't romantically involved. He had other people, and so did I, and eventually we just drifted away from each other, with no hard feelings. Love wasn't what I was after, and I don't think Rowland had it in him to be attached to a woman in that way. Not back then. It was all about sex.' She smiled. 'Actually, the idea of Rowland being faithful . . .! He only had to see a woman to want to bonk her.'

'You say he didn't have it in him to be attached?'

'Not then. He was very insecure, you know, and it was his way of proving to the world that he was worth something. The more women he scored, the better he was. Notches on the bedpost. I don't say he didn't enjoy it – that's something you can't fake – but it was a numbers game.'

'Why was he insecure?'

'My dear, I can't tell you. He was smart, good-looking – there was no reason he should be. But he was. Some people just are, you know. And once he became famous, women just threw themselves at him, so he should have been content, but still he had to have them all. That sort of behaviour can become a habit.'

'You said "back then"—' Swilley began.

Sylvia caught on quickly. 'Oh, he changed,' she said. 'I don't know whether it was age catching up with him, or that someone said something to him – he was doing more and more for the Beeb, and they're very wary of scandal. But recently he's stopped the dolly-chasing, cleaned up his image. He comes across quite the patriarch now – richly benevolent towards the whole world. My view is – and it's only my opinion, but remember I know the old fellow rather well – my view is that he's fallen in love.'

She looked at Swilley for reaction, bright-eyed, like a robin eyeing a worm.

'Fallen in love?'

'Yes, at last. The old faker hooked! The fisherman turned fish! Caught, line and sinker. You see, I don't think this new image *is* an act. I think he's actually become a nicer person, and of course that's one of the sure signs of real love, as opposed to mere sex.'

'Fallen in love with who?'

'Ah, that's the question,' Sylvia said, frowning in thought. 'Whoever it is, he's become terribly discreet, and that's another reason I think what I think. Chivalry. He wants to protect her from the eyes of the world. He'd *never* have done that before. Quite the opposite – he welcomed the eyes of the world on his conquests. Craved them. Now – Mr Discretion! Despite watching him as closely as it's possible, I can't work out who it is.'

'You could be mistaken,' said Swilley.

Sylvia must have heard the impatience. 'Of course I could. I *said* it was just my opinion. More tea?'

She had offended her. Swilley rowed back. 'Do you think it was someone on the show?'

'Well, of course, I've wondered about that,' Sylvia said, somewhat mollified. 'But who? For him to fall, really fall at last, it would have to be someone with something about her. Not just a daffy little production assistant or a fluffy gofer. And the only women of substance on the show – apart from me, and I can assure you it isn't me – are Felicity Marsh, the presenter, and Bunny. You know, Julia Rabbet?'

'I know,' said Swilley.

'Well, Bunny's lovely, but they've known each other for yonks, and they're really more like brother and sister. And she's not the type to have an affair – very straight-down-the-middle, Bunny. From a very old family, Roedean, Oxford, country house parties, hunting, Ascot. Even if she wanted an affair, I can't see her having it with Rowland. There's something a bit shabby-genteel about him, a bit middle-class and trying-too-hard, if you know what I mean. She'd have to stoop a long way to get down to his level.'

'He went to her funeral,' Swilley said.

'Did he? Well, they were friends,' she said.

'Was he upset when she died?'

'We all were. She was a lovely lady. But him more than anyone else? Not that I noticed. There was no rending of hair. He seemed quiet and thoughtful the last time I saw him – but as I said, that's been the way he was for the past two years or so. Since he fell in love.'

'So, if not Bunny—?'

'Well, that leaves Felicity – assuming for the moment that it was someone on the show, which it needn't have been at all. But Felicity – yes, I could see him going for her. She's smart, hard, ambitious, glamorous. A glittering prize. And very sexy, I have it on authority from chaps who've worked with her. But not an easy conquest. Yes, she'd be just the sort of woman he'd fall head over heels for. And of course, if it *was* her, secrecy of the first order would be necessary, because they're both in the eye of the media. Especially, they'd have to be discreet on the show.'

'Would she go for him?'

'Well, he's a bit older than her, but women like her often do fall for the slightly fatherly chap, the experienced lover who knows how to treat a woman properly. Men her own age can be infuriatingly self-centred. And he's famous and getting famouser, and he's got a very good *in* with the Beeb, and also now with independent television, with that Royal Palaces series he did, all of which would count with her. She'd want someone well-connected, because her career's very important to her. And I *have* seen them quite a few times with their heads together, and sitting together at the breaks. You know how you can tell when there's some connection between two people – the way they catch eyes across the room, significant looks. I wouldn't be a bit surprised if there was something going on with them.' She looked at Swilley thoughtfully. 'If it was her, she must be devastated now. Have you spoken to her?'

'She's out of the country,' Swilley said.

'Ah,' said Sylvia, as if that was significant.

'Doing a documentary,' Swilley added.

'The show must go on,' Sylvia said, nodding. 'Work helps in these circumstances. Have some more cake.'

'No – thank you,' Swilley said. All this was very nice and filled in a lot of gaps in Egerton's life, but it didn't get them any closer to the murderer. 'I suppose,' she tried, 'his sexual antics made him unpopular on the show?'

'Oh no,' said Sylvia. 'When it's someone famous like him, it just adds to his appeal. They think he's a hell of a fellow. No, it wasn't *that* that people disliked. It was his pushiness – grabbing the limelight.'

'Who, in particular, disliked that?'

Sylvia didn't answer, thinking.

'There was a row between him and Rupert Melling,' Swilley tried.

'Oh, that! I can tell you all about that. I was standing just a few feet away, heard the whole thing. They didn't notice me, or they might have shut up.'

'There was something about a snuffbox,' Swilley suggested.

'Oh, that was the recording before last. I thought you meant last week.'

'Tell me about both of them.'

'Well, the snuffbox caused real bad feeling between them. Rupert was very upset, and Rowland just wouldn't back down. I don't know why he was being so stubborn – and right was clearly on Rupert's side. But then Rupert lost his temper and started calling him names. Called him a thief and a fake and a crook, suggested he rooked the punters, played on their ignorance. Rowland got very angry about that, and eventually Gavin had to come over and shut them down.'

'And what about last week? Gavin didn't say they'd had another row.'

'He wouldn't have known, because it wasn't a shouting-match. As I said, I was standing just behind them, otherwise I wouldn't have known either. Anyway, Rupert had been trying to make a move on one of the shoulder-cam boys, a young, willowy lad with long hair and *very* thin shirts. Called Tarquin, or Torquil, or some such name. I'd seen that myself. And Rowland must have too, because he came over to tell Rupert to lay off, because *Antiques Galore!* was a family show and if that sort of thing got out it would ruin its reputation and all their livelihoods. Rupert of course said what business was it of his, and Rowland said it was everyone's business to keep the punters and the Beeb happy. Rupert said he was a fine one to talk, after his years of sexual antics, and Rowland said that was all in the past, that it was different now, that he didn't do that sort of thing any more. Then Rupert said Rowland was just jealous because he fancied Tarquin himself – the old tease, you see, but he said it with real venom. I suppose he was angry with Rowland because of the snuffbox and just wanted something to taunt him with. But – and I was very impressed – Rowland kept his cool. He stepped closer and said to Rupert very quietly that if he didn't lay off the cameraman he'd tell Alex – that's Rupert's current live-in.'

'Yes, I know. How did Rupert react?'

'Rowland walked away before he could say anything else, and Rupert went back to arranging his table, but I could see he was furious.' She paused. 'But, you know, these things happen. Words are exchanged, but they pass. We all went out for a meal and a drink after the show and everyone was quite chummy again.'

She was back-pedalling, realizing she was dropping her colleague in it. Swilley let it go, rather than draw attention to it. 'Why did Rupert call Rowland a fake and a crook?' she asked instead.

'Oh – I don't know. I think he meant his public persona was a fake – all that charm, and oiling up the punters, flattering them. I suppose it *is* a bit false, though they all do it to some extent. It's part of the act.'

'And crook?'

'I think Rupert had found something out about him. You see, I happen to know that Rowland had a lot of dealings with the art copyist, Pat Duggan.'

'Patrick Duggan? Wasn't he a forger? I've heard of him. Didn't he get sent down for forging a Renoir in the late seventies?'

'It was a Degas, actually. Yes, he was put on trial for conspiracy to defraud, though he always claimed he was innocent. I mean, he certainly painted it, but he said it wasn't meant to defraud anyone. He served about three months, something like that, but then he was let out on condition that he helped the police crack a criminal ring that was making a lot of trouble with fake Old Masters. Anyway, after that, he apparently went straight, and became quite a celebrity in his own way, exposing the tricks of the trade.'

'So how did Rowland have dealings with him?'

'Oh, it was quite a bit later, when he and I were having our fling, and Rowland was busy with his interior design firm. He'd met Pat Duggan somehow, and liked him – he was a very likeable rogue, I understand – and decided to put some business his way.'

'What sort of business?'

'Painting pictures for his clients, as part of the decor.'

'Forgeries?'

'No, no. Pat was a good painter in his own right, and he could copy any style, so he could come up with just the right painting for any interior, and the clients loved it – as good as an old master but a fraction of the price and no trouble with insurance.' She smiled. 'But of course, he *had* been in prison, and if you want to blacken a man's name you can always stick the old label on him. And on his friends. Something I overheard between Rupert and Rowland made me think he knew about Pat being Rowland's friend. And he did like to taunt him with being a fake, or a faker.'

She fell silent, thinking. Swilley thought she was realizing that, again, she had dropped a colleague in it. But as she was getting ready to speak, Sylvia went on, revealing a different train of thought. 'First Bunny, then Rowland,' she said sadly.

'It's what you always dread, this dropping-off-the-perch business. When your own generation start to go. You suddenly feel – exposed. "Grow old along with me! The best is yet to be, The last of life, for which the first was made." All very well, but even after Elizabeth died, Browning had a son living with him. And people were never alone then the way they are now.'

Swilley felt a shiver. Out of the corner of her eye she could see the window, with a small view of the country road outside and a hedge and field on the other side. What on earth would persuade anyone to live out in a place like this, least of all someone who didn't want to be alone?

'I must be getting back,' she said, and it wasn't just a conventional lead-in to leave-taking.

ELEVEN

More in Zorro Than Anger

'I'm not sure that gets us any further forward,' Slider said. 'Even if he was having an affair with Felicity Marsh – which is pure supposition at this point – where's the motive for murder?'

'Jealous husband?' Gascoyne suggested.

'She's not married,' Swilley said. 'First thing I looked up when I got back.'

'Jealous significant other, then,' Atherton said. 'Wasn't she supposed to be hooked up with that newsreader?'

'John Colley,' Swilley said. 'But according to the gossip mags that's over. They split amicably eight months ago. Apparently, to concentrate on their separate careers. She'd just got that new series, you know, about the Nazi art thefts. That's what she's doing in Paris at the moment.'

'Isn't there a co-presenter who's a bit of a bob?' Connolly said. 'Curly hair. Posh. Can't remember his name, but he's definitely ridey. I wouldn't chuck him out of bed for dropping crumbs.'

'Benedict Cowper,' Swilley said. 'With a "w". He's quite a bit younger than her, though.'

'No reason that should stop them,' said Atherton. 'And a hot-blooded young man might well get worked up about an older rival. No man ever understands what women see in other men – I speak from experience – but when he's old into the bargain . . .'

'Yes, age is the ultimate crime in the eyes of youth,' Slider said. 'Well, not much we can do about Felicity Marsh until she comes back from Paris.'

'I could sniff about, see if there's any rumours about her and romantic entanglements,' Swilley suggested.

'Yes, do that. The other strand is the ill-feeling between Melling and Egerton. That seems a bit more substantial.'

'But enough to make him want to murder him?' Atherton said.

'The actual killing looks like a blow struck in sudden anger, rather than a premeditated plan,' Slider said. 'And it seems as though Melling is capable of impulsive behaviour.'

'But wasn't it him provoking Egerton rather than vice-versa?'

'There was the business about Egerton threatening to tell his lover about the cameraman,' Swilley said.

'Blackmail!' Connolly said. 'We like that. That's grand for a motive. I can just see your man Egerton as a blackmailer. I always thought he was kind o' creepy.'

'Let's not get carried away,' Slider said. 'How far have we got on confirming Melling's alibi?'

'I was going to do him after Lavender, guv,' said McLaren, indistinctly through a mouthful of Cadbury's Fruit and Nut. 'I was prioritizing.'

'All right,' said Slider. 'Tell us about Lavender, then.'

'It's looking tasty,' McLaren said, swallowing with difficulty. 'I got on to Waitrose and traced his till receipt. He paid cash, but there was only one basket that matched his exactly.'

'What about CCTV?' Mackay asked.

'They've got cameras trained on the tills, o' course,' McLaren said. 'Matching the till number and the time, it's a tall man who could be Lavender. Definition's not very good, but I'd say it was him all right.'

Connolly said, 'Please tell me he was wearing a trilby, Maurice, or I'll be forced to killya.'

'No hat,' McLaren said.

'A gentleman takes it off when he goes indoors,' said Atherton.

'Can a murderer be a gentleman?' Swilley asked.

'Can a cat look at a king?' Atherton countered.

'That's not the important bit,' McLaren said impatiently, recapturing his audience. 'It's the time. The till receipt says one thirty-eight.'

'Interesting. If he didn't leave his shop until one thirty, there's no way he could have got to Waitrose and done his shopping in eight minutes,' Atherton said.

'But if he left the shop at one,' Swilley objected, 'that's too much time. What'd it take – eight minutes to drive to the supermarket? Ten minutes tops.'

'Allow him fifteen, faffing about at either end,' Atherton said. 'He looks like a faffer to me.'

'He could easy take fifteen minutes to do his bit o' shopping,' said Connolly. 'You should see my dad, God love him! Has to read all the words on the back of every packet before he puts it in the trolley. And he picks up things he's no intention of buying and reads *them* an' all. Finds it interesting, he says, the dote! Drives me mammy nuts, so it does.'

'Lavender probably goes through every piece of fruit and vegetable to find the perfect one,' Swilley said. 'I've seen 'em, squeezing and sniffing – it's always men on their own.'

'Were there queues at the checkout?' Atherton asked McLaren.

'Yeah, it was busy.'

'Well, there's five minutes. So that makes one thirty-eight credible if he left the shop at one or soon after.'

'What's not credible is that he could be One Forty Man at the house,' said Slider.

'Not unless he wears his underpants over his tights,' Connolly said sadly. 'He's got to get back to his car, get out of the car park and drive to Blenheim Terrace. That's ten minutes give or take.'

'One Forty Man was walking from the end of the street, not driving,' Swilley said. 'I never thought he could be Lavender.'

'How are we on confirming the times of these sightings?' Slider asked Mackay.

He looked apologetic. 'They're all approximate. People don't look at their watches every time they pass someone in the street. The one forty witness says it could have been a bit earlier but not later. He was walking from the tube station, and I've checked the log and the station CCTV. The train he must've been on arrived at one thirty-one, and there's a man in a trilby coming through the barrier a few seconds after, so it must have been nearer to twenty-five to that the witness saw the man in the hat.'

'Well, either way, that couldn't have been Lavender,' Swilley said.

McLaren had been looking more and more impatient. 'The point *is*,' he said loudly to get their attention, 'that Lavender says he went straight from Waitrose to the house and got there at twenty-five past two. If his till slip's timed at one thirty-eight, where was he in between?'

'That's three quarters of an hour,' Swilley said. 'You're right, Maurice. Do you need to sit down?' she added sympathetically. 'All this thinking – you must be exhausted!'

'Ah, Janey Mac, why're you always so mean to the poor oul divil? Isn't he as smart as the next man?'

'Only if he's standing next to a tailor's dummy,' Atherton answered. 'Did you know if you put your ear to McLaren, you can hear the sea?'

'They don't bother me,' McLaren told Connolly with genuine serenity. 'My back's broad.'

'Three quarters of an hour needs some explaining,' Slider said, recapturing the thread. 'You're looking for his car on traffic cameras?'

'Yes, guv. No luck so far. Trouble is, there's nothing he's *got* to pass from there, especially if he goes through the back streets. I'm going to try TfL's bus cameras, but that takes longer, o' course, cos with no number plate recognition you've got to do it the hard way.'

Fathom spoke up. 'I can't see it matters where he was, if he wasn't at Egerton's house.'

'Have you been working without a helmet again?' Swilley demanded impatiently. 'We don't know he *wasn't* at Egerton's house. And if he was there earlier than twenty-five past, he could be the killer.'

'Oh,' said Fathom.

'Any word on Lavender at Banbury?' Slider asked Atherton.

'There was a message for me when I got back,' Atherton said. 'A bloke in Banbury CID knows one of the private security guards at the fair, and asked him to check. Lavender turned up all right this morning. He's going to let us know when he leaves.'

Slider nodded. 'All right. Well, there's work to do – let's get to it. McLaren – find where Lavender's car was, then check out Melling. Swilley, you can look into Felicity Marsh if it doesn't take too long. You've still got the finances to sort out. Connolly, you're still looking through Egerton's computer? Keep an eye out for mentions of Patrick Duggan. Fathom, Gascoyne – get back out and canvass some more. We need more reliable sightings of our killer going in and, if it wasn't Lavender, leaving. I don't need to remind you we've got nothing so far, except a putative hat.'

'All hats are hollow mockeries,' Atherton said.

'Sure, a hat wouldn't be a lot o' use if it wasn't hollow,' Connolly observed. 'Nowhere to put your head in.'

The afternoon was wearing on when Slider had a telephone call from Peter de Wett.

'How are things going?' de Wett asked politely.

'Making slow progress,' Slider said circumspectly. It didn't do to forget that however nice he sounded, he was an unknown quantity and a Yard man at that. You didn't tell outsiders it was actually going as smoothly as a grand piano through a garden shredder.

'Well, I think I can help improve your average. I believe we've found your Morisot.'

'Really? That was quick. Where?'

'It's turned up in Chipping Norton,' said de Wett. 'We put out the word to all the dealers on our list, and one of them, the Ronald Hindlipp Gallery, has just contacted our agent to say someone's offered him a painting that looks very like it.'

Chipping Norton was in the Cotswolds, and only ten or twelve miles from Banbury. Slider almost held his breath. 'Who was the person who was trying to sell?'

'Hindlipp says it was an elderly man, well-spoken, who gave his name as John Smith. He thinks that might be a false name.' He sounded amused.

'Some people have no talent for deception,' said Slider.

'Actually, I once knew a chap who really was called John Smith. Had to change his name by deed poll in the end because no-one ever believed him.'

'So what happens now?' Slider asked.

'Hindlipp asked the customer to leave the painting with him

so that he could examine it, and come back later. That's the usual routine when we've put out an alert.'

'Later?'

'About seven. Told him the shop would be shut but he would be there, just to ring the bell and he'd let him in. But he said the chap seemed nervous, so he might not come back. Or if he does, he might want to take the painting away. He's awaiting instructions. What do you want to do?'

Slider looked at the clock. 'If we leave now we can just about make it by seven.'

'I'll tell Hindlipp.'

'If the man comes back before we get there, can he try and stall him?'

'Is he dangerous?' de Wett asked doubtfully.

'I'm pretty sure not. But if it is our man, I'd rather he wasn't spooked into running. Did Mr Hindlipp recognize him, by the way?'

'He says he has a feeling he's seen him somewhere, but can't place him.'

'Well,' said Slider, 'if it *is* our man, he'd naturally avoid going to a dealer he knows.'

'*If* it's your man,' said de Wett, 'and if it *is* the Morisot. Chances are, you know, that the whole thing is perfectly innocent.'

'I know,' said Slider.

But Atherton was jubilant. 'It's him. It's it.'

'Remind me – are we us?'

'He can't talk his way out of this one. We've got him.'

'We haven't got him yet,' Slider said. 'Can't you drive faster?'

'Your word is my command,' Atherton said as they reached the near end of the M40; the road widened, and he could put his foot down. 'So much for the security guard keeping an eye on him,' he grumbled.

'He may have had his own work to do,' Slider said.

'Don't be reasonable. The man's a slacker and a nogudnik.'

'If he *had* said Lavender was leaving, there wasn't much we could do about it,' said Slider. 'We weren't in a position to follow him. And we don't know if this Chipping Norton bloke *is* Lavender.'

'Being reasonable again,' Atherton warned, skimming past the home-bound traffic at a hundred plus. A moment later, 'We've got company.' An unmarked police car had fallen in behind them, keeping an interested distance. 'Where are you when we need you?'

Slider turned in his seat and held up his warrant card, and they dropped back. They'd radio the other patrols now with their reg number and give them free passage.

'If it *is* Lavender,' Atherton said, 'what on earth is he thinking, trying to sell the painting like that? Openly, to a legit dealer? What a clot!'

'If he's an otherwise innocent man, he probably doesn't know any illegal fences,' Slider said.

'Why sell it at all?'

'Why steal it in the first place?' said Slider. 'Maybe it isn't Lavender.'

'You'd better hope it is. It will solve all our troubles.' They drove on through the dark countryside. The stretches of snow looked oddly luminous. 'Something I've often wondered,' Atherton said conversationally. 'Why is there as much water where sponges grow as everywhere else in the ocean?'

Slider shook his head. 'Potty,' he said. 'I knew it would happen.'

'I like to have something to think about while I drive,' said Atherton.

Chipping Norton, which sometimes called itself the Gateway to the Cotswolds with an unflinching disregard for the kind of tourists that would attract, was fairly quiet on a cold winter's day after shop closing time. It was a pretty place of medieval buildings in golden Cotswold stone, some extremely attractive pubs, and the usual complement of tea shops, cafés and restaurants. It, and its surroundings, housed a long list of wealthy celebrities and old County families, so there were quite a few antique shops, from the entry-level to the 'if you have to ask the price you can't afford it' type, plus the sort of food shops – delectable delis and bespoke butchers – patronized by people with green wellies and Labradors.

The Ronald Hindlipp Gallery was in a stone-flagged alley just off the prettier end of the High Street, and was obviously of the pricier sort, with not a print in sight and no mention of framing services. The windows were velvet lined, with dinky little easels for displaying a few choice piccies on to which halogen downlights would shine during the daytime, but the pictures had been removed for the night and metal-mesh shutters were down, though the lights were still on.

Slider rang the bell and, seeing an entry camera above him, held up his warrant for the lens to inspect. In a moment the door was opened, and a conspiratorial voice murmured, 'He's not here yet. Come in. Come through to the back where you can't be seen.'

It was warm and still inside the shop, with a smell of expensive carpets and a cloistered feeling, as if no voice would ever be raised here. There were paintings around the walls, well-spaced and artfully spotlit, and Slider knew without even glancing at them that they were of the 'don't ask' variety.

Ronald Hindlipp himself was a lean, very dark man, with straight black hair slicked back, so smooth that it looked as though it had been painted on, brown eyes behind dark-framed glasses, and a faintly blue chin. His dark-blue suit was exquisite, his tie a nicely judged balance between the artistic and conservative. He seemed nervous, and walked catlike as he led the way through, as though the floor might suddenly turn aggressive. The back office was a businesslike place, except that the desk was a beautiful piece of antique mahogany and the chairs velvet-upholstered. On a side table a painting was lying on the brown paper and string it had been wrapped in.

'This is it,' Hindlipp said. 'Is this your painting?'

'It looks like it,' Slider said. He brought out the copy of the photograph from the computer system, compared it, and gave it to Hindlipp.

'*La Fille au Toilette*,' he said. 'That's in order. And it's signed Berthe Morisot. Of course, there's the possibility it's a copy, but on the face of it, I'd say it was your picture.'

'What did John Smith say when he brought it in?'

'He said it had been left to him by an uncle who died recently, but he didn't want it and would like to sell it. I said there would have to be an authentication process if it was to realize its full price, and he said he was in rather a hurry for the money, and asked what I would give him for it without going through the process. Of course, I was already looking out for this particular painting, but I would have been made suspicious by that. Although,' Hindlipp added, puzzled, 'he didn't seem the sort. Very well-spoken, sixty-ish, rather old-fashioned overcoat and shoes. Not the sort to steal a painting and try to sell it.'

'Do you have CCTV?' Slider asked.

'Oh – yes, of course! You'll be able to identify him. I'll just bring it up.' He went to the computer and began tapping. 'If I hadn't been alerted by SCD6,' he went on, 'I might have thought he had bought the painting in good faith and was now having doubts about it and was trying to offload it. That would have seemed sufficiently out of character for a man like him, but I never would have thought it stolen. Here we are.' He brought up the image and stood back for them.

'That's our man,' Slider said with a sense of disappointment. There had never been much doubt from the time he took de Wett's call, but he had really not wanted it to be Lavender. But there he stood, a little fuzzy and fish-eyed, but right there in black and white and caught red-handed. 'How did he seem?'

'A little awkward, perhaps,' Hindlipp said. 'But not as much as one would have expected if the painting were stolen. He seemed, rather, as though he had something on his mind. Rather absent.' He paused hopefully, but Slider did not fill him in. 'How is this going to work?' he asked. He looked at the clock. 'He could be here any moment.'

'We'll stay out of sight in the back here, with the door open so that we can hear. When you let him in, lock the door behind him. Then tell him you are very interested in the painting. That will be our cue to come out.'

Hindlipp regarded them carefully for a moment. 'He won't become violent, will he? Or draw a gun on me? I'm not cut out for heroism, and he's quite a big man.'

'He's not that sort,' Slider said. Though he did wonder. There was a vein of suppressed passion that he sensed in Lavender – and he had killed once already. There would be no gun, but the man might fight to get away. Would three of them be enough to hold him if he did? 'Put the Morisot somewhere he can see it when he comes in,' Slider continued. 'That will distract his attention for an instant.'

'I'll hang it on the wall opposite the door, with a spotlight on it,' said Hindlipp. 'It'll be the first thing he sees.'

He went to see to it, while Slider and Atherton drew back so that they were out of sight through the open doorway. Hindlipp reappeared, about to say something, but cocked his head suddenly, listening. 'I think I heard something,' he whispered. An instant later there was the sound of a door buzzer, harsh and threatening like a wasp with a headache.

He gave them one wide-eyed look and went out again. In the tense silence Slider and Atherton waited. There were no footfalls on that velvet carpet, but they heard the sound of keys and of bolts being drawn, a bright ting-ting-ting from the bell over the door at it was opened, then a deep voice saying something too low to make out. 'Yes, come in, come in!' said Hindlipp's voice. Slider winced slightly. Too cheery by half. The man was no actor. 'Horrible cold evening, isn't it!'

Another basso rumble. Slider's overactive imagination saw the tall, dark shape of Lavender, shoulders bulky under his overcoat, too big for his surroundings, head almost brushing the ceiling, like a massive garden statue brought inappropriately indoors. A statue come to life, with a granite fist and Hephaestian muscles. He heard rapid breathing and thought it was his own, then realized it was Atherton, close beside him and taut as a wire, ready for action.

'There's your painting,' said Hindlipp's voice – oh good man, drawing Lavender's eyes to it. 'I must say, now I've had a closer look, I'm very interested in it. Very interested indeed.'

Slider was on a hair-trigger, but Atherton moved so fast they almost got jammed together in the doorway. Both Hindlipp and Lavender jumped at the sudden eruption from the back room. Lavender was wearing the dark-brown trilby, on which Slider noticed a few white flecks of snow just melting; there were spots glistening on the shoulders of his dark overcoat, too. His face registered astonishment, recognition and sick dismay in quick succession, but he did not move – seemed rooted to the spot, thank the Lord. And the expression that came over his face, as Slider reached him and Atherton went quickly behind him to his other side to grab that arm if he should look like trying anything, was one of horror.

He said, in a raw voice, 'Oh, what have I done?'

The sound of it was so painful that Ronald Hindlipp, who had stepped hastily away when the detectives emerged, looked at him with something like pity, and said, as if the words were involuntary, 'I'm sorry.'

'John Lavender,' Slider said, 'I am arresting you on suspicion of the murder of Rowland Egerton. You do not—'

Lavender made a sudden movement that had them both reaching for him, but he had only clapped his hand to his nose. His face was like grey crêpe, and the red was in startling contrast. He started fumbling at his pocket, presumably for a handkerchief, but Atherton stopped him and put his own into his hand.

Slider continued with the caution, thinking of blood – Rowland Egerton's let out of him without his consent, and John Lavender's fleeing his body of its own accord, as if restoring some cosmic balance that had been disrupted.

He telephoned Joanna, to tell her it would be a long night.

'Shouldn't you sound a little happier about it?' she said. 'You've got a result.'

'I know. It's just . . . It was a bit like shooting a sitting duck. It was such a stupid thing to do, to try to sell the painting like that.'

'Well, it isn't sport, it's criminal justice,' Joanna reminded him drily.

'I know. I think I'm just tired. Everything all right your end?'

'Fine. I have some news, as a matter of fact. Good news.'

'Oh yes?' he invited.

'No, I'll wait till I have your full attention,' she decided. 'Go, be a policeman. Do your stuff.'

'Is it snowing there?' Slider asked.

'Yes, like billy-oh. Is that relevant?'

'Not really. I just wanted to hear your voice again.'

'Don't worry about us – we're fine,' she said, as if that was what he had asked.

'Well, thank God for that,' Porson said. 'Good to get it sorted so quickly. He said, "What have I done?" did he? I reckon you ought to get the whole story, then. That sort don't play out the end game, your nobs – reckon caught is caught. Old school-tie. Put your hand up and get it over with.'

'Let's hope so, sir,' said Slider.

'What's up with you?' Porson said sharply. He cocked an eye at Slider. 'No, no, don't go there, laddie! I can see through you like a book. You've developed a soft spot for him. Want someone else to interview him?'

Slider bucked up. 'No, sir, of course not.'

Porson jabbed him a bit more. 'I'll do it. It's coals off a duck's back to me.'

Water to Newcastle? Slider thought, puzzled. 'Thank you, sir, but I don't have a soft spot. Far from it. I saw the body.'

Porson nodded approvingly. 'Sword of justice, that's us.' He made a little swishing movement with his forefinger, carving a Z in the air. 'Leave sentiment to the lawyers.'

Lavender, in an interview room now and not the soft room, looked no less out of place. In his shirt sleeves, cufflinks and tie removed according to regulation, he sat hunched, a box of tissues at his elbow and an untouched cup of tea beside him. His eyes were red as though he had been crying. His nose was red, but had stopped bleeding for the moment. His comb-over had slipped, and he looked utterly pathetic. Big, but pathetic, like some large animal stuck uncomprehendingly in a bog.

'I understand you have waived your right to have a solicitor present,' Slider said.

Lavender shrugged, staring sightlessly at nothing.

'For the tape, please. Will you confirm that you do not want a solicitor present at this time.'

'I don't want anyone,' he said.

He had also waived his right to a telephone call. 'Who would I call?' he had said. 'There isn't anyone. I have no family.'

But before they had done processing him, Georgia Hedley-Somerton had turned up, asking after him, visibly upset, and accompanied by her husband. Slider had naturally wanted to know how she knew Lavender had been arrested, and she had said blankly that someone had telephoned her, saying they were from the station. Either they had not given their name or she didn't remember it. It was a leak, which Slider deplored, but of a curious sort – not to the press, or for gain, but, it seemed, out of an untypical compassion. She had been told she could not see Lavender, and had eventually gone home, having left him a message to call her if there was anything she could do.

He had shown no interest when this was relayed to him and refused, again, both telephone call and solicitor.

'You understand, don't you,' Slider said now, 'that this is a very serious matter.'

'I've been a fool,' Lavender said, but not as if it was an answer to the question. 'Such a fool. I don't know how I could have been so stupid. I see it clearly now. I could hardly have made worse choices – and for what?' He sighed, a terrible dragged-up-from-the-feet sigh, and a trickle of blood re-appeared at his nostrils. He took a tissue and pressed it to his nose with weary patience.

'You understand, don't you,' Slider said, trying again, 'that being in possession of that painting clearly implicates you in the murder of Rowland Egerton. Trying to sell it—'

'It was mine to sell,' he said sharply. 'I bought it. I have the sale receipt and the receipt from the restorer who cleaned it, the report from the evaluator at Sotheby's that I sent it to and the certificate of authentication, all clearly showing my title to it.'

'But you gave it to Rowland Egerton as a present,' Atherton said.

'There is no documentation to prove that. Any paper trail you undertake will show the Morisot is mine.' All this was said firmly and righteously. He seemed braced by the recital. But then his mouth bowed down, and his shoulders sagged again. 'He never liked it, anyway,' he said bitterly. 'He never appreciated it. The trouble I went to to get it for him, and he barely thanked me. Hung it up with the rest of his trash, didn't even bother to find a good place for it, just stuck it in the bottom row of a wall of paintings that had no coherence. Paintings have to be carefully placed, with other works that harmonize. They should sing! But the Morisot wept, where he put it, like a caged finch. He didn't care! Do you know,' he added, with an accusing glare at Atherton, 'how hard it is to buy a present for someone like him, who has everything? I'd been racking my brains for weeks. Searching, scouring the country. Then I found it. I was so happy! It was exactly right, it was perfect. But he just looked at it and practically *shrugged*.'

'That's very hard,' Slider said sympathetically. 'It must have been upsetting for you. But that was some time ago, wasn't it?'

'His fiftieth birthday. We had a big celebration for it. His half century. I wanted something special for him, something he'd get pleasure from for the rest of his life. That he'd look at and think of me. He stuck it on the wall, and I don't think he looked at it again from that moment on.'

'I can see that you would be annoyed,' said Slider. 'But there must have been something else that drove you to kill him – some other reason. Something more immediate – or was it an accumulation of things? He'd behaved so badly to you that in the end you couldn't take it any more?'

Lavender dabbed at his nose, examined the tissue, decided it had stopped bleeding, and folded his hands in front of him. He stared at them and said, almost indifferently, 'I didn't kill him. I would never do such a thing. I know I've behaved like a fool, but I'm not that, not a murderer.' Slowly, he clenched his big, purpled hands into fists and looked at them as they rested on the table; then relaxed them again. 'I didn't kill him,' he said. 'He was dead when I got there.'

Slider's heart sank. He caught Atherton's glance and knew he was thinking the same thing. *Damn, he's going to go that route. The hardest thing to prove or disprove.*

TWELVE
Loved and Loft

'**M**r Lavender,' Slider said sternly, 'it is necessary to tell us the truth now. Your lies have been found out. Your only hope of any leniency is in telling us exactly what happened, and why.'

'I'll tell you the truth,' he said, and he sounded almost surprised that it should be in question. 'I behaved like an utter fool before, but I wasn't thinking clearly. And I was – upset.' He seemed to know how inadequate the word was. He looked at Atherton, briefly, and then at Slider. 'You must be so habituated to it, you perhaps can't understand what a shock it is to an ordinary person to come upon a dead body like that. Particularly the body of someone you – cared about.'

Slider guessed he had been going to say 'loved' but pulled the word at the last minute, perhaps because of Atherton's presence. He probably reminded him a bit of Rupert Melling. Slider smiled inwardly and vowed to pass on that thought to Atherton some time.

'You are still claiming that Mr Egerton was already dead when you arrived at the house?' he said.

'I'm not "claiming" anything. I'm telling you,' Lavender said, annoyed. 'I've said I'll tell you the truth.'

'You also said you arrived at the house at two twenty-five.'

'That was a lie,' Lavender said.

'I know,' said Slider. 'Would you like to start again, beginning with when you left your shop – remembering that we know when you are lying.'

Lavender frowned at that word, and the hands clenched slightly, but perhaps he realized he had earned it, because he relaxed them deliberately, and said, 'I left when Georgia came back from lunch at one o'clock. I suppose, by the time we talked a little and I'd put on my coat, it was about five or ten past. I didn't look. I drove straight to Waitrose, to shop for things for the evening.'

'I imagine you're a careful shopper,' Slider said. 'Slow and methodical.'

Lavender studied the remark for offence. 'I don't dash around throwing things in the trolley, if that's what you mean.'

'You reached the till at one thirty-eight,' Slider said. 'So it must have taken you fifteen minutes or so to do that bit of shopping.'

'It may have done,' Lavender said indifferently. Then, 'One thirty-eight? How do you know that?'

Slider waved the question away. 'Carry on. You paid for your shopping. What then?'

'I went back to the car, of course.' He hesitated, and Slider braced himself for the lie. Lavender said, 'This is going to sound ridiculous. I'm afraid it will all sound very foolish from now on. But I said I would tell you the truth. When I got in the car and turned on the ignition, the radio came on, of course. I have it tuned to Classic FM – a poor compromise. I hate having music torn into meaningless gobbets, but there's no alternative, is there? The piece that was playing was the Brahms violin concerto. A great favourite of mine, and the centrepiece of the first concert Rowland and I ever went to together. And it started me thinking.'

He stopped, his stare gone into the past.

'Thinking about what?' Slider prompted in the end.

He roused himself, but his eyes were still far away. 'I sat listening to the music, and thinking about Rowland, and myself, and all the years we had been friends and partners. Much of it – most of it – good. But you can't think about the good things and not remember the bad. Rowland is – was – a diffi-cult person. He always was, but the little faults that were forgivable, even endearing, when he was younger have hard-ened as he's got older, and particularly so since he's become famous. He really was the last person who ought to have gone into television. It's made him something of a monster.'

'In what way?' Slider slipped the question in as smoothly as possible, sensing Lavender was on a roll.

'In the ways you associate with a spoiled Hollywood star

– the conventional, hackneyed ways. Stardom makes you believe you are more important than "ordinary" people, that everyone else is there to do your bidding, that your wishes must be paramount and anyone else's feelings are unimportant. He was demanding, arrogant, selfish, thoughtless and devious. And I was finding it harder and harder to be dependent on him.'

'You sound as if you were starting to hate him,' Atherton suggested.

Lavender didn't look at him, so deep in his memories that he was hardly aware of his surroundings. 'No, never that,' he said. 'If you once truly love someone, that never changes at bottom. I was starting to hate what he was becoming.'

'In what way were you dependent on him?' Slider asked.

'Business was bad,' he said. 'The recession hit the antiques trade hard. Overheads keep going up, you have to hold on to stock for longer, and the public are getting tougher about haggling over prices – partly thanks to those same television programmes that Rowland stars in. That's an irony. If it wasn't for his television fees, we couldn't have kept going through the recession. And I didn't want to go on like that indefinitely.'

'Did you think he might be going to withdraw that support?'

'No, on the contrary. He *liked* the fact that I – that the business was dependent on him. He crowed about it – made a point of reminding me whenever the opportunity arose. "If it wasn't for me," he'd say, "where would you be?" And I was supposed to pour out my gratitude. I was never allowed to say to him, "If it wasn't for me, where would *you* be?" Because the fact of the matter is,' he went on, anger bringing colour into his ashen face, 'I *made* Rowland Egerton. He knew nothing about art and antiques when I met him. All he had was charm and a way with words – the gift of the gab, as the Irish say. He could talk anyone into anything. He used to say he could sell freezers to Eskimos.'

'That's quite a talent, isn't it?' Atherton said.

'Oh yes,' Lavender said. 'I always acknowledged as much. But you see, he didn't want to sell to Eskimos. He was a social climber. He wanted to sell to the upper-middle classes. Even to the aristocracy. He wanted to be accepted as one of them. Rather pitiful, really. But those people don't respond to the same triggers. You can't behave like a second-hand car salesman. You need the right manner, the right vocabulary. And you need to know what you're talking about. That was where I came in.'

'You trained him.'

'I taught him everything he knew. Not just about art and antiques but about his customers, too, and how to get on with them. I even gave him his new name, indirectly. You know what his real name was?'

'Phil Harris,' Atherton supplied.

'Not smart enough for him. So he changed it. Two of my old addresses in South Kensington – Roland Gardens and Egerton Terrace. I had a flat in each of them at one time.' His mouth turned down. 'But he didn't like being reminded of it. I had to learn not to call him Phil, even when we were alone.'

'So you were sitting in your car, thinking all these resentful thoughts,' Atherton prompted.

'I told you it would sound ridiculous,' Lavender said dully. 'You must be thinking me a poor specimen. But these things build up over the years. And things had been particularly uncomfortable at the last recording at Wykeham Hall.'

'How was that?' Slider asked.

'Oh, he'd been in a bad mood for a couple of weeks. First there was Bunny dying – they'd been good friends – and then the ridiculous scene at her funeral.'

'He told you about that?'

'He said Philip had asked him to leave. He was furious that he'd been humiliated, as he saw it. I'd told him not to go, but there was an example of his "star" mentality, if you like! I said he should respect Philip's wishes, but he thought he was more important than a minor MP, so his friendship with Bunny gave him greater rights than her husband and family. He brought that on himself – I had no sympathy. And then he'd had a letter from the television company about *Going, Going, Gone*, saying they were considering getting him a female co-presenter for the next season to boost ratings.

The idea that he couldn't hold up the ratings on his own, without some simpering female tagging along, infuriated him.'

'Were those his words? Some simpering female?'

'Yes. He was sure they wanted to bring in a pretty face with no knowledge whatsoever.'

'Which was rather ironic, really,' Atherton suggested, 'given that that's what he was, before your make-over.'

Lavender shuddered. 'Don't use that expression – "make-over". It encapsulates what's wrong with television today.'

'So what happened at Wykeham Hall?' Slider asked.

'He was in a bad mood to begin with. And then there was that ridiculous Rupert Melling annoying him with his vulgar jibes. And of course he took it out on me, as he always does. He complained I wasn't finding him anything interesting on the trawl. Then when the Aldburys invited us to supper – the owners of Wykeham Hall – he wanted me to excuse myself so he could go alone. He said, "You're not very good company, you know. You just sit there without opening your mouth. Better leave them to me. I can have them eating out of my hand." Mrs Aldbury was quite young and attractive, and I suppose he wanted to flirt with her to soften her up. There was a pair of early Georgian wine-coolers he'd spotted, and he thought he could get them to sell. I lost my temper a little and told him he needed me with him because his ignorance would betray him unless I gave him his cues. And we had a bit of an argument.'

'Understandable,' Slider said.

He looked shamefaced. 'It was sordid. I've seen him do it with other people, but I've never indulged in that sort of thing – throwing up every insult and bad memory you can muster. I could see he was rather surprised. The biter bit, I suppose. When I realized, I stopped myself. I said if he wanted to go alone he could, and he said no, I was right, we should go together. But there was an awkward feeling all evening.' He stopped.

'And that's what you were thinking about, sitting in your car in the car park?' Atherton prompted.

'Yes,' he said. 'And it crystallized something I'd been

half-thinking for a while – that it was time we broke up the partnership. The lease on the shop was going to fall in soon, anyway, and the landlord was bound to put up the price, probably to a level that would make the shop unviable. I was tired of being dependent on his television fees, and running around fetching and carrying for him. I decided I was going to tell him that evening that we should wind it up. He'd hardly miss it anyway, with his TV career, and I could set up on my own. Not with a shop – there's no future in that, and I haven't the capital anyway. Just doing sourcing – bespoke work – and restoration and valuation. You can do a lot of that from home on a computer. You don't need premises, all you need is knowledge, and that's what I have. That's all I have,' he added with a hint of bitterness.

'You were going to end up rather badly off from the split,' Atherton suggested, 'while he'd carry on living in luxury. The house and everything in it was his. You'd even lose your flat over the shop.'

He managed a sort of shrug. 'The flat was nothing. I don't care where I live. Anyway, better to be poor and have your self-respect.'

'So, thinking all these angry thoughts, you were driving – where?' Atherton asked.

Lavender looked up. 'I told you, I was sitting in the car.'

'How long for?'

'I don't know. A long time. I was lost in thought.'

'Can you make a guess at how long?' Slider asked. 'Ten minutes? Longer?'

'I don't know, really. I didn't look at the time.'

'Weren't you expected at Mr Egerton's?'

'Not at any particular time. We were going to have a meal together, but not until the evening. He was going to cook for me. I think he felt bad about what happened at Wykeham Hall, and it was his way of making it up to me. I'd said I'd be over in the afternoon, that was all.'

'Very well. Carry on,' Slider said. 'You were sitting in the car, in the car park . . .?'

'I'd been sitting there thinking for some time, and I suddenly resolved that I would talk to him that day about breaking up.

I'd see what sort of a mood he was in when I arrived, and either tell him straight away, or wait until after dinner when we'd had some wine and he might be in a more mellow mood.'

'You anticipated that there'd be a row?' Slider queried.

'I thought he'd try to talk me out of it. He liked to get his own way. And if he couldn't get it by charm, he was capable of being very nasty. But I'd thought long and hard and I was ready.'

'So you drove over to the house. Every detail now, please.'

'There was a parking space right outside, which was lucky. I went in, called out, "It's only me," and took the shopping straight downstairs to the kitchen. I went back upstairs to see if he wanted a cup of tea. Took my coat off, hung it in the cupboard under the stairs. Looked into the study – I thought he'd be working there. But he wasn't. I knew he was in, because his overcoat and scarf were in the cupboard. So I went into the drawing room. And there he was.' He stopped, swallowing hard. He put a reflexive hand up to his nose, but there was no blood this time. Perhaps now he was telling the truth and there was no need for the pressure-valve.

'What did you do?' Slider asked quietly.

'Nothing, at first. I stood there, staring, trying to make sense of it. I knew he was dead; there was no need to go near him. But it was such a shock, such an awful thing to be looking at. I saw straight away that the malachite box was missing, and it came into my head that a burglar had stolen it and killed him when he got in the way. I don't know why I was so convinced that was what had happened, but I was. It seemed the only explanation.'

'What then?' said Slider, to keep him going.

'I don't know how long I stood there. But then I started thinking of all the trouble this was going to cause. It was one thing to decide to split up and wind up the business, but another to have it thrust upon me. The business debts – would I be liable for them? I had no money, nothing saved, and all his wealth would go to his daughter now. I could be ruined. And I was angry with him. For getting himself killed in this stupid, pointless way. For making me so dependent on him that I didn't know what to do next. Angry for all the slights and insults and playing second fiddle, and having him take the credit for everything when *I* was the one with the real expertise. Then suddenly I thought of the painting, the Morisot, and it somehow encapsulated all my feelings. I realized that it would go with the rest of the contents, and that Dale would probably sell everything via a house-clearance, because she cares nothing about art or antiques.'

'So you decided to take it,' said Slider.

'I thought if I sold it, it would at least give me some funds to tide me over. I could probably get eighty to a hundred thousand for it. And in justice, it was mine really, anyway – he'd never cared for it. If I took it now, everyone would think that the burglar had taken it along with the box. So I took it into the study to wrap it up, then out to my car, put it in the boot. Then I came back in. Looked at the clock. It was nearly twenty-five past. I knew I had to call the police. I realized that I'd been there a long time, and it would look suspicious if I hadn't called the police straight away. So I had to work out my story.'

'That's when you decided to say you had left your shop at half past one?' said Atherton.

He looked embarrassed. 'I didn't think anyone would believe me, if I said I was sitting in the car thinking all that time. So I had to have left later.'

'Very ingenious,' said Atherton.

Lavender frowned, sensing irony. 'I was trying to think – what would I naturally have done? I didn't want to arouse any suspicions. I thought perhaps I would have gone to him, to see if he was still alive – though I knew from the beginning he wasn't. So I went and knelt down beside him and touched him. I got blood on the knees of my trousers. I thought that was probably a good thing.' He looked at Slider. 'My thoughts – it was like being in a fever, when everything seems terribly clear and yet utterly surreal. It was a kind of madness. I can't explain any other way why I did what I did, but I assure you it seemed rational at the time.'

Slider nodded. 'Go on.'

'There isn't any more. I telephoned the police and went back downstairs to wait. You know the rest.'

He stopped, and the silence felt like a dark hole opening up. While the narrative was going on, Slider had been there, in that house, with Lavender, seeing and feeling what he had seen and felt. He had to shake himself back to the here-and-now and ask the question that had bugged him most from the beginning. 'Why did you rearrange the paintings on the wall where the Morisot was?'

Lavender put a hand up to his forehead in a helpless sort of gesture. 'I don't know. It seems mad now, when I think of it. I suppose I thought if there wasn't an obvious gap in the arrangement, it might not be missed. So I moved the still life to fill it.'

'But,' said Atherton, 'you *wanted* it to be missed. You wanted us to think the burglar had taken it.'

'I know,' said Lavender. 'I can see that now, but at the time it seemed to make sense.' He shook his head. 'It must have been the shock. I was standing there with my closest friend dead at my feet and my life in ruins, and I did the most idiotic thing. No,' he corrected himself with a touch of bitterness, 'the most idiotic thing was being scared into trying to sell the painting. After your visit to the flat I was afraid you might come back and search it, so I thought I'd better get rid of it at once. The sale at Banbury gave me an excuse to get it away. I should have known you'd have some way of looking out for it. I was a fool, an absolute fool. I behaved like a complete idiot.'

Lavender rubbed his hands together slowly, as if they were cold. When he looked up now, it was with appeal, his worn, pale, craggy face uncertain, afraid. 'I know there must be consequences for what I have done. I misled you. I tried to steal the painting. Will I – will I be sent to prison? I am,' he added in a low voice, 'very afraid of that.'

'I don't know,' Slider said, and Atherton was surprised at the lack of sympathy in his voice. He thought Lavender a venial ass, but he'd expected his boss to feel for him. 'That's not for me to decide. You have committed at least two criminal offences – obstructing a police officer, and theft. You may well be prosecuted.'

The cheeks trembled, and Lavender clenched his hands and

forced himself to sit up straight, taking his lumps like a man, as they taught you at school. 'But you believe me?' he asked. 'I didn't kill Rowland. Whatever happened, I could never have done that. He was dead when I got there. You do believe me?'

'Interview terminated at—' Slider said, looked up, and added the time. He stood up, glanced at Atherton, and walked away without answering.

Outside, Atherton said, 'Well, *do* you believe him?'

Slider sighed. 'I'm afraid I do. It's screwy enough to be the truth. And it answers all the questions.'

'Except the big one – if he didn't do it, who did?'

'Ah yes, except that one,' said Slider.

'He still had the best motive,' Atherton said. 'A lifetime of service, and he ends up living in the attic on the scraps from the table like a sort of mad maiden aunt.'

'Your imagination!'

'Still, resentment,' Atherton urged. 'Best of all the emotions for fuelling murder. It's a good, slow burner; it'll keep you warm for years.'

'But was this that sort of murder?'

'Let's not get too particular,' Atherton advised.

Porson was sitting down for once, looking almost as grey in the face as Lavender – but strip lights were nobody's friend. He listened to the story in neutral silence. 'Mad as a March hatter,' he remarked at the end. 'That's a lot of barminess for one painting.'

'Quite a valuable painting,' Slider pointed out. 'But it wasn't just the money. He'd tried to buy his friend something special, and his friend had scorned it. It was the symbol of all his woes.'

'I can't get my head round those two,' Porson grunted, scratching his bumpy poll. 'What a weird relationship. Are you convinced Lavender didn't do it?'

'I'm halfway there,' Slider said. 'Egerton's death was going to leave him at a big financial disadvantage, so he had no money motive for killing him. He could still have done it in sudden anger, but there was no spatter on his clothes. And his story holds together in its own terms.'

'Nutty terms,' said Porson disapprovingly. 'He had a key, you can't get over that.'

'No, sir. That's against him. But it'll be hard to prove either way.'

'It's the worst,' Porson said. 'What are you going to do?'

'He's given us the route he took from Waitrose to the house. We're going to try to find him on camera somewhere, to confirm the timings. Look for more witnesses, of course.'

'And search his flat while we've got him, see if he's got that box thingy stashed away.'

'Yes, sir. That would solve a lot of headaches,' Slider said.

'And if Lavender didn't do it, you'd better start trying to find out who did. What else have you got? There was that one forty man.'

'He's the one thirty-five man now. We've got someone in a hat coming out of the tube station, just after half past, that we think could be him. We'll have to try and trace his journey back, see where he came from and if we can get a squint at his face on any of the TfL cameras.'

'And probably find he's nothing to do with it and went into a different house altogether,' Porson sighed. 'Anything else?'

'Very little,' Slider acknowledged. 'Egerton wasn't a very popular man among people who knew him, but no-one seems to have hated him enough to kill him.'

'Except that if it was a spur-of-the-moment thing, he could just have said something very bloody annoying and – wham.'

That was true, Slider thought. But it was neither help nor comfort to him.

'Go home,' Porson said with sudden sympathy. 'We'll keep Lavender overnight, search his gaff, have another crack at him in the morning. If he's decided to stop lying, he might have something interesting to tell us about the victim's other relationships. But all that'll keep. I'm going home myself in a minute. Sufficient unto the day is the wassname.'

'That's very true, sir,' Slider said, without the least irony.

He drove home over a crunchy new layer of snow that had fallen since the roads cleared of home-time traffic. The skies were clear, and it was freezing hard, but he was too tired when he got home to bother with dragging out the tarpaulin to cover the car. He'd just have to deal in the morning with whatever fell overnight, like most people did.

Joanna had gone to bed, but she got up and came downstairs when she heard him come in.

'Are you hungry?' she asked.

'Starving,' he discovered. 'But you don't need to hang around here getting cold. Go back to bed – I can manage.'

It *was* cold – obviously, the heating had gone off for the night some time ago. She went before him into the kitchen and turned on the little heater by the table, and headed straight for the gas stove. 'Omelette all right?'

'Wonderful. Thanks.'

'I'm going to make myself some cocoa,' she said. 'Would you like some, or would you rather have tea?'

'Cocoa?' he queried.

'Just suddenly had a yen for it. Must be the combination of snow outside and midnight feasts.'

'Cocoa sounds good to me.' He sat down at the table, watching her track back and forth, hearing the comforting sounds – the pop of gas, the crack of eggs, the glug of milk, the clink of stirring spoons and forks – which meant someone was taking loving care of him. His thoughts brushed the edge of Lavender and recoiled from the dry, fruitless loneliness of his love, or whatever his attachment was, for Egerton. *It's good to be me*, he thought fervently – and then remembered the miscarriage, and fell back into his uneasy, questioning sadness for Joanna and what she must be feeling. Being happy made him feel guilty; forgetting, for long periods of the day when he was busy, made him feel guiltier.

'So, how was your day?' he asked.

He knew even from the back that she was smiling. 'What a dutiful question,' she said. 'It's a terrible give-away, you know.'

'Give-away of what?' he asked warily.

'It's what the man says when he comes home from work and realizes he hasn't given his wife a thought the whole day, and wonders if she knows that.'

He didn't know what to say. 'I just asked,' he said feebly.

She turned her head. 'I wasn't being nasty. I should jolly well hope you do forget all about me when you're working. I forget about you when I'm playing, and it doesn't mean I don't love you.'

'Do you?'

'Love you?'

'Still?'

'Would I cook omelettes in the middle of the night for someone I didn't love?'

'A Victorian sense of duty might make you do it.'

'True,' she said, turning the omelette out on to a plate and bringing it across to him, along with bread and butter. 'But in this case, it's love.'

She went back for the cocoa and sat down with him.

'Eat,' she said. He ate. She sipped cocoa and watched him. 'It's very satisfying, anyway,' she said after a while. 'Feeding the animals. Basic human instinct. Look at zoos.'

'And pigeons in Trafalgar Square,' he added, mopping the loose bit in the middle with the bread.

'And George.'

'How is George?'

'We're just coming into hurricane season. The Terrible Twos. He had an attack of fury today, didn't know what to do with it, or himself. I wanted him to get ready to go to the shops, and he wanted to finish his playing. He hadn't the vocabulary to tell me why it was important. So he lay down on the floor and raged.'

'You mustn't let him wear you out,' Slider said, looking at her with concern, trying to see if the depredations showed.

'Bill, it's seven weeks now. I'm all right. Back to normal.'

'I know the doctor signed you off—' he began.

'You've got to stop trying to wrap me in cotton wool,' she said, and there was a tautness under the words.

'I'm not. I don't.'

'You do.' The smile was gone now. 'You don't dare touch me. You hardly look at me. When you do, you look at me as if I might go off, like a defective grenade.'

'I'm naturally worried about you,' he said. 'It was a terrible thing you went through.'

'I know,' she said. 'But you're making it worse. It's bad enough I lost the baby, but if I lose you, too—'

'You haven't lost me,' he exclaimed, shocked she should think so. 'You won't. Never.'

'You won't even hold me in bed,' she said, from a world of sadness. 'I can feel you lying there rigid, trying not to touch me. It makes me feel as if I'm no use any more.'

He was dumbfounded. 'I didn't want to put pressure on you. Your body . . . I mean, obviously making love was out. I didn't want you to think I was trying to hurry you into anything before you were ready.'

'But you could have held me. We could have cuddled. We always did that a lot, and I miss it. I miss *you*.'

He stared at her, stricken that she could have thought he didn't want that too. 'If I cuddle you in bed,' he said in a low voice of embarrassment, 'I'll get an erection. I can't help it. It's automatic. And you'll think—'

Then she smiled. It was one of her old smiles, from Before, and it made him go hot all the way down to his toes, like a draught of cocoa. 'I can cope with that. I promise I won't regard it as bullying. I might even see it as a compliment.'

'Oh, Jo! I'm sorry.'

'So am I. I've not been much company for you these past weeks. And I'm not very good at explaining my feelings. Mostly because I'm not used to having them. I'm like George, really – don't know what all this emotion is, or what to do with it.'

'You lost a baby—' he began.

'It's hormonal,' she said, stopping him. 'Not really me at all. I just want to get back to normal now. Can we do that?'

He still looked doubtful, his mind full of sub-vocal warnings and old wives' tales. The mysteries of womankind – the terrible ways in which they could suffer and die that men couldn't know about. And however much she wanted not to lose him, you could double that at least for him, losing her.

'We can certainly try,' he said.

They finished their cocoa and went up to bed, where he took her very carefully into his arms, hoping he was too tired to get an erection. It didn't help when she murmured, 'Stop stiffening.' Then he realized she just meant he was tense. He tried consciously to relax, and in the middle of the process sleep ambushed him, and he fell out of the world like a stone down a well.

THIRTEEN
Fairy Moans

The papers on Tuesday were full of Lavender's arrest, and TV teams had doorstepped the Hedley-Somertons, resulting in a clip from the photogenic and distressed Georgia saying he was the kindest man and she knew he was innocent, which was played over and over on all the channels. In the absence of anything concrete from the police, the papers were repeating everything they had on Egerton and speculating in guarded terms as to what Lavender's relationship with him had been.

'Which is a pity, if we *are* on the brink of letting him go,' said Atherton. 'The hounds of hell on felon's traces. They won't let him go now.'

'He shouldn't have lied to us,' Slider said.

The search of the flat had not turned up the malachite box, or any bloodstained clothing, or anything else of interest as far as the case went. The shop, though closed, was now a focus of attention, not only for the press but for a constant stream of sensation tourists, probably hoping that it would reopen and allow them to buy something – anything – that could be a souvenir of the famous TV star or the weirdo who killed him. The local police had put their most imperturbable uniform on the door, who was pretending to be one of those soldiers on palace guard who weren't allowed to move their faces.

Lavender looked exhausted in the morning, said he had not been able to sleep, and was evidently starting a cold, which made him look even more unappetizing: grey, pouchy and ever so old. He had no objection to being questioned again and answered everything without hesitation, but dully, like a man whose battery is almost spent. He had nothing new to tell, however, beyond what they had gleaned from other people.

He knew nothing about the specifics of Egerton's recent love-
life, or of anything he might have been involved in outside
what was generally and publicly known. Despite the amount
of time they had spent together, they had kept the rest of their
lives separate. Egerton was adored by his fans and generally
not much liked by his colleagues, but there were no long-
standing feuds or hatreds that he knew about. He knew of no
reason anyone should have wanted to kill him.

There were several phone calls from Georgia Hedley-
Somerton that morning, asking if she could see him, or at least
speak to him, offering her own solicitor to act for him, and
finally, on being told he was being released on police bail,
offering him a billet in her own house. 'He can't go back to
the flat,' she asserted, 'and he hasn't any family.'

Atherton, who took the call, said, 'Haven't you got a lot of
press hanging around your house?'

'Yes, that's true, but it's a big house, and they can't get
round the back. He could be private there. And my husband's
pretty good at handling reporters. He'd be better off here than
on his own.'

'I can but relay the offer,' Atherton said, thinking Lavender
would be unlikely to accept. But in fact he did, looking
surprised and grateful, or as much so as was possible for a
man with a face like the Eiger's.

'Just as well to have him where we can find him,' Atherton
said to Slider. 'She can let us know if he looks like bolting
again.'

'He won't,' Slider said. Where, after all, was there for him
to go, now?

Now that he had the route, McLaren found Lavender's car on
a bus camera turning into Blythe Road, which put him two
minutes from Egerton's house at eight minutes past two. That
meant, if he had told the truth, that he had sat in the car
brooding for ten or fifteen minutes, and spent fifteen minutes
in the house being shocked, wrapping up the painting and
working out his story. It probably had been him that the witness
saw coming out of the house at about twenty past and going
to the boot of the car. Beyond that, they were not in a position

to prove or disprove Lavender's movements. It was all most unsatisfactory.

'Shall I carry on looking?' McLaren asked.

'No, I'd sooner you started on TfL's tapes and try to trace back One Thirty-Five Man. That's more important. I'm not sure Lavender's peregrinations are going to tell us much more.'

'His what, guv?' McLaren frowned. 'That's some kind o' big bird, isn't it?'

'Skip it,' said Slider.

McLaren went back to his desk and hunched over another endless series of grainy images. It was painstaking and tedious work, examining TfL's tube station footage, looking for the man in the trilby and hoping against hope that he hadn't taken it off during the journey.

'Anyone who thinks policing is glamorous'd only want to take a look at old Maurice to put sense on them,' remarked Connolly, who had brought him tea. 'Sure it's the dog's job. Someone's going down to Mike's for banjos, boss. Will they get you anything? Rasher, sausage, cheese'n'ham?'

Before he could answer, Swilley came to the door. 'I've got something, boss,' she said.

It was Melling's afternoon for doing public valuations at Christie's. Slider and Atherton arrived to find him – in the absence of any paying customers – being terribly amusing before a rapt audience of a young man and a young woman who from their exquisite thinness and intimidatingly expensive grooming could only be Christie's employees. They melted away at the sight of the warrant cards, leaving Melling, retro-chic in a double-breasted suit and co-respondent shoes, to his fate.

He became markedly less sprightly in a room on his own with the detectives, but still did his best to keep up the party spirit. 'You again!' he cried gaily. 'Have you developed a taste for my company?'

'We just wanted to ask you some follow-up questions,' Slider said with suitable gravity.

'I saw in the papers that you've arrested poor old John Lavender for the murder,' Melling went on quickly. 'I must say I was surprised – or perhaps not? No, now I think of it, I *can* see him as First Murderer. I always thought he was deliciously creepy, lurking silently in the background in that sinister way – the Mrs Danvers of the antiques trade. What put you on his trail?'

Slider ignored all this. 'I'd like you to cast your mind back to last Friday, when I interviewed you at your home.'

'How can I forget it? You turned down a perfectly delectable lunch that I'd gone to considerable trouble to put together. And champagne!'

'You told me then that on Thursday you had spent most of the day at an auction at the Guildhall in Northampton.'

'Did I?' he said lightly. 'Then I suppose I had.'

'Would it surprise you to know there was no auction at the Guildhall on Thursday? In fact, there was no auction anywhere in Northampton.'

Melling looked taken aback, but he kept his end up. 'Well, silly me! I must have got confused. I expect it was a different day, the auction. It's so easy to muddle dates, isn't it?'

'What did you do yesterday, sir?' Slider asked.

'Yesterday?' Now he was startled. 'What's that got to do with it?'

'Answer the question, please.'

'Well, if you must know, I went to see my publisher in the morning, then had lunch with an actor friend in St Martin's Lane—'

Slider interrupted. 'So you don't generally have difficulty in remembering what you were doing twenty-four hours earlier. But somehow, last Friday, you were confused about what you were doing on Thursday.'

Melling grew sulky. 'All right, you've made your point. You don't have to be so humourless about it. Goodness! Anyway, how was I supposed to know you'd go and check up?'

'We check everything,' Slider said. 'Where were you on Thursday?'

'If you want to know, I was at home all day, alone. There. You see? No corroboration – is that what you people call it? I thought I'd have you on my back if I said that, so . . .' He shrugged.

'So you lied to the police. That's a very serious matter,' Atherton said.

'Oh, the Brothers Grimm from Grimthorpe or what?' Melling cried with desperate gaiety. 'A teeny harmless embroidery, nothing more. What are you going to do – arrest me for being a stay-at-home?'

Slider ignored the question. 'You had a history of bad feeling with Mr Egerton, isn't that true?'

'I teased him a bit, that's all. It wasn't serious.'

'You were very angry about the snuffbox,' Atherton said. 'That wasn't just teasing. You were outraged by his behaviour, as you had every right to be.'

Melling looked uneasy at being sympathized with. 'Well,' he said cautiously, 'perhaps I was a bit cross with him, but it all blows away, you know. It doesn't mean anything.'

'And on the following show, you had another row with him,' Slider said. 'That's the last show before he was killed, just to be clear.'

'What are you talking about?'

'A row about a certain cameraman,' Atherton said. 'You'd been flirting with him, and Egerton came sticking his nose in. You told him in no uncertain terms to mind his own business.'

Melling was gobsmacked. 'I – what?' he managed.

'The whole thing was witnessed,' Slider said smoothly. 'Someone standing close by, unseen by either of you, heard it all.'

'You accused Mr Egerton of being interested in Tarquin Pelly himself,' Atherton took it up. 'That was the young man's name. The shoulder-cam operator. Apparently, quite a looker. And there must be lots of opportunities for flirting when a handsome young man is following you around doing close-ups of your face.'

Melling was pale, but there were spots of anger in his cheeks. His mouth opened and shut a couple of times, and then the outrage burst from him. 'It was none of his damned business! What the hell did he mean by telling me what to do? Who made him Lord High Morality? It would make a cat laugh to hear him dictating to the rest of us – him of all people!'

'Oh, quite,' Slider said. 'I can see it would be intolerable. Especially in view of what came next. He threatened to tell your live-in partner about it. Mr Melling, was Rowland Egerton blackmailing you?'

Melling groaned. 'Yes,' he said, closing his eyes and his fists in pain. 'He was! I couldn't believe it. It was excruciating!'

'How much money did you give him?' Slider asked.

The eyes flew open. 'Money? Oh, he wasn't interested in money. It was power he wanted,' Melling said with bitterness. 'To have me squirm under his foot, knowing he could crush me or not, any time the fancy took him. Alex is wildly jealous – the Russian temperament, you know. He can't bear me to look at another man. Any hint that I was seeing someone else and he'd go mad. Rowland knew that, the bastard. And he loved it. He had to have power over everybody. That was his thing.'

Slider spoke kindly now. 'Blackmail is a hideous crime. And people who are being blackmailed often feel the only way out from under is to get rid of the blackmailer.'

'Wait, wait! What are you saying? You don't think *I* killed him? You've arrested John Lavender! I had nothing to do with it!'

'You lied to us about your alibi,' Atherton said. 'In fact, now, you don't have an alibi at all. Alone at home all day – that's a classic. And blackmail is the best motive in the world. Things are not looking so good, wouldn't you agree?'

'I—' He stopped, biting his lip. Then seemed to decide. 'I *was* at home all day on Thursday. But I wasn't alone.'

'Is this another story?' Slider asked sternly. 'Because you know now that we *will* check.'

'No, it's true this time! I swear it. I didn't want to tell you before because – well, it was Tarquin. Tarquin Pelly. I've been seeing him. But Alex mustn't find out. Oh, swear you won't tell him! He'll just go crazy if he gets so much as a hint—'

'What time did Mr Pelly arrive?' Atherton interrupted.

'*I* don't know. It was about eleven, eleven thirty, I should think. He was there until about five-ish. Then he went home because it had to look as if he'd been at work. He's living with someone as well, you see. He'd got the day off, but he

told his partner he was working and – well, you get the picture.
Then after he'd gone I got ready to go out and went to meet
Alex from rehearsal, and we went for a meal with some friends
at the Café des Amis. That bit was true.'

'We know,' said Atherton. 'We checked.'

'You checked?' Melling said blankly.

Atherton nodded. 'With the restaurant.'

Melling looked from one to the other with a sort of pathetic
appeal. 'But that's me off the hook, then, isn't it?' he cried.
'I mean, now you know where I was, and I've got witnesses.
You can't think now that I had anything to do with Rowland's
death?'

'There's still the matter of your lying to me before,' Slider
said. 'That is a serious offence. Obstructing a police officer in
the performance of his duty. That can attract a custodial
sentence.' Melling looked sick. 'I shall have to ask you to come
with me to the police station and make a full statement.'

'I'm – supposed to be working,' Melling said faintly. 'Can't
I come later?'

'We can't risk having you contact Mr Pelly and agree a
story with him,' Atherton said. 'I'm sure you understand *that.*'

'But I'm telling the truth!' Melling cried.

'Perhaps you are *now,*' Atherton said unkindly.

'Another dead end,' Slider said as they trod up the stairs to
the office again, having left Melling to be processed.

'Oh, I don't know,' said Atherton, ever cheerful. 'There's
still the sinister Russian, Boris the Slasher. The smouldering
Cossack in the background. Suppose Melling told him Egerton
was being beastly to him, and Boris decided to take revenge?
That single stab to the throat is very John Le Carré, don't you
think?'

'I think you need to take a pull on the reins. Boris has the
best alibi of all. Those dancers are accounted for every minute
of the day.'

'If he was actually there.'

'Well, we'll check that, obviously. That's the easy part.'

Atherton grunted agreement. They pushed through the swing
doors at the top of the stairs, and he said, 'I think poor old

Melling's in trouble, even without any charges from us. There's no way on earth he's going to be able to keep Boris from finding out about little Tarquin. He's going to ask why Melling's here and why we're sniffing around the ballet company, and it's all going to come out.'

'Not our problem,' Slider said.

'It will be if he cleaves Melling's head with his sabre in a jealous rage.'

'Cossacks use shashkas, not sabres,' Slider objected.

'The things you know,' said Atherton.

'I used to read *The Hotspur* when I was a lad.'

'Ah, the golden age, when boys' comics were designed to inform, educate and entertain!'

'You could learn a lot from them,' said Slider. 'All human experience encapsulated in the three-colour process.'

'You could say the same of bathroom walls,' said Atherton.

Lavender had departed under bail, red-eyed and hoarse with his oncoming cold, in the rather tight-lipped care of the Hedley-Somertons. Atherton, being the most *au fait* with ballet, was out checking Alex Anton's alibi, while Gascoyne had gone to interview Tarquin Pelly, who was fortunately working out at Elstree, so he could be questioned away from his entanglement.

Slider had his head down, reading back through everything they had so far in the hope that something would spark an idea, or at least suggest a direction for him to look next. McLaren came in, looking weary. 'Any luck?' Slider asked.

'Not yet, guv,' he said. 'I've checked every station on the Central Line, both directions, but I've not got him coming out of any of them – not unless he's took the hat off.'

'That's always a possibility,' Slider acknowledged. 'But it was a very cold day, and if he wore it for warmth, or out of habit, he likely wouldn't.'

McLaren almost sighed. 'I'll have to start checking the platforms at the interchange stations,' he said. 'That's a lot of work. I could really do with some help.' He rubbed his eyes, which were distinctly red.

'I'll see if I can get you a couple of uniforms tomorrow,'

Slider promised. 'You've had a long day on the computer. Why don't you go home, before you get a hunch.'

'Could do with one of them, couldn't we?' McLaren said jovially.

Slider was impressed. Maurice had never been known to make jokes before. His New Improved Love Life, v2.1, was obviously changing him. Come to that, he noted, McLaren wasn't actually eating anything at that moment. That, too, was almost a first.

'Go on, get off, relax and refresh yourself.'

'Thanks, guv. Don't mind if I do. Natalie's Amdram club's doing auditions tonight, an' I'd like to go along.'

'You thinking of going up for a part?' Slider said – a *num* question if ever there was one.

But McLaren looked as though he would have been blushing if he had not lost the ability long ago, and said, 'Well – I was thinking of it. Maybe. Just for a bit o' fun.'

'Good Lord,' said Slider. And then, 'Well, good for you. Anything that takes the mind off.'

'Yeah,' said McLaren, and departed.

Soon afterwards, Connolly appeared. 'Fancy a cuppa, boss?'

'No – thanks. I'm all right.' He looked up as she hesitated in the doorway. 'I've just sent McLaren home. Why don't you get off as well?'

'I'd as soon be here as back at the flat.' She rolled her eyes. 'Flatmates! There's the one for ever getting the ride offa one feller or another, doing the nasty on every surface in the house. And the other's just been dumped again, streeling round the kip racked with grief. Between the two of them they have me driven mad.'

Slider suppressed a smile. 'The best defence is attack. You should get in there with a bloke of your own and drive them mad right back.'

'I'll bear it in mind,' she said with dignity.

Atherton phoned. 'I've checked Alex Anton's alibi, and he was definitely there the whole time. He was in class in the morning – general class, and then one-on-one with a coach. There was a half-hour break for lunch at one, which he spent in the canteen with half a dozen others, and then it was rehearsals all afternoon, when he was in clear sight of other dancers at all times – not that that part interests us. So there's no chance at all he could have slipped away and whacked Egerton with his shishkebab.'

'Shashka,' said Slider.

'Just giving you the opportunity to display superior knowledge, as a good subordinate should. I'm going to get off home, now, unless you need me to come back for anything.'

'No, that's all right.'

'Good. I have a hot date tonight, and I want to take a long shower. After mingling with the corps du ballet for several hours, I'm convinced I smell of feet, sweat and rubbing liniment.'

'By the way –' Slider caught him as he was about to ring off – 'did you have any words with the subject himself?'

'Couldn't really avoid it,' said Atherton. 'It's a hothouse there; you can't ask about somebody without the word getting back to them. He came over during a pause to ask me why. All hot eyes and pointy cheekbones. They have strong arms, those ballet boys,' he added, 'from hoisting girls in the air. Most men couldn't lift a kitchen chair over their heads and hold it there.'

'I take it you wriggled out of trouble?'

'He didn't swing for me, if that's what you mean. I told him it was purely routine to check everyone who knew Egerton, *and* their nearest and dearest. Don't know if he believed me, though. Is Melling still there?'

'Just waiting for Gascoyne to check in with Tarquin Pelly's version, then we'll throw him back in.'

'Lucky Alex is dancing tonight,' Atherton observed. 'At least it'll give Melling a hundred yards' start.'

The Department had never seen such glamour. From the moment the shop downstairs rang to announce in hushed tones of reverent excitement that Felicity Marsh was there, the CID room was like a kicked ant's nest. And now that she was there in his room, even Slider felt a rather shameful frisson. What *was* it about celebrities? Just because someone had appeared on a television screen, they were suddenly different from ordinary mortals, their most casual word treasured, their ideas and preferences of palpitating interest. What did you have for breakfast, Miss Marsh? At least half the population, maybe more, would pause to listen to the answer. Why was that more interesting than what Slider had for breakfast? But it was. It was one of the mysteries of life.

There was no doubt that she *was* glamorous. The pheromones she exuded could have melted breeze-blocks. There she stood, taller than him in her six-inch nude platform heels, wearing one of her trademark tailored suits, this one in cinnamon, over a slightly darker silk round-necked top. She was so thin, she appeared not to have any breasts at all: she could have turned sideways and disappeared. Her dark hair, cut in a twenties-style bob, was sleek as a rook's wing. Her make-up was perfect, as if it had been sprayed on. Well, perhaps it had, Slider thought – he fancied he had read somewhere that studio make-up artists use spray cans nowadays.

He greeted her, invited her to sit down, offered her a beverage, and took his place on his own side of the desk.

'We weren't expecting you back in England until tomorrow,' he said.

'That was the schedule,' she said, 'but we finished early.'

Her faintly husky voice – which sounded as if she was talking about sex even while reading out something like 'the GDP figures, out today, show a slight decline in the last quarter' – was startlingly familiar, giving Slider the spurious feeling that he knew her.

'We had a couple of meetings this morning, then flew back,' she went on. 'Maggie – my agent – told me you wanted to talk to me, so I thought I'd better come straight in on my way from the airport.' She folded her long, long legs.

Slider, following the direction of her gaze, saw the entire staff jammed in the doorway to the CID room – it was like a view of a Central Line tube train at Oxford Circus in rush-hour. He got up and quietly but firmly closed the door.

'Thank you,' she said.

Passing her on his way back to his seat, he got a closer look at her face. Under the delicately tinted enamel she was older than her first appearance, and she looked tired.

'Of course, I read about Rowland Egerton's death,' she said. 'And you arrested John Lavender for it, didn't you?'

'Did that surprise you?' Slider asked.

'I don't know. Did it?' She considered. 'I suppose it's always surprising when it's someone you know. You always think murder happens to other people, people very different from yourself. Yes, I was surprised about John,' she concluded. 'I always thought he was devoted to Rowland. But I suppose that kind of devotion can go either way, if the circumstances are right.'

There was something very polished about the way she spoke, Slider thought, as though what she said had been thought out, written down and learned well beforehand. She had been a newsreader before branching out into other kinds of present-ation. Perhaps the manner had stuck. Or perhaps, being a celebrity, she had to prepare answers to all sorts of questions she thought she might be asked. It aroused a strange dichotomy in Slider. The fact that it sounded rehearsed made him want to disbelieve what she said, while the fact that it was *her* voice saying it made him want to trust it.

'I don't know that there's anything really I can help you with,' she went on. 'The last time I saw Rowland was at the recording of *Antiques Galore!* on Wednesday last.'

'You went to Paris on Friday, I believe,' Slider said.

'Thursday night, actually. We took a late flight.'

'And what were you doing before that, on Thursday?'

She frowned, ever so slightly. 'I met with Maggie in the morning, had lunch with her and a publicity agent, then in the afternoon it was script and pre-production meetings with various people from TV Raisonné – that's the company that's doing the Nazi Art show. Then off to the airport. Why are you asking me that?'

'It's purely routine. We have to ask everyone who was close to Mr Egerton or who had recently been with him.'

'Well, I wasn't either,' she said, with a hint of annoyance. 'As I told you, I hadn't seen him since Wednesday. And we certainly weren't close. The only time I had contact with him was during the recording of *Antiques Galore!*'

Slider captured her gaze and held it steadily. 'I'd like you to be very careful about answering the next question. What was the exact nature of your relationship with Rowland Egerton? Because it has been suggested that you and he had – shall we say – a special understanding.'

He had thought she might redden with anger, but instead she became rather pale and still.

'I don't know what that means,' she said at last, without moving her lips.

'Let me be direct, then,' Slider said. 'Were you lovers?'

Her face crumpled in distaste. 'God, no!' she said with feeling.

'You were often seen talking together, apart, as if sharing secrets. He made a point of sitting next to you for meals or drinks. There was an air of connection between you, observed by someone on the team – eye contact and significant glances.'

'And from that you conclude . . .' She shook her head. 'I can't believe it.'

Slider waited impassively.

'Look,' she said – the word of capitulation. 'I suppose I'd better tell you what was really going on.'

'That would be nice,' said Slider.

FOURTEEN
Arts and Crafty

'I hated him,' said Felicity Marsh. 'He was a hateful, hateful person.' It was said with real feeling, but then she corrected herself, retreated behind the mask and the trained delivery, and said, 'Oh, he could be very charming. Wonderful company. That was what the public saw – they adored him, you know. That was how he seemed when you first met him – that smile, the crinkling eyes, the impression he gave you that he was uniquely interested in *you*. He could make you feel terrific. That's a real talent, you know. A genuine talent. If you've got that, you can go a long way in television – in show business in general. Half the job is *getting* the job. You can be the best actor in the world, or the best singer or musician or whatever, but if you can't get past the audition, it counts for nothing. You have to make the producers or directors want *you*, and if you can do that, it doesn't matter that scores of other people are better than you. They won't even get heard.'

All this, while interesting enough in itself, and probably true, Slider reflected – he had heard the same from Joanna about orchestras, and it applied to some extent in the Job as well – seemed to him designed to distract attention from the first unruly outbreak.

'How long have you known him?' he asked, hoping a direct question would winkle her out from behind the screen.

'I met him for the first time when I took over presenting *Antiques Galore!* I knew *of* him before that. I've always been interested in art and antiques – Dad was quite a collector – so I'd seen him on the television. And when I joined the team he was very nice to me. Took the trouble to talk to me, showed me round, asked if I needed any help, that sort of thing. Gave me some tips about how things worked. I liked him. I thought he was kind and genuinely concerned.'

'What about John Lavender? Did you like him?'

She frowned slightly. 'He wasn't the sort of person you liked. He was just *there*. He never made any effort to be friendly. He looked after Rowland's interests, and that was that. To tell you the truth, I thought at the beginning that they were in a relationship. That they were gay. I soon learnt that wasn't the case, when Rowland started coming on to me.'

'How did that happen?'

'The usual way. First he was attentive, then he started flirting with me. I was used to that – it's a hazard that goes with the territory,' she said, with the mental shrug that a beauty soon learns. 'And of course, gay men will flirt with you too. That's just fun. But I realized Rowland meant it, and he was very persistent. Kept asking me out. I'd just broken up with my partner of five years at that time – you know, Mike Shaw, the BBC political editor?'

Slider nodded.

'So I was a bit raw and wasn't interested in a relationship anyway. But when Rowland wouldn't take no for an answer, I had to tell him I wasn't interested in *him*. He obviously didn't like that.'

'He didn't take it well?' Slider suggested.

'Oh, he pretended to. Smiled, shrugged, said no hard feelings, made all the right noises. But I got the impression he was pretty miffed about it. He had a lot of women chasing after him – most of the females on the show and *all* the female punters – and I think it hurt his pride to have me reject him.'

'What did he do that made you think that?'

'Well, for a time he avoided me. He was polite but cold – very different from the way he'd been at first. He sort of – brooded. I'd catch him staring at me across the room. Then one day he came to see me.'

'Came to see you where?'

'At home. I had a flat in St John's Wood at the time. He turned up on my doorstep one day. I was startled to see him – a bit nervous, in fact, though he was smiling and behaving the way he had at first, as if we were the best of friends. He'd brought a bottle of wine. I told him I didn't think it was appropriate for him to come to my home. He said he had something to talk to me about, and he thought I'd want to be sure we weren't overheard.'

She stopped, and her face was bleak now. Slider waited. At last she went on, 'He'd found out something about me. Something I've gone to great trouble to keep secret. God knows how he found out. But it's something that the media and the gossip magazines would go mad for.'

'What is it?'

She looked at him for a long moment, but she shook her head. 'I won't tell you. If *you* know, then – I don't know who else will get to know. I'm sorry. It would make my life a misery if it got out. And – someone else's. Someone who doesn't deserve to be hounded by the press. It's nothing illegal, or anything like that. Just something very personal that I don't want known. I've a right to my own privacy, haven't I?'

Up to a point, was Slider's internal answer to that, but he let it go for now. 'So he came to blackmail you, did he?'

'That's what it amounted to.'

'He asked for money?'

'No,' she said. 'That was my first question. He gave me a sort of pained look, as if I'd impugned his honour. He said, what do you take me for? So I asked him, what *do* you want? And he said, nothing, nothing at all.'

A very odd sort of blackmail. But Slider had no temptation to mock. He was seeing a pattern emerging.

She bit her beautiful lips and stared in appeal. 'How do you cope with someone who says that? He *must* have deliberately searched out the information. Then he made a point of telling me he knew. He wanted *something*. But he kept just smiling and saying, how could I think such a thing? He said, how about a glass of wine, and when I said no, he went away and left the bottle. It was a very expensive claret. In a restaurant it would cost you a couple of hundred pounds. I was so confused.' She shook her head slowly, like a goaded bull.

'What happened after that?' Slider prompted her.

She gave him a look of great bitterness. 'That was the start of the new era. We were "friends" again, like at the beginning. He'd greet me with a kiss, sit beside me at breaks, take the chair next to mine when we all went out after the show. He'd lay a hand on my shoulder and smile every time we passed. He'd come over and gossip with me in a low voice when the cameras were off us, so that it looked to everybody as if we were great pals and had lots to say to each other. And I had to put up with it.'

'Did he mention your secret again?'

'Never. Not once. But it was there all the time, in the back of my mind, every time I saw him. It was like waiting for the guillotine to drop. Gradually, over the years, I came to think he wasn't going to blow the whistle on me as long as I was nice to him. But I could never be sure.'

'Nice to him? Did he ask you for sexual favours?'

'No! He didn't even ask me to go out with him. It was just that whenever we met, I had to pretend we were friends.' Her eyes blazed with sudden anger. 'He was *torturing* me! Like a cat playing with a mouse. It may look like fun, but it damn well hurts.'

'So what he wanted,' Slider said, 'was to have power over you.'

'Yes!' she said eagerly. 'That's exactly it. He had power over me, and there wasn't a damn thing I could do about it.'

'I believe you are in another relationship now?'

She frowned – the old imperious frown – but then seemed to realize she wasn't in a position to object to his impertinence any more. 'Benedict Cowper. My co-presenter on *Nazi Art Thieves*.'

'What was Mr Egerton's reaction to that?'

'I thought he might make a fuss, but he never mentioned it. I didn't know if he just didn't know about it, or he didn't care – or if it was just another part of the torture, leaving me wondering all the time if he was going to find out and lower the boom on me. I've tried to be as discreet as possible with Ben, but I can't go on like that. I love him, we want to get married, and with Rowland's threat hanging over me—'

She stopped, her eyes widening a little, as perhaps she remembered that now the threat was hanging no longer.

'Does Mr Cowper know about it?'

'About the blackmail, or my secret? Neither. I've never told him either.' Her lips tightened. 'I hope now I won't have to.' Slider was silent, and after a moment she met his eyes with a mixture of fear and defiance. 'I realize you now know I had a motive for wanting Rowland dead. But there must have been lots of people who felt the same way. And I don't believe, if he behaved that way towards me, I was the only one. Everyone has secrets.'

Slider maintained the silence as she looked at him with the question hanging in the air: are you going to take this any further? Are you going to crack open my secret and destroy my life? She had a powerful motive for getting rid of Egerton – a stronger one than Melling by far. But she didn't flinch in the face of his not answering, seeming to grow more steady as the seconds passed. He didn't think she had killed Egerton, or had him killed; but what about Benedict Cowper? She said he didn't know, but she might have let something out in the course of pillow-talk, or he might have observed for himself. And she was a woman to kill for.

He saw in an instant what a hellish life she must have been leading under Egerton's thumb; and in general, what a hellish life any celebrity must lead, especially a female celebrity, walking that tightrope between adulation and exposure. No wonder she looked tired under her perfect make-up. No wonder she was thin enough to slice bresaola.

He remembered a photo he had once seen of Princess Di, on a yacht in the middle of the ocean, sitting on a diving board. She was supporting her weight with her hands, so that her thighs wouldn't look fat. She knew that the odds were that a telephoto lens somewhere was trained on her. And of course she was right. Why on earth did anyone crave that sort of public eye?

He felt very sorry for Felicity Marsh and hoped that it would not be necessary to probe any further into her life. He thought, a little wearily, that they would have to check on Cowper, as they'd had to check Melling's weak point. As for Egerton – he wanted to feel sympathy for the victim, as in every case, but it was becoming harder not to think that getting rid of him was a form of pest control.

The excited clamour about Miss Marsh's visit was only just dying down when Slider was summoned to Mr Porson's office.

The old man was pacing back and forth behind his desk, talking – or rather listening – on the phone. Porson's contribution seemed limited to, 'Yes, sir. No, sir. Yes, sir.'

When he slammed the phone down, he whirled round on Slider in what was practically a fouetté. 'Bloody Nora, that's all we needed! That was Mr Wetherspoon on the blower.' All bosses were a pain, but Mr Wetherspoon was a particular thorn in the ointment.

'Has something happened, sir?'

Porson's eyebrows collided in the middle like two hairy caterpillars mating. 'Happened? The spit's hit the spam, that's what's happened! One Rupert Melling, TV celebrity, one of your suspects, has ended up in hospital. Also a certain freelance TV cameraman. And one of the dancers in the Royal Bally has been taken into custody for assault and actual bodily harm.'

'Good God!' Slider said. 'What happened?'

'The bally dancer went on the rampage. According to Melling, he came home in a temper because the police had been asking questions about him. Apparently, he's Russian, and they don't have the same warm, friendly relationship with the police we do over here.'

'He beat Melling up?'

'Broken nose, broken cheekbone, black eye, three cracked ribs and a hairline skull fracture. Apparently, he threw him at the wall as part of the assault. Then he pranced off and ran down the other character in this cosy *menarche ah troy*. Name of Pelly. Got one good punch in before Pelly managed to slam the front door shut. Carried on pounding the door, trying to break it down, until the police arrived and nicked him. Pelly also went to hospital, but was released after treatment for a split lip and swollen nose when an X-ray revealed no underlying fractures.'

Menarche was the *mot juste*, Slider thought, with all that blood around. 'It's hardly our fault, sir,' he defended himself. 'Atherton didn't tell Anton anything about Pelly. Melling must have caved in and confessed.'

'Caved in is about right,' Porson said. 'Bally boy just about caved his bloody face in. Now he wants to sue us for reckless endangerment.'

'They all watch too much television,' said Slider. There was no such crime in the UK.

'What's more to the point, Mr Wetherspoon wants our cockles in a seafood sauce for showing him up in posh company. You perhaps don't know,' Porson went on with elaborate sarcasm, 'that *Mrs* Wetherspoon is best chums, gawd 'elp us, with Mrs Redbridge, as in Assistant Commissioner Gordon Redbridge of Scotland Yard.'

'Oh dear,' Slider said. He was one of the top bods in the Met hierarchy. Two steps further up and you got to God.

'And further to the point, Mrs Assistant Commissioner is one of the leading lights of the Patrons of the Royal Bally, and the Redbridges and Wetherspoons have a box for the season. I expect they pay a lot for it, and they like to get their money's worth.'

'I'm getting the picture, sir,' said Slider.

'Now one of the soloists is banged up in the nick, the whole company's upset, last night's performance was forty minutes late starting – I can't remember the whole lottery of sins because frankly I stopped listening after the first ten minutes. That's what happens when you're on the wet end of a shit shower. You get numbed to it. But Mr Wetherspoon is not happy; and, guess what, his not-happiness gets traced back to his favourite operative at the far end of the food chain – again. So, what have you got to say for yourself?'

Slider tried to remain sturdy, though the images that were flooding through his brain as a result of Porson's imagery were pushing him towards laughter. Actually, it was no laughing matter, upsetting Mr Wetherspoon, whose skills all lay in the general area of making people's lives a misery. But it was a cheering thought that despite the Wetherspoons being bosom buddies with the Redbridges, he had never risen higher than Borough Commander, which surely proved he had a deficiency in some department or other. Slider suspected personality. Mr Wetherspoon, in his observation, had all the charisma of a vacuum flask.

'As I said, sir,' Slider replied to the charge, 'I don't see how I or my firm can be held to blame for the domestic upsets of anyone we question.'

'You're going with that, are you?'

'What else can I say, sir? We have to do the job as it comes.'

Porson nodded. 'I said the same thing to Mr Wetherspoon, the first two times he rang. Shit happens. You can't break eggs without straw. You understand, I'm only speaking to you like this on his bequest.'

'Reprimand accepted, sir,' Slider said.

Porson sighed, and his brow furrowed like the result of a drunken ploughing contest. 'All the same, I wish we could keep on good terms with the powers that be for more than two minutes at a time. I'll try and keep everyone off your back, but you'll have to pull off something spectacular to row back from this particular pile of *merde*. Like a quick result on this Egerton case. Do I need to tell you that Mrs Redbridge and Mrs Wetherspoon are also fans of *Antiques Ahoy!* or whatever it's called?'

'I could have guessed that, sir.'

'So get someone for the murder, and get 'em quick. And preferably some low-life who's never been nearer the bally than the one-and-nines at the Roxy for *Billy Elliot*.'

'I'll do my best, sir.'

'You'll want to do better than that,' Porson warned him.

A miracle would be nice, Slider thought as he trudged back to his office. Or, failing that, a bit of evidence and a nice confession.

'It's a bit rich, criticizing us for that,' Atherton said when Slider told him the reason for the carpeting.

'You have to look at it from Mr Wetherspoon's perspective: Mrs Wetherspoon and the AC's wife both unhappy with him. Domestic bliss it ain't.'

'There's an old saying which I think applies in this case,' said Atherton. 'Before you criticize anyone you should walk a mile in their shoes.'

'How wise.'

Atherton nodded. 'That way, when you criticize them, you're a mile away, and you have their shoes.'

The phone rang, and Slider waved him out.

'Mr Slider?' An unfamiliar voice, slightly husky,

medium-weight London accent, as of someone who had started off a bit Shepherd's Bush and worked their way towards Notting Hill. 'My name's Harris. Jim Harris.' Hearing Slider's blank pause, he added, 'Lenny Picket thought I might be able to help you.'

'*Crafty* Harris?' Slider enquired.

The wince was almost audible. 'I used to be called that, many years ago. It was just a bit of fun, but I don't like it now. Doesn't give the customers the right idea.'

'I'm sorry, Mr Harris. What can I do for you?'

'More a matter of what I can do for you. Lenny said you were looking for a certain Fabergé box, green malachite, gilt and unpolished diamonds.'

'Have you found it?' Slider asked eagerly. Just when he'd been asking for a miracle . . .

'Not *found* it, as such,' said Crafty Harris, 'but I've got a bit of information on it. I put out feelers, d'you see, and someone's come back to me. A dealer that had it through his hands, would be about eighteen month, two year ago. Any use?'

'Anything we can find out about the box could be useful,' Slider said, his hopes sagging like chocolate on a radiator. All the same – eighteen months could put it close to the time it came into Egerton's hands. It might be useful. 'How can I get hold of him?'

Harris gave him a name, address and phone number. 'He's got pitches in a lot of different shops and marts, so you're not likely to find him at home. Best to ring him first and find out where he is. He travels a lot.'

'Thanks a lot,' Slider said, scribbling.

'No probs. You still want a lookout for the box?'

'Yes, please. More than ever.'

'Righty-oh. Just one thing – it's not trouble for anyone I tell you about?'

'If they've acted in good faith, they won't be in trouble. And helping us is the best way to make that work.'

'Gotcha. Right. I'll be in touch.'

I hope so, Slider thought, going to the door of the CID room to see who was free. His eye fell on Hollis, who was looking careworn and indefinably seedy, in the manner of a man living in a hostel who finds keeping spick and span a challenge. But perhaps it was just frowsting indoors all the time.

'Hollis, d'you fancy an outing?' he called.

It didn't turn out to be much of an outing, as Arthur Abrams was servicing one of his pitches, in a mart in Upper Street, Islington, when he answered the phone, and agreed to meet Hollis there if he could come straight away. 'Only, it's one of my busy days. I've got to get out to St Albans this afternoon,' he said cheerfully, 'so I can't hang about too long.'

Still, Hollis thought, as he drove out to the Angel, it was a change of scene, and he didn't get too many of those these days. Abrams turned out to be a short, round man with a lot of tightly-crinkled hair gone gray – it looked as though he was protecting his head against CIA spy satellites with wire wool. He had thick glasses balancing on a thick nose and thick lips stretched out in a permanent smile, and he offered a handful of thick fingers like prime pork sausages to shake as Hollis introduced himself.

'Can't talk here,' he said, jerking his head towards various other pitch-holders with their ears on stalks. 'Come across the road for a cuppa tea and a sticky bun. There's a nice caff there, and I'm starving. Didn't get any breffus this morning, so my belly thinks my throat's cut, as they say in the music halls. What did you say your name was, again?'

'Colin Hollis.'

'Colin. I got a nephew called Colin, works in the meat trade. How do, Colin? It's Art, by the way, or Arty. You're a long way from home. What's that accent?'

'Manchester.'

'Ah, the granite city. Had a fantastic curry there once. Place on Deansgate. What was it called, again?'

'Akbar's?'

'No, that wasn't it. Wait a minute, I'll get it. Shimla's – that was the name. You know it? Gor! I can still taste it!'

Conversing, they crossed the road to a small, unfashionable-looking café that was clinging to life between the trendy and transient hotspots that the Angel was prone to. Hollis thought they must look ridiculous walking side by side – the beanpole and the beach ball – but you couldn't help liking Abrams, with his permanent grin and easy chat. It was why the guv had sent him to interview the witness, rather than simply talk on the telephone. You could learn so much about your source face to face. Abrams, Hollis was sure, was straight as the Mile End Road.

Tea and buns in front of them at a table in the window, Hollis let Abrams range a bit longer, swooping about like a kite enjoying the breeze, before bringing him gently down to earth.

'I'm interested in a certain green box,' he prompted.

'So you are, Colin, my old mate, and so am I. I missed a trick with that box, I don't mind telling you! I could have kicked myself after, which is why I remember it so clear, of course. I got it in a job lot at a house-clearance – up your way, as a matter of fact. Cheshire. A nice country house, out Wilmslow way. Not a stately, but a very nice manor-house, bit of Tudor, mostly Georgian, only who can afford to keep 'em up these days? And you can't get your sheikhs and oligarchs to buy so far from London. So the whole lot was going, contents *and* the house. Probate auction. Well, you can generally pick up a bargain or two at that sort of sale because the beneficiaries are only interested in the grand total, not the bits and bobs. Hence the job lots. *Any*way—' He checked himself. 'Stop me if I ramble on. I don't know how much detail you want.'

The tea was brick-coloured and invigorating, and the sticky bun was large. Outside, the sun had come out and long-haired, skinny Islingtonian girls in miniskirts and long boots were tick-tacking along the pavement only feet away. Hollis was enjoying himself. 'Take your time,' he said. 'Tell it your own way. I like detail, me.'

'Good-oh,' said Abrams. 'Well, this was a job lot of orna-ments, chucked together in a cardboard box. Mostly ceramics, couple of bits of brass – the odds and sods, nothing much of any value, which is why I missed it that the malachite box was a bit different. Also, I was in a hurry to get to another sale that day, so I chucked the lot in the boot and didn't look at it until I got home. Then I sorted out what I was going to put into which pitch. I've got several, as you know, and they're different value levels. No use putting a thousand-pound piece on a ten-quid stand.'

'I can see that. So, the malachite box?'

'Right. Well, it wasn't much to look at. Green's not a popular colour, and the unpolished diamonds just looked like white crystal beads that'd gone a bit milky. I didn't spot it for what it was, and that was my own silly fault – can't blame anyone else. But I gave it a bit of a buff, and it was a good size and the gilt sort of saved it, so I put it into my pitch in Hatfield. Quite a good class of client comes in there. I thought I'd give it a try there, then move it downmarket if it didn't sell. But as it happened, I was in there, doing my stint behind the counter, when this middle-aged couple came in and took a fancy to it.'

'Do you know their name?'

'As a matter of fact, I do. They were regulars, you see. I'd sold 'em a thing or two over the years. Mr and Mrs Arbogast. They weren't in the trade – retired couple; he was in oil, I think – but they prided themselves on having a good eye and knocking off the occasional bargain. So I ought to have paid attention when they picked up the box, but somehow or other I'd taken a dislike to it – not a dislike, really, more I just couldn't be bothered with it. I'd priced it in my head at eighty for the gilt, but o' course that sort always want a bit off so they can feel they've beaten you down, so I'd put it in at a hundred and sixty. After a bit of haggling I took a hundred and thirty off them, and we were all satisfied. And Mrs Arbogast said, as I was wrapping it up, "Well, I think this might be something a bit special, so I think I've got a bargain." And I thought, good luck to you then, my darling.'

Abrams took a draught of tea to fortify himself. 'Well, just for once the punter was right and I was left with egg on my face. Because about a month, six weeks later, they came back in, the Arbogasts, to tell me the box turned out to be Fabergé, and those damned crystals were diamonds, and they'd sold it for fifteen-hundred pounds.' He shook his head in wonder. 'How it slipped past me I'll never know.'

'Did they say who they sold it to?'

'Oh yes. It was quite a little story. You see, there was an episode of that *Antiques Galore!* programme being filmed at Hatfield House, and they'd gone along with a few things, including the box, just for the fun of it. Apparently, it caught the eye of some official who was looking round for items for the programme, and they got to show it to one of the big experts.'

'Rowland Egerton?' Hollis said.

'Yes, that was him. Of course, the programme doesn't get aired until a long while later, but I made a point of watching it when it did come on, just so I could torture myself all over again for missing it. And there he was, all smarm, and the Arbogasts smiling so you'd think their faces would fall in half. Wait a minute,' he interpolated, 'didn't he die recently? Rowland Egerton? I saw something in the paper. Well, there's a coincidence!'

'Isn't it, though? Go on about the box.'

'Right. Well, he says the box is Fabergé, blah blah blah, and the upshot is, after they've done their bit for the telly, the Arbogasts're walking away and another one of the experts comes running after them, wanting to buy the box as a present for someone, and will they sell? Well, they were pretty happy to get ten times what they paid for it, what with looking forward to telling me what a mug I'd been, so they said why not, passed it over and took the cash, happy as clams. Or a cheque, probably. Though,' he added, 'mind you, I think they could have got more than fifteen hundred for it at auction, a lot more, so they were mugs as well. If they'd brought it back to me I could probably have got them two, maybe two and a half. But I didn't tell them that. There's no future making people miserable, that's what I always say.'

'You're not wrong,' said Hollis. 'I wish more people thought like you.'

'Your job'd go down the pan if everyone was nice to each other, wouldn't it?' Abrams suggested jovially.

'You could be right,' said Hollis. 'Did the Arbogasts say who it was that bought the box from them?'

'Yes, it was that Julia Rabbet – Bunny, as everyone calls

her. I've met her a couple of times. Nice woman – posh as the queen, but never any side to her. Always gives you the time of day. Come to think of it,' he said, a rare frown creasing his face, 'didn't she die recently, as well? Good grief! What was that box, jinxed or something? There was I thinking I'd missed my chance, but looks as though I had a lucky escape.'

'You could say that,' said Hollis.

'Well, there! I always said there's a bright side to every situation if you look for it. Fancy that! The curse of the Romanovs!' He chuckled. 'I'll dine out on that one, I can tell you! Wait till I tell my wife.'

FIFTEEN
Madame Ovary

'So Bunny Rabbet bought the box as a present for Egerton?' Swilley said, when Hollis finished. They were all gathered in the CID room for the day's meeting.

'Does that mean she was the secret lover?' Connolly said.

'We shouldn't jump to conclusions,' Slider said. 'Someone else could have bought it from her before it came into Egerton's possession.'

'And we can't check, because Bunny's dead,' Atherton said. 'Gives new force to the old saying, "I hope your rabbit dies," doesn't it?'

'But Sylvia Thornton thought they were more like brother and sister,' Swilley objected.

'She also thought that Egerton and Marsh were doing it,' said Atherton. 'She's not infullable.'

'Infallible,' Hollis corrected.

'Exactly,' said Atherton.

'A brother and sister can give each other presents,' said McLaren, though doubtfully. He had one of each and hadn't seen or spoken to either of them in years.

'Yeah, but wait,' said Connolly. 'If they were just great mates, it was all innocent, why wouldn't her husband have known about it? And fifteen hundred's a lot to spend on a prezzie for a pal.'

'Not for someone like Bunny,' Atherton said. 'She comes from a moneyed background.'

'Whatever,' Mackay said impatiently, 'it couldn't have been Rabbet that killed Egerton and took the box, because she was already dead. It's much more likely Lavender was right all along, and it was a burglary gone wrong. Chummy was looking for something worth nicking, Egerton comes in at the wrong moment, Chummy whacks him, pockets the nearest object and has it away. End of.'

'No sign of a break-in,' Atherton objected.

'You don't know who had a chance to make a copy of the key,' said Mackay. 'There's Lavender at the shop, Mrs Bean at her house. Either of 'em could have left it around for long enough. And Egerton's own key – all sorts of people come to the house. What about his big parties? Don't tell me him and Lavender did all the food and drinks themselves. They're bound to've had caterers and waiters in.'

'Good point,' Slider said. 'Well, you'd better get on and check that line. And talk to Lavender and Bean again, see if they ever left the key anywhere, or lost it at any point.'

'Yes, guv.'

'Fathom and canvass team – keep at it. If One Thirty-Five Man was the murderer, someone must have seen him coming out, or leaving the area.'

'It's not easy, guv,' said Fathom, a touch resentfully. 'If we had an e-fit – even a description, apart from the coat and hat . . .'

'No-one said it would be easy,' Slider said. 'McLaren, how are you getting on with tracing back One Thirty-Five Man on the tube?'

'Haven't found him yet, guv,' McLaren said apologetically, his lips flaky from a sausage roll he was eating out of a bag. 'It's slow work.'

'Keep at it. If you can get a decent CCTV shot of him, it'll give Fathom something to work with. What else? Swilley, what about the money side of it?'

'Nothing untoward to report, boss,' she said. 'He had plenty coming in, but no suspicious, untraceable amounts. No large cash sums either way. He seems to have been fairly frugal. Spent money on his parties and eating out, less on clothes than you'd think – I suppose he had enough already to ring the changes. He was sinking quite a bit into the shop and business, as Lavender said.'

'I suppose that was his hold over Lavender,' Atherton said. 'In his little game of emotionally blackmailing everybody.'

'Anyway, he had quite a bit to leave,' Swilley concluded, 'which goes to Dale Sholto. As to Lavender, the stock in the shop should leave him with a small surplus after the business is wound up – if he can shift it on the current market. A few thousand.'

'Not enough to kill Egerton for,' Mackay remarked.

'Lavender's motive was never going to be financial,' Atherton said.

Swilley went on, 'I've found no evidence of debts. No evidence of drugs or gambling habits. I'm working my way round his contacts – I hardly like to call them friends – but so far they're all clean. Anyway, apart from Lavender, he doesn't seem to have been close to anyone, so nobody really knows how he spent his spare time.'

'Boss,' said Connolly, 'the only person we do know about that had a shady past is your man Patrick Duggan, the forger.'

'Yes,' said Slider. 'What did you find out about that?'

'Well, boss, Egerton's done a lot of work with him, and it isn't all lost in the mists o' time. I've been going through his files, and he's been doing the odd interior design job all along, one or two a year on average. The last one was eight months ago, and he gave Duggan quite a commission on that one – four big paintings.'

'Your point being?' Slider asked.

'He's the only person in Egerton's address book that we know's been inside.'

'*Honi soit qui mal y pense*,' Atherton said.

Connolly tutted. 'What's that when it's at home?'

'It means Duggan's famously on the straight and narrow now,' said Atherton.

Connolly ignored him and continued her pitch to Slider. 'Egerton'd been using him over a long time – maybe they were friends as well.'

'God knows we've got few enough leads to follow up,' Slider said. 'You might as well have a chat with him. Get all the paperwork that mentions him together – letters, invoices, anything – so you've got your ducks in a row, then give him a ring, set something up.'

Connolly looked pleased. 'Yeah, boss. I've got a good feeling about this.'

'We don't want feelings, we want facts,' said Slider. 'All

right, back to work everyone. Gascoyne, have a look through
records for anyone who does this sort of house job and check
them out. I'll goose up my snouts. Atherton, anyone on
Egerton's other shows, or his contacts in general, that he might
have been blackmailing in the same way. I've a feeling,' he
said apologetically as they moved away, 'this is going to be
hard graft.'

It was coming up for a week, and they had no strong lead.
Slider thought Mr Porson was right – it was going to take
more than trying their best.

Nothing made you feel more tired than a day's work that got
you nowhere. Slider let himself in and paused just inside the
door, sniffing the air for something comforting, like the rich
aroma of a slow-cooking stew in the oven. It was disappoint-
ingly neutral, cold and faintly dusty, carrying only the sound
of Joanna playing. He dumped his coat and briefcase and went
to find her.

She wasn't working from music this time, so he assumed
it was just practising – scales and arpeggios and other such
combinations that tested the dexterity and exercised the
muscles. He couldn't always tell from a distance. To his
uncultured ear, a lot of music sounded like practice.

She stopped as he came in and turned to him with a questioning look. 'Is it that late already?' she said.

'I'm a bit earlier tonight.'

'Sorry, I got carried away,' she said. 'You must be hungry.
It's all ready to go, vegetables cut and everything. I can
have it on the plate in fifteen minutes. I'm doing corned
beef hash.'

'Let's have a drink first,' Slider said. 'I could do with a
sharpener.'

'You look tired,' she said.

'So do you,' he countered.

'I'm all right,' she said sharply.

He stepped round the pothole. 'I'm remembering that you
said you had good news and didn't get round to telling me
what it was. I'm sorry. I should have asked. Tell me now.'

'I'll get the drinks first. Go and sit down. Put some music on.'

He was too weary to search for anything in particular and grabbed the first CD that came to hand, which happened to be Respighi, *The Pines of Rome*. OK. Undemanding. He put it on, turned down low; loosened his tie and pulled off his shoes; and sat down on the sofa. Joanna came back in with two tumblers, ice cubes clinking, a half-moon of lemon, delicately beaded, bobbing between them. It looked as if it was smiling at him.

'Ah, there is life after work,' Slider sighed. 'I'd heard a rumour, but I wasn't sure.' She sat, tucking a foot under her. He lifted his glass to her. 'Cheers.'

'Be well,' she responded, and took a mouthful.

'So what's your good news?'

'I hope you'll think it's good,' she said. 'I'm going back to work.'

He felt instant alarm, which he concealed as well as possible. 'Are you sure?'

She cocked a humorous eye. 'I think I'll notice when it happens,' she said.

'I mean, are you sure you should?'

'I know what you meant.' She sipped again. 'I rang Tony Whittam,' she went on. He was the fixer for the Royal London Philharmonia, in which she had sat at number four in the firsts. 'He said he couldn't give me anything before the middle of March, but after that I could come back regularly, though not to my old position. Obviously, they had to replace me there. He said I'd have to work my way back up over time.' She gave a little shrug. 'I don't really care about that. The extra money was nice, but I'll be happy to sit nearer the back and have a bit more flexibility.'

Slider felt relief. 'So you won't be going back to work until March?'

'I didn't say that. Not with the Phil until March. But I rang round a few other fixers, and some old friends, and I've got a few things lined up. Sid Cohen's offered me some sessions next week. And you remember Phil Redcliffe? I used to share a desk with him years ago. Well, he's got a long run in a West End show, and he's given me a lot of dates to dep for him. You know what it's like when these shows go on for ever – you end up with the entire pit full of deps.' She gave a slightly nervous smile. 'It's only Lloyd Webber, and it's only second violin, but it's work. Reminds me of the old joke – how many second violins does it take to change a light bulb?'

'How many?' Slider said automatically.

'None. They can't get up that high.' He only managed a smile, and she looked at him with embryo annoyance. 'You ought to be pleased for me.'

'I am – if it's what you want,' he said quickly. 'But I don't want you doing too much too soon.'

'I'm ready. It's time,' she said shortly.

'Don't feel you have to go back,' he said awkwardly. 'We can manage without the money.'

'It's not about the money,' she said. 'At least,' she added honestly, 'not mainly. It's about what I do with my life. I can't sit at home and do nothing.'

'What about George?' he asked.

'Your father and Lydia will babysit when necessary. You know that. They can't get enough of him. And on the occasions when they can't, well, we'll fix something else up. People all over the country manage to find babysitters.'

'I didn't mean that. I meant – don't you want to stay home with George?'

'I don't see you fighting to stay home with him.'

'I have a career.' The instant he said it, he knew what she would say.

'So do I.' She locked eyes with him for a moment. 'You're gone all day, and in a year or so George will go to nursery school and he'll be gone most of the day. And then what?'

'You can have another baby,' Slider said. 'You know the doctor said there was nothing wrong with you, it was just bad luck, no reason to think it would ever happen again—'

'I don't want another baby,' she said flatly.

There was a silence, filled with a complexity of pain; his and hers, and theirs.

'It's natural that you should be a little bit afraid . . .' he began.

She sighed. 'Bill. Please. Understand. I don't want another baby. I love George. He's my son, and I love him more than life. I love *you*. But I'm not a *hausfrau*. That's just not me, and you've always known that. I *need* to work. My work is who I am. You accepted that before George came along. You have to get back to accepting it again. We never planned this baby. If I'd had it, I'd have loved it too, but things didn't turn out that way. Now we have to move on.'

'I want you to do what makes you happy,' he said. He hadn't meant it to sound the way it came out: it sounded resentful and sulky. She raised an eyebrow, and he tried again. 'I'm not some kind of sultan. I never expected to lock you up in my harem and breed from you. I married Joanna the musician.'

'Well, then?' she asked.

'Compromise has always been difficult, given our two careers,' he said. 'I thought you were going to settle for rather more domesticity and rather less career, that's all.'

'I'd have had to, with two babies,' she said. 'But now I don't.'

'I understand. I'm not disapproving of your going back to work. Truly, I'm not.'

'What, then?'

'I'm anxious about you, that's all. Your well-being. I want to be sure that you're ready for this. I know how tiring it can be. The strain. The long hours. The late nights.'

'I'm ready,' she said. Her voice and face softened. 'Don't worry,' she said, 'I won't crock myself. And,' she continued, going to the heart of his unspoken fear, 'I'm not running away from the miscarriage, if that's what you're thinking. I'm not hiding all sorts of mental anguish from myself by burying myself in work. I've been through the anguish. It's done with. I'm out the other side.'

'But,' he said reluctantly, 'I've never seen you cry.'

She gave him a slow, amused, loving smile. 'Is that what's bothering you? When did you ever see me cry?'

'I've never seen you lose a baby before.'

She put down her glass and hitched along the sofa to him, drew his arm round her, nestled her head into his neck. He kissed the crown of her head, held her against him, loving her so much it gave him an ache in his stomach.

'I cried inside,' she said.

* * *

The papers went mad over the Melling assault. The front pages were ablaze. The *Telegraph* and the *Mail* had those tedious headlines lazy journalists love, based on the movie title *The Cook, the Thief, His Wife and Her Lover* – a movie no-one now living had ever actually seen. The *Telegraph* headline was 'THE BALLET DANCER, HIS LOVER AND THE CAMERAMAN', while the *Mail* went with 'THE TV STAR, HIS LOVER AND THE CAMERAMAN'. The *Sun* had 'TV STAR BALLET BOY BUST-UP' and the *Star* had 'TV GURU LOVE-RAT PUNCH-UP SHOCK'. The Express's headline was 'DANCER IN TV STAR ASSAULT SPARKS IMMIGRATION ROW', and the *Financial Times* went with 'G8 TENSIONS THREATEN DOHA ROUND'.

It would have been a welcome distraction, except that Melling was eagerly giving interviews in which he blamed the police for his current condition, which meant the papers had to explore the fact that he had been questioned and released over the Egerton case, leading to sub-headings along the lines of 'Police Baffled' and 'Police Have No Leads'.

Things were so bad that Hammersmith Headquarters set up a press conference, at which the assembled journos were addressed by no less a figure than Detective Chief Superintendent Morgan, Commander Wetherspoon's right-hand man and Brown-Noser in Chief. His principle skill was in talking at length, fluently and plausibly without actually saying anything – invaluable in this case, since there was nothing to say except 'Police Baffled'. Porson came back from it almost tearful, begging Slider to get him something – anything – to show Mr Wetherspoon before the end of the day.

'He says we're showing him up. They're laughing at him down the golf club. Tell me you've got some leads you're following up. Somebody you've got suspicions of.'

Slider had to tell him they had nothing; upon which Porson's capacity for supplication split under the pressure, and he bellowed that Slider had better bloody well go and get something then, and double-quick, or they'd all be watching daytime TV tomorrow.

When Slider got back to his office, Connolly was there, not bearing tea this time, but a piece of paper. 'It's about Patrick Duggan, boss,' she said. 'The forger.'

'Copyist is what we call him now, I think,' Slider corrected.

'Whatevs.' Connolly shrugged. 'I was getting all the papers together, like you said, going through the computer records and printing stuff out. And I found something a bit odd. It's a letter, but it wasn't in the correspondence file. It's not really correspondence at all. Look.' She handed him the sheet of paper. It was a printout of what was obviously a photocopy of a letter, which was neither from Egerton, nor addressed to him.

'Where did you find this?' Slider asked.

'It was in the folder that lists all the art and antiques in the house. They've each got a separate file with a photograph, description and valuation. This file just had this photocopied letter in it.'

Slider examined it. The letter heading, in large letters, said 'Patrick Duggan. Fine Art Restoration and Copying'. The address, below that, was in Little Missenden, and the letter was addressed to Philip Masterson at his home.

'Interesting,' Slider said. He read on.

Dear Philip,

I enclose my invoice for the copy of the painting in your office, 'Girl with Embroidered Reticule' by Joest van Wessen (1480–1539).

As you know, it is my custom, when copying an Old Master painting, to introduce a deliberate small variation from the original, in order to guard against any accusation of fraud. You will see that in my copy of your painting, there are six gilt tassels on the reticule, as opposed to five on the original.

I would appreciate settlement of my invoice within thirty days as discussed. Thanking you for your esteemed patronage and hoping to be of service to you again in the future,

Yours truly,
Pat Duggan

'Well,' said Slider, 'that *is* interesting. Why would Egerton have kept a copy of this letter?'

'Why would he even have it in the first place?' Connolly went him one better.

'I think a visit to Mr Duggan would be in order,' Slider said.

'Yes, boss. I'll see and get out to him this morning.'

'I meant me,' Slider said.

Her face fell like rain on a Bank Holiday.

'But you can come with me,' he added. 'Only fair, since you found it.'

The address – Mistletoe Cottage, Christmas Lane, Little Missenden – was almost unbearably picturesque. 'It makes you sound as if you've got badly fitting false teeth,' Slider observed as he drove out into the countryside. The snow had mostly gone in town, but in the fields there were still wide patches, and white lines of it lingered along the cold side of walls and hedges.

The cottage itself turned out to be much less romantic than its name, sitting all alone and rather tumbledown in a wide vista of dull fields, and blighted by the widened and straightened A413 that allowed traffic to Brands Hatch past about fifty feet away. It was a plain grey-stone cottage with several less-than-lovely brick extensions and a couple of ugly sheds in a long back garden dedicated otherwise to Brussels sprouts and the skeletons of sunflowers and teasels.

'Strange,' Slider said as they pulled up in the muddy lane outside, 'how someone who makes his living as an artist can put up with such unaesthetic surroundings.'

'That's your average genius,' Connolly observed. 'So deep in their own world, they never notice what class of a ganky kip they're living in.'

The door (paint peeling off, brass Lincoln Imp door-knocker in desperate need of a polish) was opened by a short, stout woman in trousers and a bulky home-knit Arran cardigan, with faded blue eyes behind rather startlingly green framed glasses, and a perm so tight it looked as though she'd had a tin of beans poured over her head. She gave them the sort of happy, trusting smile that tells the door-to-door scammer they've rung the right bell. Slider hastened to show his brief and introduce himself.

'Oh yes,' she said, the smile not changing a whit. 'Come in. Pat's expecting you. He's in his studio. Mind your head – that beam's a bit low.'

The narrow passage had bulging walls, an uneven brick floor that bucked like a frisky pony, and a low beam right across it in just the spot best calculated to catch you as you turned from shutting the door. The air was cold and damp and the cottage smelled of mould and dogs, two of whom – a collie and a Lab – came advancing to meet them with tails swinging.

Mrs Duggan squeezed past Connolly and Slider, saying, 'It's this way. Better let me go first or you won't find it.'

She was right. The original small, rectangular cottage had been built on to in such a haphazard way that they were led through rooms, across passages and round corners on a route they would not have been able to guess without help. The three of them, plus the two dogs, made an unwieldy mass for some of the sharp turns, and the light was so dim that it was hard not to stumble on the uneven floors and raised thresholds. Finally, they stepped out of doors and across a three-foot gap to the door of one of the large sheds, into which Mrs Duggan ushered them while repelling the dogs with waved hands and a certain amount of hooshing.

'Pat, it's your visitors,' she announced.

The shed was brick built with large windows and was refreshingly light after the house, and much less cold and damp, and there was no mould smell, but instead the penetrating odour of paint and turpentine. It was spectacularly untidy. In the near left corner there was a cheap office desk with a computer on it and a filing cabinet behind it, but the desk's entire surface was covered in letters, bills and other paperwork, and there were two overstuffed wire trays on top of the filing cabinet carrying on the theme. The rest of the room was given over to art. There were battered wooden tables covered with tins of paint, bottles of turps, brushes soaking in jam jars, scrapers, rags, boxes of charcoal and chalk, Oxo tins full of odds and ends, heaps of cartridge paper, drawings, and reference books; and on easels and propped around the rooms were canvases in various states

of completion or in process of being scraped off. There were
various chairs and stools scattered about, their surfaces
equally inhabited, and the theme was carried on over the
wooden floor, where things seemed to have been put for want
of anywhere else to leave them.

In all this visual cacophony it was hard immediately to
identify the owner, but Slider's challenged eye finally picked
him out in a corner between an easel, an old-fashioned tailor's
dummy and a large artificial ficus plant in a pot. He was
holding a palette and working on the painting on the easel,
and did not seem to notice that he had been invaded. He was
short like his wife and stocky where she was round, wearing
thick cord trousers and another bulky home-knit sweater with
the sleeves rolled up, over which he had tied a pinafore in
dull-blue cotton, liberally specked and smudged and dribbled
with paint. He had an upstanding mass of grey hair, a bushy
beard, grey except for two dark dabs at the mouth corners,
and thick-framed glasses, which left little of his face visible
between them. He looked a lot older than Slider had expected,
though that might be the effect of all the hair; but studying
the face as he continued to be ignored, he saw the deep folds
and lines and guessed Duggan must be in his seventies at
least.

Mrs Duggan, standing beside them, must have detected
some difference in her husband's movements because after a
silence she suddenly said, 'Pat! Visitors!' and this time Duggan
turned at once, put aside his brush and palette and came towards
them. Behind the glasses his eyes were deep blue and aware,
and his smile was lively. He picked up a cloth from one of
the tables he passed and wiped his hands as he advanced.

'Hello!' he said. 'You must be the detectives. I won't shake
hands because I'm rather painty. Are you the young lady I
spoke to on the telephone?'

'Yes, sir. Detective Constable Connolly.'

'Ah, lovely accent! Dublin, isn't it? I've a bit of Irish in me
myself, as you can probably tell. What part are you from?'

'Clontarf.'

'I know it. My mother was from Raheny. My father was
from Donegal, though. And you are?'

'Detective Inspector Slider. I'm the investigating officer in the enquiry concerning Rowland Egerton.'

'Right. Right.' Duggan looked sharply from one of them to the other. 'Let me clear you a couple of chairs.' He did so by unceremoniously scraping everything off on to the floor – now Slider knew how it got that way. He and Connolly sat, rather gingerly. Duggan perched on the end of the table nearest them, folding his arms across his chest, making himself look even more spherical, while Mrs Duggan remained where she was, standing by the door, vaguely smiling. 'So,' said Duggan, 'what did you want to know?'

The Irish in his voice was so diluted that it was hardly more than a slight softening of certain vowels and a rolling over of the 'r' in some words.

'You had quite a long association with Mr Egerton, I understand,' Slider began.

'I've known him for years,' said Duggan. 'Twenty or thirty, it must be. He's put a lot of work my way over the years – good, paying work. One thing about Rowland, he knew how to pick the right customers. People who wanted the best and never questioned the bill. We'll certainly miss him, won't we, Sheila?'

Mrs Duggan nodded.

'Will you be missing him any other way?' Connolly asked. 'As a friend, maybe?'

'Well, we haven't seen so much of him over the last couple of years. You know how it is – you get set in your ways as you get older, don't get out so much, go round in the same small circles. But yes, I'd still call him a friend; I shall miss him. I read what happened in the papers – not that they said much. It was very shocking. How did it happen?'

'That's what we're still trying to find out,' Slider said.

'Hence your visit. I get it. Going round all his old pals. Well, he and I had some pretty wild times together when we were both younger. Drinking, chasing girls – sorry, Sheila! Obviously, after I got married, I was doing the drinking and he was chasing the girls. He had an amazing strike rate. Women couldn't get enough of him. And of course his telly career only helped. It's like catnip to women, fame. Any sort of fame.

You'd be amazed the letters I got from women after I was jugged for fraud. Offers of marriage and everything.'

'Do you know who he's been going out with recently?' Connolly asked.

'No, I can't say as I do. As I said, I haven't seen so much of him lately. It must be – oh, what? – a year since I saw him.'

'You did a job for him last May,' Slider said. 'Four paintings.'

'That's right – for a house in Onslow Square. Russian businessman. Wanted four large oils in the style of Chagall. Was that only last May? It feels like longer.'

'Did you see Mr Egerton at that time?'

'Once at the client's to size up the job. Once when I delivered the paintings. And we went out for a drink afterwards. He seemed in good form.'

'What did you talk about?'

'God, I can't remember! Nothing in particular.'

'Anything about his television work? His current love-life?'

Duggan shook his head. 'Nothing that sticks in the mind. It was just old-pals talk, you know? This and that. I think we may have mentioned his Royal Palaces series, but more from the point of view of the paintings he featured in it. There's such a lot of great art shut away in those places that never gets seen. I think I told him he was a lucky pup to get the chance. We, the British Public, are the biggest art-owners on the planet, but we only get to see a tenth of it, if that.'

'There's a lot of art in government offices, I believe,' Slider said, glad he had come to the point on his own penny.

'God! Yes. The Whitehall treasure trove. The state owns so many fabulous pieces; the government seeds them round the various department offices. It's a cheap way to store them – security built in, a stable environment, and at least they're look-at-able, even if the poor old wage slaves generally don't bother.'

'But I believe one particular wage slave, at least, *did* bother,' Slider said. 'Tell me about your dealings with Philip Masterson.'

Duggan stared at Slider with an intensified interest, as though cogs were whirring and clicking behind those bright eyes. 'Philip Masterson! There's a name I haven't heard for a long while. I'd forgotten about that job.'

'Tell me,' said Slider.

SIXTEEN
Swindler's List

'How did you come to meet him?' Slider asked.

Duggan almost shrugged. 'He was Minister for the Arts. We bumped into each other on occasion. You know that after my little bit of trouble I was consulted by the police and the government on various cases – authentication, advising on forgery techniques and so on. I made as much of my contacts as I could, you can bet on it. I didn't want anyone thinking my copies were anything but copies any more, so I made good and sure everyone knew what I was doing.'

'Can you really copy anything?' Connolly asked, unable to help herself. 'I mean, they're all different styles and everything.'

'Copying is copying,' he said with a shrug. 'Once you see how they've done it, you can reproduce it. Manet, Van Gogh, Constable, Vermeer, Picasso – they all had their little tricks. My trouble as an artist was always that I can be anyone except myself. I have the talent all right – bags of it – more than most successful artists – but I haven't the single eye. As soon as I try to paint something for myself, it falls into pastiche. It's as if I can't take myself seriously. And when you see the rubbish that's sold in the galleries, and the damned extortionate prices they charge for something I could do with one hand tied behind my back – well, you see that the whole art world is in fact a great big joke, with the punter and his pocket the butt of it.'

Interesting though this was, Slider knew a hobby horse when it stepped on his foot, and invited Duggan to dismount. 'You were saying how you knew Philip Masterson.'

'Right. Well, because of the cooperation with officialdom, I got invited to the occasional bash, as a pat on the head for being a good boy. Had drinkies at Number Ten once. It was at a Christmas party at the Department for Culture, Media and Sport that Philip approached me about the painting. Said he had a bit of private business he'd like to put my way, and would I be interested in a commission. I said yes, of course.' He smiled. 'Curse of the freelance. You can never say no.'

Slider had heard the same from Joanna. She had tales of trumpet players who'd do the first half at the Albert Hall then tear across London to do the second half at the Festival Hall, all because they couldn't say no.

'Go on,' he said.

'So we slipped out of the party,' Duggan said, 'and he took me across to his office. There was a painting there – government property, of course – but as I said, they have these works of art seeded around all the buildings. I'd been in his office before and noticed it. Quite a pretty piece – "Girl with Embroidered Reticule" – by a sixteenth century Dutch painter, Joest van Wessen. One of the minor masters, if such an expression is allowable. Anyway, he said that his wife had been visiting him in his office one day and she'd fallen in love with it. Her birthday was coming up, and he wanted me to paint a copy of it as a present for her.'

'Had you met his wife?'

'No. I'd never met him outside of business. I knew nothing about his home life.'

'Did he say anything about her?'

'Nothing, except that he wanted to surprise her with this painting, so it all had to be kept a secret. I said thank you very much, named my price, and we shook hands.'

'How did you manage, working in a busy Whitehall office?' Slider said.

'I didn't do the actual painting there,' Duggan said. 'It would have been too disruptive on both sides. I did the work in my own studio. But he arranged several visits for me so that I could study the painting closely, do some sketches and make notes, and take as many photographs as I wanted. Of course, he wanted it in time for the birthday which didn't leave me a great deal of time, but I'm one of those people who works better under pressure. I said I could deliver on time, on condition that he paid me on time. People can be amazingly vague about paying their bills once they've got the actual goods. Anyway, I took a decent deposit off him, just in case. But he paid up like a lamb, so that was all right.'

'Where did you send the painting to when it was finished?' Slider asked.

'He came and fetched it himself. It was a pretty good piece of work, though I say it myself.' Duggan smiled complacently. 'He seemed very impressed with it, said his wife would love it. I sent him the invoice, he sent me a cheque, and that was that.'

'Did you ever see it in place, in his house?' Slider asked.

'No. As I said, I had no contact with him outside work. And as a matter of fact, it wasn't long after that that he got reshuffled out of the Arts and I had no work contact with him either. Valerie Agar was the new Arts Minister, God help us!' He rolled his eyes. 'So, what's all this about? Why are you asking about Philip Masterson, and what's it got to do with Rowland Egerton?'

'That's what we're trying to work out,' Slider said. 'Did you ever tell Mr Egerton about this commission?'

'No,' said Duggan. 'Philip wanted it kept a secret, so I didn't discuss it with anyone.'

'Did you generally discuss your work with Mr Egerton?' Connolly asked.

'Obviously, the stuff I was doing for him. And yes, we'd chat now and then if I had anything interesting on.'

'So how can you be sure you didn't mention this one to him?' she said.

He gave her a frosty look. 'Because I'm a professional, young lady. The same way you know you haven't talked about something at work that has to be kept secret.' He looked at Slider. 'Why are you asking that?'

Slider shook his head, thinking things through. 'Did you ever discuss Philip Masterson with him?'

'Why on earth should I? He wasn't exactly an interesting person, Anyway, as far as I know, Rowland didn't know him from Adam. Look, I think you'd better come clean with me. Maybe I could help you if I knew what it was you wanted to know.'

Slider nodded to Connolly, who produced the photocopied letter in a clear folder and handed it to Duggan. He looked at it, and a faintly puzzled frown crossed his face. 'Where did you get this?' he asked.

'We found it in a file in Mr Egerton's computer,' Connolly said. 'Is that your signature?'

'Yes. It's the letter I sent to Philip, all right.'

'Any idea how Mr Egerton came to have a copy of it?'

'None at all. *I* certainly never gave him one. He must have got it from Philip, I suppose,' said Duggan. He turned the folder over as if the back of the letter might have the answer. 'It's a mystery,' he said. 'But why is it important?'

Slider shrugged. 'Probably, it isn't. We have to follow up anything unusual, and this seemed odd, that's all. Well, thank you for your cooperation.' He started to rise, and Mrs Duggan, still standing silently by the door, stirred.

'Pat, didn't you lose that letter?' she said. 'The first one, I mean.'

'What are you talking about?' Duggan said with a hint of impatience.

'I'm remembering now,' she went on, 'that when you came to posting it, you couldn't find it after all. Didn't you have to print out another one?'

Duggan frowned. 'Did I? It's possible. I'm not the tidiest of people.' He waved a hand towards the desk under its snow-drift of papers. 'I'm always misplacing things. They usually turn up again, though, given time.' It sounded like an oft-repeated justification.

'That one didn't. You got in quite a temper,' Mrs Duggan went on serenely, 'because you said if you didn't get the invoice out before that so-and-so got cold you'd never get the money. So I said for God's sake print out another one and stop your fussing.'

It was all delivered in a voice so colourless, it was almost deadpan, but Slider could imagine a much fierier scene. He could almost see Duggan throwing papers up in the air in a fury and bellowing at his wife to be more of a help and less of a nag.

And now a sheepish look came over Duggan's hairy face, and he said, 'It's ringing a bell, my love. Definitely a bell. I think you're right. But even if that's a copy of the missing letter, how could it have got into Rowland's hands?'

'Did he ever visit you here, in your studio?' Slider asked.

'God, yes! Any number of times. We used to hang out here and gas.'

'And drink,' said Mrs Duggan. 'And get noisy. Good job we don't have any neighbours to complain.'

'Those days are long gone,' he said, fixing her with a look. 'I'm a reformed character now. And Rowland—' He stopped and went on seriously, 'Rowland is dead. God, in all this chatter, I'd forgotten. Poor old Rowland. What a rotten thing.'

Slider got up to go. Connolly retrieved the folder from Duggan, Mrs Duggan opened the door, and the dogs surged in as if they had been leaning against it, and were hooshed out again. 'No dogs in the studio!' Duggan bellowed them. 'No hairs on my paintings!'

At the door, Slider turned back and said, 'Just one last thing, Mr Duggan – you said you never met Philip Masterson's wife. Do you know who she was?'

'Mrs Masterson, I suppose,' he said. 'Why, was she someone different?'

'Did he ever mention her name to you?'

'No, I don't think he did. Just talked about "my wife". He sounded as if he was very fond of her, though. Must have been, to spend that much on her birthday present.'

'How much?' Connolly asked.

'Five thousand,' said Duggan.

'Not enough,' said Mrs Duggan, 'once you've taken materials into account.'

'Ah well,' said Duggan lightly, 'it was fast work. I didn't labour long over it. Easy come, easy go.'

'That's your trouble,' said Mrs Duggan.

Despite her blancmange-like appearance, Slider was getting the impression she wasn't nearly the pushover she appeared, and that Duggan didn't have nearly as much rope as his surroundings suggested.

'Well,' said Connolly on the drive back, 'that was a wasted journey. I can't see it helps us with the murder at all.'

'I'd still like to know what the letter was doing in Egerton's computer,' said Slider.

'Sure, we've all got loads of rubbish in our computers. And on our desks. And in our drawers. If I was killed in a car smash right now, I bet there'd be some heads scratched over what I've got in me handbag. Some poor sap of a detective'd be puzzling himself to an early grave saying, "What in the name of *arse* does that mean?"'

Slider wasn't listening. He was thinking. 'He could have picked it up from Duggan's desk during one of his visits there. That could be why it went astray. But the question is, why?'

'Maybe he knew from Bunny that that's what she was getting for her birthday, and he was interested.'

'Masterson said it was a secret present.'

'Ah, sure God, women always know about these things,' said Connolly. 'There never was a secret present that stayed secret.'

'Even so, it doesn't explain why he'd take the letter. Much more likely that he'd just discuss it with Duggan.'

'Maybe he didn't want Duggan to know he knew. Maybe he wanted to compete with a big oul present of his own.'

'Still doesn't explain.'

'No,' Connolly admitted. 'It's queer, all right.'

'The queerest thing,' Slider said, 'is that it wasn't the letter itself, but a photocopy of the letter. Where would he get that from?'

'That,' said Connolly, 'is a real mincer.'

Slider fell into a brooding silence, and Connolly wisely let him alone.

Atherton, perched on the radiator in Slider's room, considered the new information, as far as it went, and then said, 'Well, if nothing else, we've got another connection with Philip Masterson, which is more than we've got with anyone else. There's the altercation at the funeral, and the letter addressed to him in Egerton's computer.'

'Photocopy of the letter,' Slider corrected.

'And the fact he was getting the ride off Masterson's oul lady,' Connolly added. 'That's three.'

'We have no evidence at all that they were having an affair,' Slider said.

'Still,' said Atherton, 'the letter must have been significant to Egerton in some way for him to have preserved it. Maybe he had an interest in that particular painting. He didn't care for Lavender's Morisot, so maybe his taste was more towards the representational. His collection, as far as we've seen it, wasn't hot for Impressionism.'

'But when would he ever have seen it?' Swilley asked. She was propping up one side of the door and Hollis the other, like a pair of gargoyles representing Heaven and Hell. She was golden and beautiful as an angel – a later Disney representation of an angel, but still – and he certainly looked like hell these days.

'He might well have visited Masterson's office at some point, when he was Minister for the Arts. Or he might have seen an image of it in a catalogue or a book or on the Internet,' Atherton said.

'I know what the Mona Lisa looks like, but I've never seen it in real life,' Hollis said.

'That's a bit more famous than this Van Weasel joker,' Connolly pointed out.

'Or he could have seen it somewhere else altogether,' Slider said. 'Those paintings get moved about.'

'We could ask your contact in SCD6 – what's his name? De Wett? – if it's been anywhere else,' Atherton suggested.

'I wouldn't mind having a look at it now,' Slider said. 'Connolly, see if there's an image on the Internet.'

She went out to her desk and in a very short time called them over. 'Here it is. From a site about Dutch Old Masters. There's three Weasel paintings on it.'

Everyone crowded round to look. It was typically Dutch, with the light falling from an unseen source at one side, the background simple. A golden-haired girl in a yellow robe was sitting at a table covered with a brown plush cloth. Her face was turned towards the artist, and she was holding a piece of paper in one hand, as though it was a letter she had been reading. There was a cream-coloured vase on the table and an earthenware bowl containing red and yellow fruit. The girl's eyes were brown, very striking with the gilt hair, which was crinkled in front into fine corkscrew curls hanging about her brow.

'It *is* a pretty piece,' Slider said. The limited palette of brown and yellow tones gave it a harmony that seemed designed to emphasize the girl's colouring and beauty. The reticule itself was lying on the table, half hanging over the edge, a flat square bag of deep crimson velvet covered in elaborate embroidery of coloured silks, gold threads and pearls, the bottom of the bag finished off with gold tassels that hung down against the brown plush of the tablecloth. Though not large or prominent in terms of the rest of the picture, it nevertheless caught the eye because of the richness of the embroidery – hence, Slider supposed, the title. The subtext of the picture, he thought, was that this was a love-letter she carried around in the bag and took out to read from time to time.

'You can see why someone might like to own a copy,' said Swilley. 'It's rather nice.'

'Hasn't got the precision and technique of a Vermeer,' Atherton remarked. 'But still.'

'Make a nice prezzy,' Connolly agreed.

'I wonder what it's worth,' Hollis said.

Slider straightened and sought Atherton's eye, and found the same thought there. 'I think perhaps you'd better go and visit Masterson's old office in the DCMS,' he said. 'Have a look at it.'

'Yes,' said Atherton.

'Be discreet.'

'Right.'

'As of now, I'm promoting checking Philip Masterson's alibi to the head of the list,' Slider announced. 'Mackay – this committee. Find someone who was on it and check he was actually there. Connolly, contact his secretary, whatever she knows about his movements that day. Hollis, find what officers were on duty on the entrances to the Palace of Westminster.'

'Yes, guv.'

'McLaren? Where's McLaren?'

'Here, guv.' He was right behind him, having left his own

desk to join the party. His breath smelled of artificial strawberries – he was eating an individual tub of jelly trifle.

'Tracing One Thirty-Five Man. Concentrate on the route between Shepherd's Bush and Westminster in both directions,' Slider told him. 'Take as much help as you need. I want this done quickly. And Swilley, in case he took a cab, get on to all the taxi firms you can find locally and around Westminster, see if anyone took him anywhere on Thursday last.'

'Yes, boss. Are we thinking—?'

'We aren't thinking anything until we know something,' said Slider. But of course they were. *He* was. Things were falling into place.

'It's nasty,' said Porson. 'The last thing we need is more aggro of that kind.'

'It's still just a theory, sir. We don't know yet there's anything in it.'

'Well, what're you telling me for, then?'

'I just thought I ought to prepare you, sir. If I'm right, there'll be a media storm.'

'Everywhere you blasted well go there's a media storm,' Porson grumbled.

Slider looked hurt and said nothing.

Porson went on, 'Well, keep me informed. The instant you've got something. And don't go plunging in irregardless, like a bowl in a china shop.' !Argh

'No, sir.'

'I want all your ducks in a row before I go in to bat. This is a whole new kettle of worms you're opening up.'

'I know, sir,' said Slider. It was never a good sign when Porson's imagery started to fracture. Along the fault lines were deposits of deep shit, which could go anywhere in an explosion.

The Department for Culture, Media and Sport (go figure what that lot had to do with each other, Atherton thought) lived at 100 Parliament Street, one of the grand, elaborate white buildings just along from Downing Street – Parliament Street was in fact the end part of Whitehall. It was the kind of architecture that reminded one of an iced wedding cake, for which reason Slider had named the style 'gâtesque'.

In the modern climate of paranoia, getting access to any government building was a painstaking process. Atherton had to establish his identity and state his purpose to more than one Cerberus, and his bona fides were verified by a phone call back to the station. It all took an inordinate amount of time. Glaciers around the world had moved and stalactites and stalagmites inched closer to union before he breached the citadel and was escorted by a minion to the correct floor. On exiting the lift he was handed over to the charge of another minion who actually worked there.

This was a very thin girl with her hair drawn back into a bun, all except the obligatory one strand which fell annoyingly over one eye, making Atherton's fingers itch to push it back for her. He wanted to shout at her, 'Get a grip!'

'The Minister's not here,' she said. 'She's at the House, and the PPS is with the Permanent Secretary over at the Cabinet Office, so there's just me.' She looked very young and seemed nervous about having so much responsibility. 'I don't know that I ought to let you into her office, when you're not in the diary.'

'It's police business,' Atherton said sternly, though he was trying not to laugh. 'Very important. I must warn you not to obstruct a police officer in the performance of his duty.'

The girl lifted frightened eyes to him, but still chewed her lip with indecision. 'Couldn't you come back later, when the Minister's here? I could make you an appointment, if you like.'

'No, I couldn't.' He tried kindness. 'I just want to look at the office, that's all. It's nothing for you to worry about.'

'Anything in particular?'

'You haven't been here very long, have you?' he hazarded.

'Six months,' she said. 'I was at Work and Pensions before. I liked it much better there. It's too quiet here. What d'you want to look at the office for?'

'I can't tell you that,' Atherton said importantly, and being refused information seemed to reassure her, as though she was back on familiar ground.

They reached a tall, mahogany door, and she seized the

door knob and opened it. 'I hope I'm doing the right thing,' she murmured to herself.

'I won't touch anything,' he told her.

A moment later they were out again and she was closing the door behind them with an air of large relief. 'Was that it?' she said.

'That's it. I told you it was nothing to worry about.'

She walked him back to the lift. 'I wish you could tell me what it's about,' she said wistfully. 'It's really quiet here, after Work and Pensions. There was always something going on there, a real buzz, and lots to do to keep you busy. This is like a morgue. I could do with a bit of excitement.'

Murder in the Rue Morgue, Atherton thought. 'Oh, I don't think you'd find it exciting, even if I could tell you,' he said kindly.

Mackay reported first. 'There was a meeting of the Deregulation Committee, whatever that is, on Thursday, starting at eleven a.m., and Masterson was there all right. I talked to the chairman, Doreen Freeling, MP. Masterson arrived with two other people from the Department of Energy and Climate Change about a quarter past eleven. They were giving depositions and answering questions. She said the notes show that Masterson was speaking from about twelve to twelve fifteen. But they finished that business around half past twelve and moved on to a different topic, and all the DECC people left.'

'Masterson definitely among them?'

'Yes, he went all right. It was a good alibi, though,' Mackay went on. 'Officially, the Committee met from eleven till two, and Masterson was definitely there. If we'd not enquired specifically, we'd have thought he was covered.'

'It's easy to get caught out. That's why we're paid to do the footwork. All right, you'd better get out there, find this Freeling person, get a statement. Ducks in a row, Mr Porson wants.'

Connolly was next. 'Your man said he had lunch in Portcullis House. There's a cafeteria sort of yoke downstairs in the atrium.'

'We saw it when we were there. I think there's more than one.'

'That's right, boss,' said Connolly. 'Woeful daft names they've given 'em. There's a sit-down restaurant called the Adjournment, a caff called the Debate and a coffee shop called the Despatch Box. Can you imagine saying to someone, "Meet me in the Adjournment at one"?' She rolled her eyes.

'We're not here to discuss nomenclature,' Slider reproved her.

'I know. But you'd crease yourself laughing, sure you would. Anyway, your woman was having her own lunch in the Despatch Box.' She paused to snigger. 'She was just leaving around half two when her boss comes in, saying he's going to get a quick sandwich, then he'll work in his office. She assumed he'd just come from the House, from the committee room. So he comes up to the office around three, asks if there's any messages, then says he wants to be left alone, he's not taking any calls, and he goes into his own office and shuts the door. She doesn't see him again until she goes home half five, when she sticks her head round the door to say she's off, and he's in there reading. So,' she concluded, 'she doesn't know if he was there all the time, because he can go out his own door without going through her office.'

'It doesn't really matter,' Slider said. 'We're not interested in that part of the day. Did you ask her how he seemed?'

'Yes, boss. She said he's been in flitters since his wife died, so she didn't notice any difference that day. He looked moody and depressed, but that's the way he's been. And saying he doesn't want any calls is just par for the course. But if he had just been at Egerton's and done the biz, he might be too shaken to talk to anyone.'

Hollis joined in. 'I checked on the entrances, guv. The usual way in and out from the House for the MPs is the Carriage Gates, and o' course they keep a log. Masterson left by the Carriage Gates at twelve thirty-nine that day.'

'I suppose it would take him a few minutes to get from the committee room to the gates.'

Hollis nodded. 'And, look, guv, if he leaves the House at twelve forty and doesn't get to the caff until half two, that's plenty o' time for him to get to Shepherd's Bush and back. If he were One Thirty-Five Man, it gives him fifteen minutes at

Egerton's house and forty to get back to Westminster. Long enough.'

'Long enough,' Slider agreed. 'But we've got to be careful here. We'll have to trace him. Both ways. I want everything dotted and crossed. I don't have to tell you how important it is to be invulnerable on evidence when you're going after a minister.'

'Even a minister nobody likes,' Hollis agreed. 'You're thinking he done it, then, guv?'

'I'm just waiting for one more piece of the puzzle,' Slider said.

Atherton returned at last. Slider heard his voice in the outer office, speaking quietly to Hollis, then he appeared in the doorway, clutching a cardboard container of coffee from some outside source like Costa or Starbucks. What Slider always thought of as exocoffee, as distinct from the endocoffee from the canteen.

'You were a hell of a long time,' he said.

'Penetrating the sanctum takes time and skill, especially if you don't want to leave a mess behind you. Carter and Carnarvon had it easy.'

'And?' Slider prompted.

'I got in. The painting's still there.'

'*And?*'

Atherton met his eyes with the light of the hunt in his own. 'Six tassels,' he said.

SEVENTEEN
The Kindly Ones

S lider phoned home, to say that he would be working late. 'The hunt's afoot,' he added, with an attempt at humour. 'Not in this house,' Joanna said. 'Diarrhoea's afoot. George has got the bellyache.'

'What's caused that, then?'

'Alimentary, Watson,' Joanna said. 'Now *that*'s a joke. You know what he's like for picking things up and putting them in his mouth. Don't worry, it's not too serious. All helps to build up immunities. Are you on the verge of a result?'

'I think so,' he said. 'But we've got to be sure before we move, and the last bits of evidence are the tedious ones to track down. Expect me when you see me.'

'All right. Good luck. And,' she added as he was ringing off, 'eat something!'

'Ditto to you,' he said. He rang off and telephoned Peter de Wett.

'You just caught me – I was going home. Working late tonight?'

'Yes, we've got things breaking.'

'Good for you. Anything I can do to help?'

'I just want to pick your brains,' said Slider. 'Are you by your computer? Can you look at this image?' He sent the URL to him.

'Right, got it,' said de Wett. 'Yes, that's very nice. I don't know the picture personally, but of course I know of Joest van Wessen. Is this another one you've lost?'

Slider put aside the implication that he was always losing things. 'No,' he said, 'I just want to ask you what you think it's worth.'

'What it would fetch, you mean?' de Wett corrected delicately. 'You know there's no definitive answer when it comes to auction value. It depends very much who's there on the day. But if you want my personal opinion, for what it's worth, I'd say between two and three million.'

'And what if it was stolen?'

'You mean, if it had to pass through a fence? Well, that would lessen its value enormously. You can't sell stolen art with its provenance, if at all. It would have to go to a private collector, and they would only pay a fraction of the auction value.'

'What sort of fraction?'

'You might get eight hundred thousand for it. But then you'd have to pay the people handling it, and they don't come cheap. You'd be lucky to clear half a million.'

'Still, a goodly sum,' Slider mused. 'Especially if you need the money.'

'Don't try it, that's my advice,' de Wett said, sharply humorous. 'Not worth it, to be looking over your shoulder for the rest of your life.'

'Thanks,' said Slider. 'I'll stick to the day job.'

Swilley found a taxi driver. He worked out of one of the local black cab garages – not Monty's, with which they had had fruitful previous encounters, but a new kid on the block, Central Line Cabs, which appropriately had a garage down Sterne Street, behind the Central Line Station. They hadn't the same history of cooperating with the police, but once convinced of the urgency of the enquiry they put it out over the radio.

The driver in question was on evenings this week and came in to the station between fares. Swilley went down to him. He was a lean young Asian man with a shiningly-shaved head and a small gold earring in one ear. His accent was Shepherd's Bush, his demeanour sharp and his eyes quick.

'Yeah, I picked up a geezer in a coat and hat on Thursday afternoon. On the Green, corner of Rockley Road. He waved me down, asked for Parliament Square.'

'What time would that be?'

'I've looked at me log. Picked him up at ten to two. I drove to Parliament Square, and he tapped the glass and said to drop him at the corner of Parliament Street. So I did. He got out;

I did the rest of the square and went back up Victoria Street, caught meself a fare at the station.'

'Did you see where he went when he got out?'

'No, sorry. I was looking at the traffic. You know how it is.'

Swilley nodded. 'And what time did you drop him?'

'Twenty past two.'

'And now the big one,' she said, producing a photograph of Masterson. She'd had it photoshopped to be wearing a brown trilby. 'Is this the man?'

He studied it gravely and responsibly. 'Yeah, I reckon that's him, all right. Near as I can say.'

She took it back and looked at him curiously. 'You didn't recognize him, then?'

'No. Should I? Is he someone famous?' A light of eagerness came into his eyes.

'He's an MP.'

The light died.

'A minister, in fact.'

'I don't know much about that lot,' the cab driver said, disappointed. 'Football, now, that'd be different. I had that Roberto Soldado in the back of my cab once. You a Spurs supporter?'

Swilley eased him away from footy and into making an official statement.

Looking through TfL security camera footage was painstaking and tiring work, even when you had a specific route to check on. Thousands of passengers exited and entered hundreds of trains, milled along platforms, through passageways and up and down escalators, all in grainy black-and-white and jerky *Shaun of the Dead* movements. McLaren and his team had their work eased when Swilley came up with her taxi driver, so they only had one journey to check out. It was very late when a bleary-eyed McLaren came through to Slider's room.

'Got him, guv,' he said. 'Going into Westminster Station, at the barrier. On the Jubilee Line platform, northbound. Bond Street interchange. Central Line platform westbound. Shepherd's Bush getting off the train and at the barrier coming out of the station.' He handed over a fistful of stills and rubbed his face wearily with both hands.

Slider looked through them. 'You don't get a decent sight of his face in any of these.'

'No, guv,' McLaren admitted. 'It's the hat. All them cameras are mounted high. Course, you could argue it's not him. You could argue it's not the same hat all the way. He's not the only bloke in London with a trilby, especially around Westminster. But that's the best we can do.'

Mr Porson hadn't gone home. 'I thought you were up to something,' he said when Slider came to see him. 'I've got a second sense for when something's going down.' He surveyed Slider's face and the folder of evidence in his hand and said, 'Looks like a long job. You'd better sit down.' And, surprisingly, he sat himself, opposite Slider, resting his big, chalky hands on the desk and fixing attentive eyes on Slider's face. For all his oddities, the old boy was a policeman through and through and had a mind you could fillet fish with.

Slider went through the whole case as he had assembled it, and then waited while Porson cogitated.

'You've still not got any direct evidence he killed him.' He put his finger unerringly on the weak spot.

'No, sir. But I think if we rattle him sufficiently, he'll break and put his hand up. He's in a state anyway with his wife dying, and when we went to see him, he was pretty nervy. He must be strung out like wire, wondering when the other shoe will drop.'

Porson nodded. 'All right. What do you want to do? Go out and interview him tomorrow?'

'No, sir. I want to bring him in.'

Porson looked uneasy. 'The powers that be won't like that. He's a government minister. Like the garbage man, he's got friends in high places.'

'It's important to get him off balance. He'll have more confidence in his own environment. And if we arrest him, we can search his house. We may find the malachite box hidden there.'

Porson stirred. He'd taken a dislike to the whole box issue.

'And,' Slider went on, 'clothes with traces on them. There must have been some spatter when he stabbed Egerton, but if it was fine he may not have noticed it. Even if he did notice, and had the clothes cleaned, the date will be significant. It'll add to the pressure on him.'

'Right,' said Porson. Blood spatter was evidence a straight-forward man could get his teeth into. 'All right. Get a warrant out and pick him up tomorrow.'

'Tonight,' Slider said stubbornly. 'It'll throw him much more than a polite, leisurely call in the morning when he's had his eggs and b.'

'They won't like it,' Porson said, with a jerk of his head to signify Hammersmith and all points east right up to the Yard. Slider kept an insistent silence, and finally Porson made an exasperated movement. 'All right,' he said. 'Do it your way.' He hesitated, and then confided. 'Mr Wetherspoon as good as hinted he thought we did the stuff that annoys him to court publicity. I don't like having my bony Fridays questioned, or my officers'. You do it, and I'll back you up.' He stood up, muttering to himself. 'Mrs Assistant Commissioner Redbridge my arse. We're not here to drink tea and dispense doilies.' He caught Slider looking at him enquiringly, and bellowed, 'Well, what are you waiting for? Get on with it! You've got to go and wake up a muppet to get the warrant. You know they sleep like the deaf.'

Slider hurried away.

Philip Masterson, sleep-bleared and rumpled, would have been a sorry sight anyway, hauled into the police station in the middle of the night. But underneath that there was another layer of degradation. He was pale, hollow-cheeked, bag-eyed. He had the look of a man who had heard the leathery creak of the Erinyes' wings in the darkness, smelled the chthonic reek of their breath, felt the clammy touch of their lips on the back of his neck. Slider felt a little surge of triumph. It was always most productive to kick a man when he was down.

The young, smartly-suited solicitor, Martha Maitland, looked a degree less perky when she had heard the evidence summarized, but she did her best with poor material. 'I'm not going to allow any fishing expeditions,' she said. 'If you're hoping my client will incriminate himself—'

Slider gave her a kindly look. 'The evidence against him is so solid, there's no need for that.'

'Then why don't you charge him? Because you know you haven't got enough, and you want a confession to beef up your case.'

'Miss Maitland, we found traces of blood on Mr Masterson's overcoat. The lab's typing it now. Once that result comes back we won't need a confession, and he will be charged. Now, if your client wants to plead provocation – and I do believe he was mightily provoked – this is his chance. There's a window of opportunity for him to gain some Brownie points. Once that closes—' He shrugged.

She had a long conversation with Masterson, before accompanying him to the tape room. He looked at Slider with victim's eyes as he came into the interview room and sat down opposite him. Atherton took his place beside Slider, and Masterson logged him as well. His two previous persecutors.

'My client has agreed to cooperate with this enquiry,' Maitland said, sitting down beside him. 'I wish that to be taken into account.'

'It will be given all due weight,' Slider promised, and turned his attention to the sorry object she was representing. 'Mr Masterson, let's begin with the matter of fraud, concerning the oil painting by Joest van Wessen, "Girl with Embroidered Reticule",' Slider said. 'We know *what* you did. This is your chance to tell us *why* you did it.' Some flicker of doubt registered in the hunted eyes, and Slider pushed the clear folder containing the letter across the table. 'We've seen the painting in your former office. We know all about it.'

'Where did you get this?' Masterson said, looking at the letter as though it were a poisonous snake.

'Never mind,' Slider said. 'Tell us about the painting. It wasn't really for your wife, was it?'

His eyes filled with tears. 'I loved my wife. I adored her. She's the love of my life. You have to understand. *I* knew I wasn't good enough for her, her family and friends didn't have to keep reminding me. Grammar-school boy, they called me, as if that was something to be ashamed of. They thought I was leeching off her. She married me for love!' His voice went higher, as though this was an oft-repeated argument that had never worked. 'Things may have changed, but she loved me in the beginning, and I would never have done anything to hurt her.'

'So why did you?' Slider asked.

'I *didn't*! She never found out – that was the whole point of the van Wessen. Look, I was a fool, I know that. But all her circle had money to burn, and I wanted to show them I could keep my end up. They talked as though I was making her live in a council house and wear rags. I *had* to put on a bit of a display,' he said pathetically. 'It was for her sake as much as mine – she couldn't have liked having them sneer at her husband. So I bought her presents, jewellery, took her to expensive restaurants. Insisted on picking up the bill when her old circle were around. I had to dress well – they can spot a ready-made suit like a pig sniffs out truffles,' he ended bitterly.

'And you got into debt?' Atherton suggested. 'That sort of lifestyle doesn't come cheap.'

'I was a fool,' Masterson said. 'I couldn't go to her for money. I couldn't let her know I was in trouble. And I couldn't get any more from the usual sources. So I borrowed from some other people. You know what I mean.' He shrugged. 'Once you get into their hands, they've got you over a barrel. Any interest rate they fancy, and you can't argue. I *had* to get enough cash to pay them off, or they were going to make sure certain people knew all about it. They were hounding me; it was a nightmare. It would have finished me, but more than that, Bunny would have despised me. And then I met that forger at a party. Pat Duggan.'

'How long had you been planning to have the painting copied?' Slider asked.

'I hadn't,' said Masterson. 'It just came to me on the instant, when I met Duggan at a party in the building. The painting hung in a dark corner, and no-one ever looked at it. It was wallpaper, that was all. The state owns hundreds of these things. It wasn't even an important piece. Who would ever know if it was the original or not? It wasn't as if I was hurting anyone, stealing an old woman's pension or something. It was a victimless crime, and God knows I needed the money more than the state did. So I took him along to my room. Told him I wanted it copied for my wife's birthday. I think he was glad of the work. I arranged for him to be there to study it when there was no-one else around, and he did the actual painting at home. So we kept it secret from everyone.'

'How did you exchange the copy with the original?' Atherton asked.

'I came back late one night, told security I had some paper-work to collect. I had the painting in a cardboard tube. I locked my office doors and made the switch. It was easy enough. The backboard was held in by little tacks, but it was so old, they came out with a bit of twisting. Then I knocked them back in with the foot of the stapler. Put the original into the tube and that was that.'

'And how did you dispose of it?' Slider asked.

'Through an export agent I'd had dealings with. He'd been bugging me for an export licence for a van Dyck we weren't going to let go. I told him I'd sign it for him if he fenced the van Wessen for me. He didn't like me using those words, of course, but he reasoned like I did that it wasn't an important painting, so where was the harm? And we couldn't rat on each other because we were both in it equally, so he'd be safe enough. It cost me, though,' he added gloomily. 'He found a private buyer in Amsterdam, but he charged me a hefty commission on top of signing the licence. I only ended up with seven hundred and fifty thousand.'

'Still quite a big sum,' Slider pointed out, with scant sympathy.

'But it was only just enough to pay off the debt,' Masterson said fretfully. 'I'd hoped for a bit extra, to tide me over, but once I'd paid up, I was back where I started, with nothing but my salary.'

'And a wardrobe full of nice clothes, and a happy wife,' Atherton said. 'And you had the debt collectors off your back.'

Masterson agreed, but gloomily. 'It was good to be out from under,' he admitted.

'So you thought it would all be plain sailing from then on,' said Atherton.

'Until Rowland Egerton turned up with the letter,' said Slider. It was the pivotal point. He was holding his breath, afraid Masterson would clam up, or that Maitland would intervene.

But Masterson's face almost writhed with the mixture of emotions that swept through him, and he said in what was practically a gasp, 'That bastard! That utter bastard!'

Maitland whispered something to him, and he shook his head, clenching and unclenching his fists.

'He was blackmailing you, wasn't he?' Slider said with sympathy. 'Blackmailers are the scum of the earth. The worst of all criminals.'

Masterson seemed to take comfort from that. 'Nobody knew what he was really like. They thought he was this genial, charming fellow on the TV. But underneath he was a snake.'

'Tell me how he approached you,' said Slider.

'He came to me one day with a photocopy of the letter – just like that.' He nodded to the folder on the table. 'He'd been to my office and seen the painting and knew it was the copy. I remembered then that I'd come in the previous day and my secretary had said he'd been there to see me but hadn't waited. He must have gone deliberately to check. Well, I was sunk. With that letter, he could destroy me.'

'What did he want from you?' Slider asked, though he already guessed at the answer. 'Was it money?'

'I wish to God it had been,' Masterson said bitterly. 'Money would have been easy compared with—' He stopped.

'Compared with what?'

Masterson stared at the table, as though there was a crack there through which he could glimpse Hell. 'He was having an affair with my wife,' he said at last, in a low voice. It sounded not as if he was answering the question, but as if he was simply remembering the terrible fact that had ended his happiness for ever.

'Had you suspected it already?' Slider asked him gently.

Masterson's mouth bowed with bitterness. 'No. I had no idea. I adored Bunny, but I knew she didn't feel quite the same way about me – and there were always men hanging around her, flirting with her, sending her flowers. She attracted them like moths to a candle. I knew I wasn't worthy of her, and I never knew what she saw in me, but she was a very loyal person and she'd never have showed me up. I always knew that if she took a lover she would be discreet about it. It was terrible to have Rowland stand there and tell me right out, to my face. So brutal. Like someone with a baseball bat smashing up everything in your house.'

Slider nodded. 'What did he want?'

Masterson met his eyes, as though coming to the worst thing of all. 'He wanted me to go along with it. I had to accept the fact and not object to it. And I had to keep the secret. He said Bunny didn't want me to know, so I must never let on to her that I knew. If I ever let slip so much as a hint that I knew about it, if she ever found out I knew, he'd use the letter and destroy me.'

There was a silence as Masterson paused, and Slider reflected on the exquisite nature of the torture Egerton had inflicted. Not just to have power over him, but to make him suffer; to give him knowledge that poisoned him while forbidding him the outlet to be rid of it.

'What did you do?' he asked.

'What could I do? I had to go along with it. He gave me the photocopy, but said he had the original in a safe place at home. As long as I kept my side, no-one would ever see it. And it didn't come out. I suppose he kept his word. But all the time I *knew*. Him and Bunny. Oh, they were discreet. No-one else ever found out. But that only made it worse, somehow. As if I was colluding in it. That's what everyone would have thought if it *had* come out – that I didn't mind. But I minded. My *God*, I minded! Every day, every hour. It ate away inside me like acid.'

'And then,' Atherton said, 'she died.'

Masterson gave him a look as though he'd struck him. 'Yes,' he said. 'My wife died.'

'Tell me about what happened at the funeral,' said Slider. 'You weren't completely honest with me before. He wasn't there to court publicity, was he?'

'No, he came to gloat. I went across and asked him what the hell he thought he was doing, and he had the gall to sympathize.

He said he knew how I felt, said we'd both loved her, pretended his loss was as deep as mine. I wanted to hit him, but there was a crowd there, I couldn't risk anyone seeing. I couldn't even shout at him. But I made sure he knew how I felt. I told him he had no right to any feelings about Bunny. I said he was nothing but a worthless gigolo and that she'd never cared tuppence for him. *I* was her husband. I told him to get out. I told him I never wanted to see his ugly face again. And he just smiled and said we'd had a bargain, and he was glad I'd kept my part of it, and I should remember he'd kept his. And then he went.'

'You didn't ask him about the letter?'

'I didn't think about it then. I was too upset. I was shaking with rage. I had a job to calm myself down so as to talk to the other guests. And for a long time afterwards, I was too grief-stricken to think much about anything.'

'So what brought it to your mind?'

'It was last Wednesday. I was looking in my diary at home to see what I was doing, and I suddenly remembered that was the day Bunny would have been doing a shoot for the antiques programme. With Rowland. And I thought about the letter. I'd kept my end of the bargain. He ought to give it back. In fact, if he didn't give it to me, it meant I was still living under the threat of it. I thought about it all day. I was half-scared to ask him, I admit it, in case he decided to blackmail me some more. I thought maybe he'd forgotten about it and I shouldn't stir up a hornet's nest. But I lay awake all night thinking about what he could still do to me.'

'And the next day, when your committee finished early, you decided to go and see him,' Atherton finished for him.

Maitland intervened. 'You don't need to answer that.'

'It's all right,' Slider said. 'As I told you, we know *what* you did. All of it. This is your chance to put your side of it. You must have been under intolerable strain.'

Masterson seemed close to exhaustion. 'More than you can imagine. The committee broke early, and I had nothing to do. My secretary had been keeping my diary free, because of my bereavement, but work was the only thing that kept my mind off it. Now it all came over me in a wave. I decided right then

I'd had enough, I'd have to go and have it out with him. I knew he'd be home – I knew more about his routines, through Bunny, than I wanted to. I hoped he'd be alone. And he was. He gave me a sinister, slippery smile when he saw me, invited me in, and then just stood there looking at me, waiting for me to speak. So I said, "I want the letter back." I said I'd kept my end, and now that Bunny was dead, it was all over.'

'And he refused?' said Atherton.

'Of course,' Masterson said, with a look of great bitterness. 'He said, "Oh, I think I'd rather keep it." I said why? And he said, "Because it amuses me." And he picked up this box from the table behind him and opened it, and showed me the letter, all folded up. He said, "Bunny gave me this box. A lover's gift. I think it's rather appropriate that I keep it in here, don't you?" I suppose I just snapped. He was grinning at me, taunting me, and I couldn't take it any more. There was this paperknife thing on the table just beside me. I grabbed it and went for him.' He rubbed his eyes. 'I didn't mean to kill him. I wasn't really thinking at all. But the knife went into his throat. He fell down and thrashed about. He made a horrible gurgling noise. And then he was lying still.' He shuddered to a stop.

'So what did you do?' Slider asked quietly. He was feeling all too much pity for the man now.

Masterson looked at him, haggard. 'I realized what trouble I was in. But nobody knew I was there. If I could get away quickly, I could pretend I was still at the committee hearing. I – I know I shouldn't have tried to cover it up. But after what he did to me – why should I be the one to suffer? And I was scared. I was just – so – scared. So I wiped the knife on my handkerchief, took the letter and left.'

'You took the malachite box as well,' said Atherton.

'*She'd* given it to him. I couldn't leave it there,' he said simply. 'I hurried out and flagged down a taxi and – well, I got back in reasonable time. I thought it was all right. I didn't know,' he added with a touch of anger, 'that he'd got another copy.'

'It was on his computer,' said Slider.

'I suppose I should have known he'd do that. He never meant to let me go.'

'He liked to keep control over his victims,' Atherton said.

'There were others?' Masterson said. 'I'm not surprised. He was a filthy blackmailer, and he deserved to die.' He obviously heard his own words on the air, and the anger drained away. 'What happens now?' he asked, almost humbly.

'If you continue to cooperate fully, I'm sure the mitigating circumstances will be taken into account,' Slider said. 'But that's not for me to decide. We found the malachite box in your wardrobe, but where is the letter?'

'I burned it.' He looked at Slider. 'I won't go to prison, will I?' he asked, much as Lavender had. Prison only worked as a deterrent on the people who were least likely to end up there.

'I'm afraid you must prepare yourself for a custodial sentence,' Slider said. 'Murder is still murder.'

As they walked up the stairs, Slider found his hands were shaking from all the vicarious emotions.

'Blackmail is a disgusting thing. I wonder what I would have done in his shoes,' Atherton said thoughtfully. 'Probably planned ahead and made a better job of it.'

'Don't tell me that,' Slider objected.

'He could still recant,' Atherton said.

'Doesn't matter. As soon as the blood on his coat gets typed, he's done like a kipper, with or without a confession. God, I'm tired,' he said, rubbing his eyes.

'No use being tired. You've got a night's work ahead of you,' said Atherton.

'If I have, you have,' said Slider grimly.

'It's a beautiful case,' Porson said, and the way he said it made Slider misgive. It was late on Friday afternoon, and he still hadn't been home. Nor had Porson, and he'd been over at Hammersmith all afternoon into the bargain. 'You've got the busted alibi, the tube journey covered, the taxi-driver's ID, the copy of the letter, that blasted box, and best of all the blood evidence from the overcoat.' They hadn't heard back from the lab yet, but it was only a matter of hours. 'Plus motive to dive for. And the confession. No loose ends. Very nice indeed.'

'But?' Slider said. 'I can hear a but coming.'

Porson regarded him steadily like a soldier facing a firing squad. 'The powers that be aren't keen to take it any further. He's a government minister, for God's sake! You can't expect the Home Secretary to be happy about stirring up a stink. The PM doesn't want another by-election. Plus the BBC top coots are putting in their twopenn'orth. They've got six episodes of this antiques programme in the can that they haven't aired yet, and a scandal about Egerton and the bunny rabbit will blow the whole programme out of the water. And the Director General, surprise surprise, is a pal of Deputy Commissioner Redbridge, and they both play golf with the head of the Crown Prosecution Service. Heads are being put together, and tuts are being tutted. So don't be too upset, laddie, if they decide it's not in the public interest to prosecute. It's a can of worms. Egerton turns out to've been an excrescence, and the thinking seems to be it wasn't so much homicide as pesticide.'

'Sir,' Slider protested, 'A man was murdered.'

'I know. I don't like it any more than you do, but the power's not in our hands.'

'And what about the art fraud, sir?'

'Old buns. Water under the dyke.'

'A victimless crime?' Slider asked sourly.

'No such thing,' said Porson. He paced a bit. 'Frankly, I can't see how they can hope to keep the whole thing buttoned up. Too many people know too much already. Even if there's no leak.'

'My firm doesn't leak,' Slider said.

'I know that. But you know what the press is like. With an MP involved they won't stop till they sniff it out. And there's always Rupert Melling. *There's* a chap who could make a hint go a long way. Anyway, you've done your job, you can be proud of that. The rest is up to the gods.'

Despite the unsatisfactory ending, Slider had to authorize the usual post-case pints party at the Boscombe Arms. It wouldn't have been fair on his people to have sulked about it. They'd all done their part and deserved to celebrate.

The weekend intervened, so it couldn't take place until Monday after work. McLaren asked if they were bringing

people, and though the answer should have been 'no', everyone
was dying to see his new girlfriend Natalie, so pressure was
put on him to extend the invitation. No-one else wanted to
bring anyone. Hollis said gloomily that he hadn't anyone any
more, everyone else's spouses avoided these things like the
plague, and Atherton said he'd arrange to meet his date *du
jour* afterwards rather than subject her to a work outing.

Joanna was working – the first of her dep dates in the West
End. Slider was both pleased and anxious for her.

Atherton didn't help. 'Second violin in a Lloyd Webber?'
he said with a delicate shudder. 'How can you let your wife
do work like that?'

Slider gave in to a bit of shameful curiosity and asked
Connolly if she was bringing anyone, but she only rolled her
eyes and said, 'Love a God, sir!' as if it were a ridiculous
question.

In spite of everyone's intentions, the mood was a little
subdued as they trooped into the bar. It was galling to work
so hard and have the rug pulled at the last minute. Still, there
was the first sighting of Natalie to cheer them up. She turned
out to be remarkable mainly in that there was nothing remarkable about her at all, and they had never thought old Maurice
would be able to land a normal mate. She was just a nice,
ordinary female, not ragingly pretty but quite all right, neither
fat nor thin but normally well-covered, evidently good-natured
and good humoured, and ready to like Maurice's work
colleagues for his sake.

He was plainly besotted with her, poor goop, but this time
everyone had a good feeling about it, and after a very short
time had settled down to thinking it might be all right after
all. McLaren beamed with proprietary pride and fussed about
her like a mother hen, plying her with food and drink. It was
really rather touching.

The second round was going in, and the platters of sand-
wiches, sausage rolls and scotch eggs were well depleted,
when Andy Barrett, the publican, beckoned Slider over and
told him sotto voce that there was someone wanting to see
him privately in the snug. Slider was at a loss who it could
be, thinking perhaps one of his snouts had tracked him down,

but he was even more surprised when he slipped into the otherwise empty bar and found Mr Porson standing there.

Porson gave him a placatory smile, while his eyebrows signalled some momentous news. 'Don't worry, laddie, I haven't come to spoil the party. That's why I came in here – I know a whiff of a boss can ruin the merriment. But I've got some good news for you.'

'Let me get you a drink,' Slider said.

'No, thanks all the same. I just came to tell you that there's been some thinking going on over the weekend, and they've decided to prosecute Masterson after all.'

'On the fraud? Or the murder?'

'Both,' said Porson. 'Bit of a job to separate the two in the circs.'

'But why did they change their minds?' Slider asked.

'Mr Wetherspoon had a word,' Porson said, his eyebrows doing arabesques. 'Pointed out how bad it would look for the government if the press got hold of it and it looked like they were protecting their own. Especially with all the media connections to make the story good and juicy and guarantee maximum exposure. The Home Secretary and the PM decided Masterson wasn't worth the risk. Apparently, he doesn't have a lot of friends in the party. Also, in case of a by-election, there's a very good candidate ready to stand for the constituency, who as luck and complete chance would have it is the godson of the Director General of the BBC.'

'Amazing coincidence, sir,' said Slider.

'So all in all, they've decided to let justice take its course and rely on mitigating circs to spin the story away from complete bloody disaster. Egerton being a worse villain than Masterson and so on.' He cocked an eye at Slider. 'You mustn't be too upset if he doesn't go away for a long, long time. They'll want the lightest possible sentence. Given it wasn't premeditated, and the provocation, he could even get a suspended.'

Slider was studying his boss. 'What made Mr Wetherspoon step in?' he asked abruptly.

Porson gave him a bland look. 'Did it off his own belt. Purely in the interests of justice. Doing the right thing, eckcetera. As a matter of fact, the DC's decided to give him a promotion as a pat on the back for conspicuous virtue. So Mr Wetherspoon'll be leaving us. He's going to the Yard. Not sure what job he's getting, but he's pleased as a dog with two willies, is our Mr Wetherspoon.'

'Good God, sir,' Slider said blankly.

Porson rarely smiled, in the interests of not terrifying people, but he smiled now. 'So pleased, he's dishing out bokays right and centre. He's making you a detective chief inspector, as a farewell gift.' He surveyed Slider's face. 'Don't look too happy about it, will you?'

'I'm still trying to work it out, sir,' Slider said.

'Nothing to work!' Porson barked. 'Give the brain a rest, Slider, and that's an order! Go and have a jar. Or two. Tell your firm well done, and—' He dug into a pocket and came out with two twenties. 'Tell 'em to have a drink on me.'

Slider rejoined his men with such a look of bemusement that the conversation died, everyone stared, and Atherton said for all of them, 'What's happened, guv? Is something wrong?'

'No,' Slider said, trying to shake off the feeling of strangeness. 'In fact, everything's suddenly right. The CPS is going to take the case after all.'

There were cheers and glass-waving and back slapping before someone asked, inevitably, 'Why did they change their minds?'

Slider thought of the oversized tale he'd been told and took it in a couple of inches. 'Mr Porson made them.'

The cheers this time made the chandeliers shake. Slider waved the twenties, managed to convey the boss's congratulations, and went and sat down before he fell down.

Atherton put a pint in front of him and sat down beside him. 'What's up, ol' guv of mine? You look somewhat poleaxed.'

'Post-case blues,' Slider excused himself.

'The bad guy got done,' Atherton pointed out. 'Both bad guys, in fact.'

'I can't help remembering that Bunny Rabbet loved Egerton. As did John Lavender, in his own way. And his fans were legion.'

'They were morons.'

'Don't be so judgemental. We're all fans of something. And no-one deserves to be murdered.'

'All right, I'll grant you that one.' He knew it was time to be serious. 'Even if Masterson doesn't get jail-time, his career's finished, his wife's dead, and he'll have to live with how the knife felt going in and the sounds Egerton made while he died, for the rest of his life. It's all over for him. Natural justice has been served. The Furies have been appeased. You can stand down.' He studied his boss's face. 'What else?'

Slider made the effort. 'Nothing else,' he said. 'It's all right, I'm ready to party now. Shove me over a sausage roll, will you?'

'Put it on the floor, and I'll gladly shove you over it,' Atherton said obligingly.

Slider took a good long swallow of his pint and chomped the sausage roll. All around him his firm – his other family – were in rare old spirits. He thought of Joanna sawing away in the pit at that moment and longed to be home with her; just to go to bed, spoon up, and sleep in the blissful heat of her body.

Mackay was proposing a toast to him. He raised his glass and smiled back at them all. He decided he'd tell them about the promotion some other time. He hadn't been able to take it in properly himself, yet.